SPEND MY LIFE WITH YOU

MONIQUE FISHER

Brief mention of child abandonment, brief mention of racial profiling.

This book is a cozy, low-angst/low conflict read that centers on the couple sharing in their love. There are scenes with secondary characters, of course but unlike Latrice and Nathan who had to hide their love, Thad and Drea get to love each other out loud and they do!

Thank you.

FAMILY

THE RICHARDSONS

AUNT RENEE UNCLE SLY UNCLE LEVI AUNT BEBE EARL JANET

KOFI TAMAR NATHAN LATRICE NADIA

KAI QUINCY

THE WOODSONS

MOMMA ERNIE

LEON AMBER

TYLER SHELLIE

TREES

THE JOHNSONS

GREYSON   VIVIAN
THADDEUS   ANDREA   MARKUS   ACACIA
JELANI   LETICIA

THE MACARTHURS

TIM   RACHEL
ELI

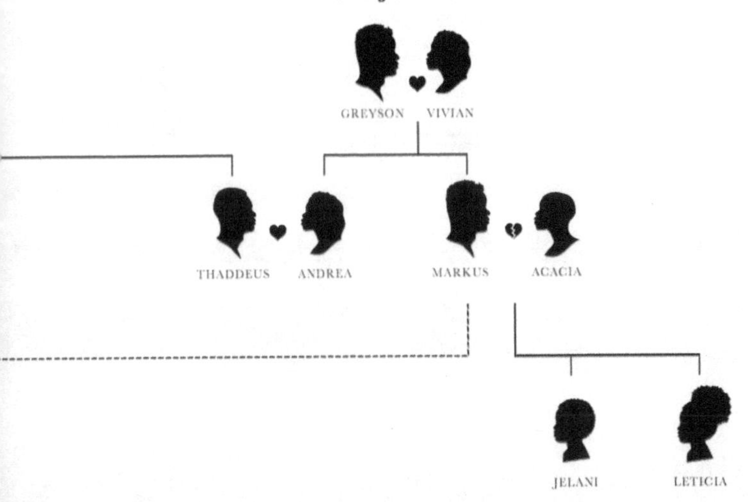

FICTIONALIZED LOCATIONS, SHOWS, & MORE!

- Tony's in San Pedro (I'm sure there is a real place called Tony's in San Pedro but the one in the book isn't real.)
- The Mauritian place on Slauson.
- The Ava Love Doll.
- The Park-Barrington Hotels (This hotel chain appears in other books in my rom-com universe too.)
- Vincente's (the food Thad and Drea had delivered when her mom visited.)
- Carver's Bakery (This place also makes an appearance in "She a Baddie.")
- LW (The restaurant makes an appearance in "She a Baddie.")

- Carter Willems Museum of African American Pop Culture (This is basically a combo of two real life museums at here in LA. One is the Paley Center for Media and the other is the California African American Museum).
- Angelo's (the pizza place from Thad and Drea's date night).
- The TV shows *Doll Face and Gumshoe.* And the film, *Scattered Ashes.*
- Florentino's (The place they go to for Thad's birthday).

SPEND MY LIFE WITH YOU

I t's August 19, 2024. Thaddeus Richardson is sitting in his car, contemplating his life. He's thirty-five. His career could not be going better. He just opened his sixth location for *We Cut Heads*, his chain of barber shops, and he hired a new barber for the flagship location. His relationship with his family is healthier and happier than ever. He loves his sisters and parents, and he tells them all the time. And his nephew Quincy may very well be his most favorite person in the whole world.

So, what's missing? Drea. Thad wants Drea by his side. He wants Drea in his bed and in his life, as more than just his sister Latrice's best friend and Quincy's aunt. More than just the woman he flirts and jokes with. He's in love with her, and he has been for the past four years. He's tried denying it and dating other women, hoping he would meet someone to get his mind off her. It's been a fool's errand. There is no getting rid of Andrea Michelle Johnson. She's embedded into his soul. She owns his heart, and he is foolish to think he can undo the spell she has him under. Thad's luck in relationships has been bad. Really bad. Comically bad. The idea of having a failed relationship with someone he feels so deeply for petrifies him. And it certainly doesn't help that she is close to his family. So, he keeps his mouth shut. That is, until Latrice goes and pushes her fear aside, showing him he needs to do the same. Latrice hadn't let a man into her life romantically since she ended things with her ex-husband, Mark. Thad heard her talking with her friends. Them encouraging her to put herself back out there and Latrice refusing, citing she was too scared of getting hurt. And then she met Nathan.

Two months ago, Latrice got engaged to the love of her life, Nathan Woodson, her son Quincy's former third grade teacher. And today, they're getting married. They spent a whole year having to hide their relationship, only for it to have been unnecessary. And now they get to love out loud and be together without fear of any retribution from the school district or Mark. Thad doesn't have to worry about such dire consequences. And yet, he's let his fear of another failed relationship keep him from saying anything for four years. He can have the type of life he craves with the woman of his dreams by his side if he just says the word. His fear of failure has kept him quiet long enough. Days like today are in his future, if he just makes it so. So today, after the ceremony, Thad is going to tell Drea that he is in love with her.

THAD GETS OUT OF HIS CAR AND OPENS THE FRONT door to his sister's house, seeing a flurry of people. The bridal party, the groomsmen—of which Thad is one—family and the rental people dropping off tables and chairs. He smiles, knowing that in a few seconds, Latrice is going to—

"Thad, there you are," Latrice says. "The tables and chairs need to be set up. Thankfully, the company already cleaned them. For now, I need you to please, please, please set them up like the tables were set up for Uncle Sly and Aunt Renee's anniversary dinner. You remember, don't you? Of course you do. After you're done, come find me, and let me know when Drea gets back."

"You got it, sis. Will do," Thad replies. Latrice gives him a warm smile before something gets her attention and she runs off.

"The florist is here!" she squeals.

Thad chuckles at the sight of her getting so excited over centerpieces. The ceremony is at four o'clock, and it's currently ten in the morning. He heads over to the tables and chairs and gets to work. By the time he has placed the last centerpiece on the table, Drea is back. She's carrying some drinks from the nearby smoothie place, so he rushes over to help her, taking the smoothies out of her hands and placing them on the counter.

"How chivalrous of you, Thaddeus." Drea beams. Her brown eyes sparkle as she looks up at him. Her mouth is so inviting with her perfect Colgate smile and her rose-colored lips. They look so soft and pillowy. He has dreamed of holding her beautiful face in his hands before leaning down and kissing her. He imagines the act to be so powerful that it would transport him to another world. She looks back at him with a curious gaze. She's given Thad this look before. Whenever they find themselves staring deep into each other's souls, one of his sisters is usually nearby and disrupts by teasing them about their obvious attraction. As annoying as Latrice and Nadia's behavior might be, Thad secretly hopes they're right. The way Drea is looking at him now, they just might be.

"It's my pleasure, Andrea. It's always my pleasure," Thad answers, causing Drea to simper. She is beyond gorgeous. If someone were to ask what his favorite time of day is, he'd answer, *Whenever Drea smiles.* He reaches up to touch her face, compelled by a force stronger than himself. She doesn't stop him. When his hand connects to her cheek, "I Only Have Eyes for You" by the Flamingos comes on. The DJ—Quincy—must be testing out the playlist for the reception. She moves closer to Thad. He embraces her, and she wraps her arms around his shoulders. He leans down. Their faces are inches apart from each other when—

"Thad!" Latrice calls out.

He and Drea separate just as Latrice walks in. Drea hands her a smoothie. "Here you go, Trice."

"Thank you." Latrice turns to Thad and playfully hits his shoulder. "I told you to tell me when Drea gets back."

"Don't go chastising Thad. I barely just got back," Drea explains.

"Come on, we have so much to do before hair and makeup arrive. Remember Fatima is doing the bridesmaids faces before she does me." Latrice pulls Drea's arm.

Drea grabs the remaining smoothies and looks back at Thad biting her lip. His eyes connect with hers as he fights the urge to say, *I love you.* Thad has been fighting the urge to tell Drea how he feels since she walked in. She disappears into Latrice and Nathan's bedroom as he takes a deep breath. His heart is racing. It's crazy that for four years he has been too scared to say anything, and now that he's decided to break his silence, he's more than a little eager to tell her. He needs to chill. This is Latrice's day, and he doesn't want to make it about him. That's why he's decided to do it after the reception is over. The plan is to get Drea alone, profess his love to her and make her his lady. He just has to be patient and wait.

Hours later, Thad smiles as he watches his sister promise forever to Nathan. Latrice looks like an angel in her white satin sleeveless gown pooling at her ankles. She has a white rose in her curly natural hair to complete the look. She's glowing. Love positively radiates between her and Nathan. It's a beautiful sight. Nathan and the groomsmen—his best friend Ronnie, Thad, his brother Leon, and a fellow teacher friend, Greg—are in classic Hugo Boss tuxedos. Black tailored tuxes with crisp white shirts and black bow ties. The bridesmaids are wearing soft yellow gowns to match the color of Latrice's engagement ring. Thad looks at Drea. The off-the-shoulder gown she's wearing looks magnificent. She looks like the sun. Bright and beautiful. Her makeup includes a shimmering lip with a slightly golden hue. Her rosy cheeks are natural and her eyeshadow and liner make her brown eyes pop while enhancing their beauty. Thad's stomach clenches, and his heart feels like it's expanding, his breath caught in his throat. He tries to look away but can't. She catches him. Their eyes connect again. Drea bites her lip once more, causing Thad to will his dick to calm down. There is a list of things that Drea does that sets him off. Biting her lip is one of them.

Latrice speaks, bringing their attention to the bride. "Nathan, you taught me to take a chance and to stop being afraid," Latrice says, tears streaming down her face. "I love you so much. Thank you for showing me real love does exist. I never thought I could be this happy. Quincy loves you, and I'm so grateful for that. I love the relationship you two have built. I don't know what else to say, but I'm so happy my sister, Nay Nay, convinced me to take a chance with a handsome stranger." Latrice smiles.

"Me too!" Nathan adds, making everyone chuckle. He continues, "Lala, I love you. I worship you. I live for you. You and Quincy are the best thing to ever happen to me since my mother adopted me. I love you both more than life itself. I will spend the rest of my life proving to you how much you two mean to me." He removes his glasses to wipe his tears. Latrice assist him. Their foreheads touch as they gaze at each other, neither able to stop their sobbing. Soon, the crying passes on to the wedding party. Thad can't help but to wipe away a few tears. He's so happy for Latrice. She deserves this.

Everyone takes a moment to breathe before the officiant continues—he even got a little choked up. Latrice and Nathan exchange rings before being pronounced husband and wife. The newlyweds walk back down the aisle. Everyone applauds as they hold hands, smiling a mile wide.

Latrice raises her hands to get everyone's attention. "Thank you all so much for coming. Nathan and I could not be happier. Our family means the world to us, and we're happy to announce that another member will join the family in about seven months. Nathan and I are having a baby!"

Everyone erupts in a combination of applause and cheers. Thad makes his way to Latrice and hugs her, lifting her up. "Wooo! Yeah." He lets out a gregarious laugh.

"Thad put me down." Latrice laughs too.

"Right, sorry. Tricey, I am so happy for you."

"Thank you."

"I get to spoil another kid." Thad beams.

"Easy, Uncle Thad. Slow down, this bun isn't even fully cooked yet." Latrice smiles.

"Don't care. I'm going to spoil the shit out that fetus."

Latrice playfully rolls her eyes. She and Thad draw their attention to Drea, who hugs Nathan then Quincy. Latrice looks at Thad. His eyes involuntarily leave Drea and go to Latrice.

"You can have what me and Nathan have with her. You know that, right?"

"Yes, I do." He gives Latrice a knowing smile.

Her eyes grow large. "When are you planning on saying something?"

"After the reception. I want to get her alone, and I'm not trying to take away from your day."

"What? Fuck that, Thad. I just announced I'm pregnant on my wedding day, and I look amazing. You couldn't steal my thunder even if you tried."

Latrice and Thad share a laugh. "The minute you have an opening, go for it," Latrice urges.

Thad nods his head. "Yes, ma'am."

The reception is beginning. Some tables and chairs have been replaced with a portable dance floor. Quincy puts on a mix of slow songs to start the evening. A few guests get up and dance, while the photographer gets the wedding party's attention and takes photos. Almost half an hour passes before he's done. Latrice and Nathan have their first dance. When they finish, dinner is served. The guests feast on their choice of boneless chicken breast with pear sauce and sautéed green beans with mushrooms or pan-seared lamp chops with cippolini onions and a spring salad. He watches Drea take a bite of her chicken. The food is delicious, but it might as well be a flavorless paste. All that matters to him is finding the right moment. He finishes his dinner and has some champagne and strawberry sorbet. Looking over, he sees Drea swaying in her seat. *Holy shit! This is it... This is the opening.*

He gets up and walks over to her quickly. "Hello, Drea," he says, smiling.

"Hello, Thad." Drea grins right back.

"Would you like to dance?" he asks.

"I'd love to."

Thad offers his arm. She links hers with his as he leads them to the dance floor. Quincy plays "Best Part" by Daniel Caesar featuring H.E.R. Thad holds Drea close as she slides her hands up his chest and around his neck. Her head rests on his shoulder. His hands rub all over her back. Drea inhales deeply. She looks up at him as he looks down at her.

"You smell so good," Drea whispers.

Thad's dick throbs in his pants. "Thank you. You smell incredible."

"Thank you. Thad?"

"Yes."

"You were going to kiss me earlier," Drea mutters.

"I was."

They rock side to side in rhythm. "Do you want to kiss me now?" Drea asks.

"I want to do more than that." He takes her hand and leads her to a quiet corner of the backyard near the rosebushes. No matter what Latrice says, he isn't going to make this day about him. Besides, Drea deserves to know how he feels without an audience. The setting sun makes the perfect backdrop. The perfect moment. He pulls her to him and wraps his arms around her waist.

She looks up at him and sighs contently, "Thad."

"Drea." He breathes. The end of the song can be heard and the line "If you love me, won't you say something?" repeats. She reaches up and scratches his beard. Drea has touched Thad whenever they flirt. Her finger will slowly graze his bicep, or she will take her hand in his. But this is more intimate. Her finger brushes his lip, and he kisses it. She lets out a quiet moan. He takes her hands and kisses them. Her eyes are glassy, as if she's about to cry. His voice is intense and husky.

"Drea, I am in love with you," he announces.

The damn breaks and a flood of tears runs down Drea's face. When she doesn't stop crying, Thad becomes alarmed, unsure if they're happy or sad tears. Drea soon assuages his fear.

"You have no idea how long I have dreamed of you saying that to me." Thad's face breaks into a smile. "I'm in love with you too, Thad."

He leans down, and his mouth captures hers. Their kiss, years in the making, is unyielding. He cannot stop. The taste of champagne and strawberries on her tongue refuses to let go of him. He's spellbound, in a never-ending trance. He doesn't know if it will ever end...

"OH, DREA. FUCK!" THAD CRIES. THE KISS DIDN'T SO much end as it moved to Thad's Range Rover and to his dick. He drove a few minutes away from the house to an empty park with an overlook. Thankfully, his windows are tinted so no one can see inside. As loud as he is, the lack of sight wouldn't matter. By now, the sky has darkened and moonlight shines into the car's sunroof. Drea's dress is off, and she's currently in nothing but her panties. Thad's pants, drawers and tuxedo jacket are in the corner with his shirt. Drea's fingers play with his nipples as she sucks his dick. His balls tighten and pre-come oozes out the tip of his dick. Drea runs her tongue along his slit. Thad stirs, the sensations coursing through his body are out of control.

"Uhhhh!" he cries out in pleasure. He's always been a vocal and loud, and what Drea is doing makes him grateful no one is around. Not that he is embarrassed by how loud he's being. Drea's mouth feels too good to care.

"I have wanted to suck your dick for a while now, Thad." Drea runs her tongue along his shaft, all the way up to the tip.

Thad hisses. "Sshhiiittt! Well, I'll tell you what, baby, you are permitted to suck my dick any time you want to."

Drea smirks and runs her tongue along his balls before taking the head of his dick into her mouth. "Mmmm."

"Ohhh, you about to make me bust." His eyes roll into the back of his head. Come shoots out of his dick, and she swallows it greedily.

Drea twirls her tongue around Thad's head, prompting him to shoot more come. "You're still hard," she says in wonder when he's done.

"Yeah, I am." Thad smiles.

She pulls down her panties. She's completely hairless down there. She must get waxes on the regular. The wetness between her legs makes his dick jump again. Drea sees this and smiles. "I've been tested recently. I don't have anything," she says.

"Me too. I got tested a year ago and haven't been with anyone since."

"I have an IUD. Do you want to come in me, Thad?" Drea asks while squeezing those beautiful titties of hers.

"Dear God, yes!" Thad begs. Drea bends until her pretty pussy brushes against the head of Thad's dick. She pushes her hips forward so her pussy tickles him before sinking down on his dick inch by inch. Thad grabs ahold of her hips. "Ahhh! Damnit, baby. Your pussy is so tight."

"Mmm, Thad. Ooooo, right there. Right there. Don't stop." Drea moans.

Thad's fingers sink into the round flesh of Drea's ass as he thrust more and keeps hitting her spot. "Shit, Drea, you keep clenching." Drea has the best pussy Thad has ever experienced. *There's no way anyone else's pussy is better than this. It's just not possible.* His senses are working overtime. Especially his nose and ears. Thad can smell their sex, and it's making him high. "Sweet ass pussy." Thad's so high his filter is gone. Drea's pussy has obliterated it. The sounds of Drea's wetness covering his dick are what's keeping him from coming. The noises are so good, he wants to keep them going. Besides, he wants Drea to come first. This is an ultimate test of wills because Drea's pussy is, "so fucking good. I can't... Drea, pussy...so good."

"Mmmm, Thad. I love your dick, baby. It's so big. You're stretching me." Thad's dick pulsates. "Somebody has a praise kink," Drea purrs. Thad's dick responds again. "Have I ever told you how sexy you are, Thad?" She giggles. She leans down and looks Thad in the eye while bouncing on his dick. "You remember last year when you won me a panda at the school fair?"

"Yes," Thad hisses. Her walls are closing in on

him. She sinks down and thrusts her hips forward, riding him. "Hoooo! Fuck." He chokes.

"You want to know what I was thinking while I was feeling on your arm?" Drea stops, and Thad clutches her ass some more. Her pussy won't stop gripping him. "You need a minute?" He nods quickly. She waits. After a minute or so, she says, "Thad, I want you on top of me, fucking me hard and deep."

Without a word, he puts her on her back, determined to fuck her into oblivion. "You were getting ready to tell me what you were thinking when you felt my arm."

Drea begins to speak. "Right, I was thinking—" Thad pushes his dick deep inside her and proceeds to pound on her pussy. "—Ohhh, fuck! This. This is what I was thinking of. You fucking me." He doesn't catch the last few words due to her voice rising. Drea starts lifting her hips, meeting him at each thrust. "Yes, yes, Thad," Drea moans into his ear before licking it. He almost loses it. *You are not playing fair, baby. Alright, I got you.* He winds his hips. She cries out in pleasure, wrapping her arms around his shoulder and nipping his earlobe. "That's it, baby. Fuck me deep."

"Mmmm, fuck, Drea. I want this to last, baby, and you still need to come." Thad strains to keep himself from coming undone. The build and the sensations are incredible.

"Your dick is too good. Uhhh, Thad!" Drea cries as Thad pumps so hard the damn car shakes. Drea's legs spread wider as she clutches Thad's shoulders. "You're about to make me come."

"Give it to me. Come on my dick." He breathes the command in her ear.

"Ohhh, fuck. Thaaaddd!" she whines as she comes.

Thad looks Drea in the eye and comes inside her. Her walls tighten around him, milking him for every drop. "Huuuhhh!" He shakes as he yells. Drea's hands slide down his back and make their way to his ass, where she grabs his cheeks. "Oh, got fucking damnit!"

Drea sniffles, and Thad looks at her. They both have tears in their eyes. She takes his face in her hands. "Why did we take so long so say it?" she asks.

"I don't know about you, but I was scared. The thought of making you mine and then losing you terrified me," he confesses.

"Really?"

"Hell, yes. I haven't had much luck with relationships—"

"Preaching to the choir."

He chuckles before becoming serious. "Drea, I began to fall so hard for you that the idea of you rejecting me, or us being together and it not working out...and then I'd have to see you all the time knowing that I lost you..." Tears fall down Thad's face, and Drea kisses them away.

"I used Latrice and Quincy as an excuse, which, in hindsight, was pretty pathetic. Whenever Trice would bring you up, I'd tell her that if we did date and it didn't work out, how would that be for her? Who would she invite to gatherings? I came up with every excuse in the book. I dated one loser after another to get you out of my system."

"I dated woman after woman to get you out of mine. It was a fruitless effort. There's no escaping you, Drea. You put something on me."

Drea smiles and plays with Thad's chest hair. "No, I didn't."

"Yes, you did, 'cause I am yours. I am all yours, baby." Drea bites her lip. Thad licks his. "Let me make you dinner tomorrow."

"That sounds divine. But I'm flying to New York tomorrow. With Latrice going on her honeymoon, I have to represent the boutique at a series of meetings. One of the perks of being the co-owner but I'll be back for the Richardson Labor Day barbecue."

Thad's heart went from fluttering to slamming against his chest with a thud. "Drea, baby, that's in two weeks. I don't know how I'mma cope."

"You're so sweet. Don't worry, we'll FaceTime every night, and it's only two weeks."

He lets out a pained groan.

"You want to go another round?"

"You know I do." He pouts.

Drea sticks a finger in his dimples. "I love you."

"I love you too, baby."

They kiss.

1

THAD

Thad takes a seat on his bed and hops on FaceTime to talk to Drea. She's due back from New York in a week, and the two of them have talked liked this every night for the past six days. The good news is she won't have to travel for a while after this trip. According to Drea, Latrice lined up a lot of meetings with some up-and-coming designers before she and Nathan left, but most can be done via Zoom. She sent Thad a text earlier today from Mexico telling him how happy she is that he and Drea are together. When he and Drea returned, they looked more than a little rumpled and it was obvious what they had been up to. The good news is that Quincy was asleep by then. Aside from Nadia—who took over for DJ duty—playing "About Damn Time" by Lizzo, after they told everyone they were finally a couple, none of Latrice and Nate's thunder got stolen. Latrice had been right. Folks had been happy for them, but the focus remained on the newlyweds.

Drea answers his call with her ass in the camera, twerking. Thad bows his head in laughter. "You tell a woman you love her ass once and she's got her booty in the camera. Heathen!"

"Shut up. You love it."

"You're right. I do love it. I'mma eat that thang when you get home."

"Is that so?"

"Yes, baby, that is so. I'mma take off every stitch of your clothing, I'mma bend you over then I'm going to town on your ass and your pussy."

"You're so nasty, Thad."

"Shut up. You love it." He growls.

They both laugh. Drea takes a seat. Her small box braids are down, and she's wearing a short multicolored kaftan. They look at each other in silence for a bit before he breaks their trance by winking at her, which causes her to giggle. Drea's smile dies, and she whispers, "I miss you."

"I miss you, too, but it's okay. You'll see me in seven days. It will go by in a breeze."

"Is that what you've been telling yourself?"

"Yes."

"Is it working?"

"No," he replies. They laugh some more. Drea takes her laptop from the hotel desk to her bed and sits crisscross applesauce. "Have you eaten today?" he asks.

"I just ordered room service before you called. Thad, I swear that was just *one* time."

Early last week, she made the mistake of telling him she hadn't eaten since the bagel she had for breakfast. At the time, it was nine at night in Los Angeles, making it midnight where she was. Thad is one of those dudes who will tell a woman to go eat her hard-headed ass some food or he will cook something and bring it to her. He immediately told her to call room service and get some food.

"Sure it was. The minute you land, I'm cooking you dinner."

"I fly back on Labor Day morning. After a shower and a nap, I'm heading to your parents' house, so technically, Poppa Earl is cooking me dinner."

"And who do you think is going to be working the smoker, my love?"

Drea's eyes light up. "You're busting out a new smoker!"

"Yes, ma'am."

There's a knock on the door. "Be right back." Drea hops off the bed and leaves. Seconds later, she's back. She moves the laptop to a nearby table where the hotel attendant placed her food.

"And what is that you're dining on, my dear?"

"Lobster ravioli."

"Remind me to take you to Tony's in San Pedro. They have some of the best ravioli I've ever had, and it comes in so many different varieties. I'm partial to the spinach one."

Drea chuckles.

"What's so funny, baby?"

"You. I swear you always know of places to eat. Someone could have a random food craving and you'd immediately know where they should go. I could say that I really want some Mauritian cuisine and you'll be like, 'I know a place near Crenshaw.' And the whole time I'm thinking, how? How does he know this?" Drea laughs.

Thad joins in her laughter. His shoulders shake, and he tries to catch his breath. When finally does, he tells her, "I actually do know a place, but it's near Slauson—and not Slauson and Crenshaw."

Drea rolls her eyes and smiles. "We were talking about the smoker."

"Yep. Just got it and a brick pizza oven."

"I love that you collect food-related stuff and actually use it. My dad bought tons of shit off the Home Shopping Network and never used any of it."

Thad chuckles. "That smoker is going to get plenty of use."

"I really do enjoy your meat in my mouth, Thad." Drea takes a bite of ravioli.

"You see now, you say stuff like that, knowing that I can't do anything to you." He shakes his head.

"What? All I said was that I love the taste of your thick, juicy meat." She sips some sparkling water.

"Don't test me, Drea." He squints at her. "Stop acting like I won't hop on a plane right now."

She laughs. "I can't help it. You bring out my inner slut."

"Do I?" Thad smirks.

Drea smiles brightly and nods.

Thad grins as she finishes her dinner. "How would you rate the lobster ravioli?" he asks.

"Not bad. They were generous with the lobster, which I'm happy about. There were big chunks in the pasta and in the dish itself, but the sauce was a little too thin. I wish it had been thicker and creamier like mine." Drea takes another sip of water.

"I love it when you talk like a judge on a food show." Thad's voice is playfully low and husky. Drea laughs. "Wait, what do you mean, thicker and creamier like yours?"

"My sauce."

"What'chu mean *your* sauce? Drea, are you telling me you can cook?"

"Yep. I've been cooking since I was eleven. Olympia, my old nanny, taught me."

"I cannot wait to try your food."

"Next time we fuck, which will be the next time we see each other, I'll make you breakfast in the morning."

"Why, thank you, and I will make you dinner."

"It will have to be when we're at your place. I don't like other people cooking in my kitchen. I'm very particular about things. I like for things to be in their proper place. Having someone in my space really triggers my control freak. Pretty soon, I'm cringing at the amount of seasoning they use and fighting the urge to take over." Thad raises an eyebrow at her statement. "What? You knew what you were getting into when you got with me."

They both laugh again.

"Speaking of your nanny, I still can't believe you're a rich kid after all these years. Part of the reason it took me so long to notice you is because the minute I met your brother and your parents, I figured you were just like them, so I didn't bother getting to know you. You existed, but I chose not to see you."

"I guess I can understand that," Drea says. She's downplaying it, but Thad can hear the hurt in her voice.

"I'm sorry, Drea. I should not have misjudged you. I wish it hadn't taken me so long to see how amazing you are, and I wish my fear of getting hurt hadn't been so strong. I will use the rest of my time on Earth to make that up to you from now on."

Drea widens her eyes. "Wow. Thank you, Thad."

"It's my pleasure. So, now that we're talking about your upbringing, I've always wanted to know something, but I didn't want to offend you."

"Go ahead."

"Why do you still speak to your parents? They seem toxic."

"You've been talking to your sister." Drea smiles.

"I mean, yeah. I apologize, but Latrice and I talked about your parents once. And based on what she told me and what I've seen, they're awful people. And if I have to, I will curse them—"

"Whoa, whoa. It's okay. That won't be necessary. How do I put this? When it comes to my parents, I'm afraid your sister is an unreliable narrator, and I think that has more to do with how my parents basically went no contact with her when she divorced Mark. I know she feels some kind of way about it because they lessened their interactions with Quincy as a result. This has caused her to see them not in the most positive light. That extends to how she sees their treatment of me."

"Oh, so they weren't bad parents?"

"Not so much bad as misguided. Latrice, God love her, makes it seem like I was chained to a radiator in the basement or something. My father would encourage competition between me and Mark, but we were the ones who usually started it. Dad just used it to motivate us. But it stopped when Mark left for college. And my dad basically just began to ignore me."

"Why?"

"Because Dr. Greyson Johnson, renowned neurosurgeon, found that despite that big, medical, sciency brain of his, he couldn't figure out how to relate to a ten-year-old girl." Drea shrugs.

"So, his solution was to pretend you weren't there?" Thad looks horrified, making Drea laugh.

"Relax, Thaddeus. And not really. He just treated me like I was a guest in my own home. He'd ask superficial questions or would talk to me about the weather. I'm not kidding. He's done that a few times."

"Yikes! The nigga didn't even try."

Drea bursts out laughing. "He didn't have to. Our family dynamic was an extension of his and my mother's marriage, and like so many other marriages within the bubble of privilege they inhabit. It was all for appearances. They made themselves the envy of every couple in their social circle, while their relationship was rooted in nothing. Our family is the same way. And my mom tried to push that on me from a young age." Drea straightens out her posture. *"Honestly, Andrea, you're not going to find a man of any real quality if you don't watch those smart remarks of yours."* She does a perfect imitation of her mother, cracking Thad up. "I was thirteen when she said that. Thirteen!"

"Oh, my God! That's insane. But for real, baby, you sounded just like her. That took me back to Latrice's baby shower. I think that's the last time I saw your mom."

"Which baby shower?"

"The one my mom threw." He gives her a knowing smile.

"Oh, right. Yeah, that was an interesting day." Drea nods.

"Your mom seriously sulked the entire day because folks liked my mom's baby shower better."

"Vivian Johnson has been the belle of the ball ever since she and my dad got married. She and my father's parties are legendary for the amount of money and detail that they put into everything. The idea that she lost to a woman who made all the food herself was unfathomable."

"Yeah, we're going to have to keep them separated from each other when we get married."

"Is it weird that I can't wait for us to enter that phase?" Drea asks.

"No, not at all." Thad smiles.

"I can't believe you wrote a speech." Lance says.

A week later, Thad is on speakerphone with Lance Greene, his best friend since eighth grade. Lance is like Thad's brother. Him, along with Thad's cousin Kofi, are the reason Thad never felt bad about not having a biological male sibling. He and Lance been there for each other throughout everything. From talent scouts coming to see Lance in high school to Lance's retirement from the NBA. From Thad giving his first cut to him opening a chain of barbershops. These two are the definition of thick as thieves. Lance played for the NBA for seventeen years. He was a point guard for the San Diego Sharks for his entire career. Not long after he retired, he married his longtime girlfriend, Jesslyn. It was a quickie wedding in Vegas, and Thad was by his side as his best man.

Thad thinks how he is ready to take the next step with Drea. As much of a romantic as Lance is, Thad's surprised he's against him giving a speech. "Look, what we have, however short, has been amazing, and I know that I will spend the rest of my life with her. So, why not propose? And if I'm going to, I need to have a speech."

"But why, T? You're not accepting an award, you're asking her to be your wife. I say speak from the heart, and keep it simple," Lance argues.

"See, that's where you're wrong, my friend. Drea is an award. She's *the* prize, and I'm going to show her that real 'I love you, and I can't live without you' type shit."

"Swoon! Don't listen to him, Thad. That sounds beautiful," Jess says.

Jess and Lance got married only three months before Nate and Latrice. Thad loves Jess to death. She's his third sister and always has been. It's been this way since they first met. He loves how much Jess fits in with his and Lance's playful roasting.

"Thank you, sis. Tell your man I'm trying to give this woman some romance."

"Romance is fine. You know I love, *love*. Which is why I think you should speak from the heart."

"We'll see."

Thad pulls up to his parents' house and takes his phone out of its holder, which is attached to the console, before exiting and opening the trunk to unload the marinating meat. Lance pulls up, parks next to him and gets out of the car. They greet each other with a half handshake, half hug. Lance is here early to help assist with the cookout. Since retiring, he has a lot of time on his hands, and he's been reconnecting with family and friends he hasn't seen in a while. Back in the day when they were kids, Thad and Lance would assist Earl on the grill. Lance asked if he could help out, and Earl, of course, agreed.

"You two are ridiculous. You knew you were going to see each other and still talked on the phone," Jess teases.

"Yeah," Lance answers as Thad nods. Both men look at her like they don't understand her point, causing her to erupt in laughter.

Lance helps Thad take in the meat. They head straight for the backyard, making a stop in the kitchen to greet Thad's mother and sisters, who are hard at work with the side dishes. Nay Nay's been assigned potato salad. Latrice is making corn salad, and his mom works on the baked beans with brown sugar and bacon. Thad and Lance place each Tupperware container on the picnic table closest to Earl before they head back in to properly greet the ladies.

"Hello, Momma." Thad kisses his mother, Janet, on the cheek. "Hello, sisters." He kisses Latrice on the forehead, then Nadia. Lance repeats these actions, saying hi as well. All three ladies smile as the men return to Earl and the meat.

Earl immediately starts giving orders. "Thad, get that chicken into the smoker. Lance, the grill is plenty hot. Start getting those ribs on."

"Yes, sir," the men say.

Hours later, after giving his assistance, Lance is relegated to a guest by order of Janet Richardson. Thad, being Earl's son, wasn't relieved of his duties, but that was fine. He loves being out in the backyard with his dad, grilling and smoking meat. He's been assisting him on the grill since he was ten years old. And next year, they'll both start teaching Quincy.

Thad heads into the kitchen to get himself and his father something to drink when he sees couples—sans Nadia—cuddled up. His father enters, washes his hands and takes his drink. "What's up, Thad?" Earl asks.

"Nothing, Pop, just noticed that, except for me and Nay Nay, everyone here is married." He smiles. "It's a club I'm looking forward to becoming a member of."

Earl smiles back at him. Thad knows he doesn't need to say any more. His father gets it.

"Well, your future wife should be here any minute. No worries, son. You'll be where all of us are soon enough." He pats Thad's shoulder.

"Thanks, Pop."

Earl nods his head and joins his wife in the living room, kissing Janet on the cheek. Meanwhile, Latrice is lays on the couch getting her foot rubbed by Nate. Hell, even his noncommittal sister Nadia is texting someone and smiling a mile wide.

Thad takes the piece of paper containing his proposal out of his pocket to go over it one last time, when the doorbell rings. Nay Nay lets Drea in. Thad and Drea rush over to each other, where Thad takes her in his arms and kisses her. She digs her fingers into his locs while he wraps his arms around her waist and kisses Thad on the lips repeatedly, like she can't stop. He doesn't blame her. He can't control himself around her, either. That's how they ending up fucking for three rounds in his car. When they break apart, Thad looks deeply into her eyes. "I missed you so much," she says.

"I missed you more," Thad responds.

Latrice clears her throat a few times before Thad turns to his family, who are amused by their blatant display of affection. Latrice is covering Quincy's eyes and looking at them like they've lost their minds. He has, though. Being around Drea makes him temporarily insane. He mouths, *Sorry* to his family, most of whom chuckle at his exuberance.

"Perhaps you two should go somewhere a little more private," Latrice suggests.

Thad turns back to Drea and lifts her up in the air. "Aiiieee!" she squeals as he throws her over his shoulder. Drea told him that she tended to date strong niggas 'cause she likes being picked up.

Shit, say less. "If you'll excuse us, we're going to follow Trice's advice. We'll be right back," Thad says. As he walks out the door, he hears his family laughing, making him grin.

2

THAD

Thad and Drea walk hand in hand to a nearby neighborhood park. Thad thought that since their first time making love was at a park, what better place to propose? He finds a secluded corner that offers views of the grassy hills, and they take a seat on the bench. She rests her head on his shoulder.

"How was your shower and nap?" he asks.

"Blissful. Catching early flights are never fun for me."

Thad turns his head and kisses Drea on top of hers.

"I thought you were taking me to your car so we drive somewhere *private*." She purrs.

"I'm afraid that's going to have to wait until after we leave my parents' house."

She lifts her head and looks at him. "It's okay, I can be patient. Besides, your dad's barbecue is no consolation prize. I'm winning either way." Drea isn't wrong. Earl Richardson has won prizes for his barbecue. Lance always joked that Poppa Earl should have stopped being a CPA and opened a barbecue joint.

"Drea," Thad says.

"Mmmm, Thad." Drea sighs, making him chuckle.

"I actually wanted to ask you something, baby. I wasn't just saying your name." Thad gazes at her.

"Oh, sorry." She giggles.

"No worries." Thad takes a deep breath. "Drea, I —uh, hold on." He takes out his prepared remarks.

"This must be serious. You actually wrote down what to say," she teases.

"Yeah, I did." He chuckles and looks down at the paper. *Shit, why didn't I memorize this, and two paragraphs! What the fuck was I thinking?* Thad fiddles around with the paper, then looks up at Drea. She gives him a toothless smile. *She is so beautiful.* He remembers Lance's word, urging him to speak from the heart. "Drea, will you marry me?" he asks, hoping she doesn't notice the jitteriness in his voice.

She looks at him with soft eyes. "Only on one condition."

He takes her hand and kisses it. "Name it, my love."

"That we get married as soon as possible."

"Done."

He takes a ring out of his pants pocket and places it on her ring finger. It's a heart-shaped purple diamond with white diamonds around the silver band. "Thad. Oh, my God! It's beautiful." Drea sighs. "This is incredible and so much better than when I used to have my Ken doll propose to my Barbies. He had a lot of wives. I only had one Ken."

Thad just listens. He loves hearing Drea talk, no matter the context.

She continues. "I wanted his last wife to be an Ava Love doll. I desperately wanted an Ava Love doll, but my mom said she was too expensive, as if we weren't rich. I sound like such a spoiled brat right now, don't I?" Tears form in her eyes. "I'm just rambling. I'm sorry. I'm just so happy. I can't believe we're engaged."

"You don't have to apologize, baby," Thad assures her.

She climbs into his lap and kisses him. There's no one around, so she brushes her tongue against his lips. He's all too eager to open his mouth. Drea's kisses make him high and a little dumb, because why are they thinking of making out in the middle of a park? A woman pushing a toddler in a stroller walks by. "Get a room."

They immediately break apart.

"Sorry, we just got engaged," Drea calls back.

"Congratulations, now get a room," the woman says over her shoulder.

Drea cringes in embarrassment. "Let's go back to your parents' house."

"Yeah." Thad nods and takes her hand.

He opens the door to his parents' house and sees his family laughing, joking and eating in the back-yard. They enter. "Yo, y'all couldn't wait until we got back?" Thad asks.

"We had no idea how long you were going to take," Latrice says.

"Point taken. Well, since everyone is here, Drea and I wanted to let you all know that we're getting married."

Lance jumps up and cheers, "Yes!" until he sees everyone has stopped what they're doing and is staring at them. He sits back down quickly.

"Wow, that was quick," Latrice finally says.

"Let me know when you want to set up a prenup," Nadia says. Latrice looks at her with an expression that says, *Really?*

"What? Who says I can't help family and get paid while doing it?"

Momma Janet gets up and walks over to address them. "I don't know, you two… It seems awful sudden. I mean, hell, you've only really been together for two weeks, and Drea was in New York the whole time."

"Mom, this is what we want. We love each other and want to spend the rest of our lives together. We don't want to waste any more time," Thad explains.

"Well then, I guess you two have my blessing. I swear you kids make everything so urgent. Latrice couldn't wait until the end of the school year to be with Nathan, and now you two are getting married." Janet turns to Nadia. "I have no idea what you're cooking up, but I've seen you snickering at your phone all day, and frankly, I'm terrified."

"I'm not going to do anything, Momma. At least not anything you'll find out about." Nadia mumbles the last part.

"What was that?" Momma Janet asks.

"Nothing. Thad and Drea are engaged, let focus on that." Nadia grins.

Momma Janet rolls her eyes and turns her attention back to Thad and Drea. "I don't know when you two plan to do this, but I'll be there." She heads back to her seat.

Thad can tell she's still not totally on board, but she's trying to be supportive. He looks over at Drea, and she smiles at him and winks.

"You know, Momma Janet, the sooner Thad and I get married, the sooner you get more grandbabies," Drea mentions casually.

Momma Janet turns around.

"You got her, baby. Keep going," Thad encourages Drea.

"Picture it, Momma J, a beautiful brown-skin cutie with Thad's dimples and my eyes."

Momma Janet cups her hands together. "You two have already talked about having kids?"

"Yep. We want to be married for at least a year before we start trying. And we both want two kids."

"A year? Suppose you two end up engaged for eighteen months? That could mean close to three years before I get my grandbaby."

"Well then, it's a good thing we're getting married in three weeks," Thad says.

Again, everyone is stunned into silence.

Thad and Drea talked on the way back to his parents' house. They discussed the basic stuff they assumed the family would ask about, like kids, whose house they'd live in, insurance, updating wills, etc. They have already started getting their ducks in a row and are going to continue combining their lives while planning a small ceremony. Aside from their eagerness to be husband and wife, Drea wants to avoid her mother's inevitable interference. She told Thad that if they had a long engagement, her mother would wedge her way in and take over. They both agreed on something simple and casual.

"Three weeks? Do you two even have a venue booked?" Latrice asks.

Thad looks at Lance. "Hey, L and Jess, can we get married at ya'll house?"

"Sure," Jess answers.

"Yeah, no problem." Lance shrugs.

"Venue booked." Thad smiles.

"Catering?" Nadia asks.

"L?" Thad looks at his best friend.

"No problem. I'm the best man, I got you covered. All you and Drea will need to do is figure out what you're both wearing and show up," Lance assures him.

"Cool," Thad says before turning to his family. "Any more questions?"

"So does this mean that once you're married in three weeks and have been married a year, you going to get started on my grandbaby?" Momma Janet asks.

"Yes, Mom."

"Okay," Momma Janet says. Based on the excitement in her eyes, Thad and Drea know they've secured her blessing.

Poppa Earl stands and raises his glass. "I would like to propose a toast to my son, Thaddeus, and my future daughter, Drea. Your love story is only beginning, and may it last a lifetime. Cheers."

"Cheers!" Everyone toasts except Thad and Drea, who are both beaming and cuddled against each other.

"Now, you two, get some food and take a seat," Poppa Earl instructs them.

The happy couple does as he says and sits next to each other. Thad takes Drea's hand and kisses it. She leans into him, snuggling close. He has never been happier.

3

THAD

T had and Drea burst through the front door of Drea's condo, frantically kissing. On the way there, she massaged his dick and balls through his jeans, so Thad is definitely ready to go. His lips are on Drea's neck as she punches in the code for her alarm system. His hands are on her ass. Her full and plentiful ass. Drea unbuckles his pants and pulls his jeans and boxers down. He undoes her jeans and pulls them down before she gets on her knees and swallows Thad's dick.

"Oh, shit, Drea!" Thad shouts. Her head bobs as she sucks his soul out of his body. Thad's hands go to the sides of her head, and he fucks her mouth. This results in Drea grabbing Thad's ass and squeezing his cheeks. "Uh, shit. Uhhhh..." Thad moans. Drea's aggression is a huge turn on. And all respect to Kirk Franklin but Drea's moans are the only melodies from heaven.

She pulls his dick out of her mouth. "I can't get over how sweet your come tastes."

"It must be my diet."

Drea licks the veins along his shaft making Thad shiver. "Fuck, baby. Damn, that feels amazing. You have a very skilled mouth, my love."

"Thank you." Drea smiles before heading back for more. She sucks the head of his dick.

"Uh, goddamn. Drea, please let me fuck you," Thad begs.

She backs up and removes her pants and under-wear. She takes his hand and turns, leading him upstairs to her room. Halfway up the stairs, Thad gently wraps his arms around Drea's thighs and bites into each ass cheek.

"Ahhh!" she squeals, then giggles. "Thad!"

"Mmmm. I told you, baby, I was going to eat your ass and your pussy, and I intend to do just that."

"I thought you wanted to fuck me."

"I do, but *goddamn*." He rubs her ass cheeks and gives them a nice smack. Drea clenches her cheeks and giggles. "You gotta big ass booty and a pretty, slick, wet pussy. You make me so fucking hard,

Drea." He licks her pussy from the back before he bites her cheeks again. *Fuck, she tastes so good!* He eats Drea's pussy like a buffet.

"Thad! Thad, oh my God. Thad!" Drea clutches onto a stair. He travels all over Drea's pussy. First starting at her folds, then tickling her clit, before his tongue is inside her. He tongue fucks her repeatedly, quickening his speed. "Oh, fuck! I'm going to come!" she whines.

Something about hearing her sound so turned on brings out an animalistic side to him. "I'mma bout to make you come hard as fuck. You heard me, Drea?"

"Yes!" He spreads her ass cheeks before he sticks his tongue in and licks her asshole. "Oooo, shit. Thad."

"You like it, baby?"

"Hell yes!"

Thad goes back to her pussy and sucks on her clit before tickling and blowing on it.

"Suck on it again."

"Yes, ma'am." Thad sucks on Drea' s ripe, juicy fruit. He always knew her pussy would taste good, but damn! And she smells like heaven. He's ready to fuck her until she passes out. His dick is so hard it hurts.

"Fuck, fuck. Thad, Thad, Thad!" Drea screams.

Thad licks up her pussy and inner thighs before wiping his beard. He inhales the scent of Drea on his face. With renewed vigor, he rises and picks her up. He carries her up the remaining stairs to her bedroom.

"I love it when you pick me up," Drea says weakly.

"I know you do, baby. I'm going to lay you on the bed, then we gon' get started. Remind me to get you a bottle of water after."

"Thank you. I was rather parched after our first time."

"Yeah, when you guzzled down that glass of water the bartender gave you, I made a mental note to have some on hand for you."

"Awww, that's so sweet. And you won't even have to leave my room. I have a mini fridge in there. I tend to get thirsty at night."

"Noted." Thad leans in and kisses her. His tongue gently collides with hers. Their tongues glide along one another in syncopation. He can't stop. Her lips feel too good, her mouth tastes too good. Eventually, he manages to stop. His head feels light, almost like he's walking through a dream. Thad places her on the bed and climbs on top of her. He rubs the tip of his dick against Drea's clit. Closing her eyes, Drea moans. Nothing has ever turned him on more than seeing her aroused. Her breath hitches, breasts rising. Thad leans down and pops a titty in his mouth. Her nipples are so responsive, making Thad even harder. He licks the very tip of her nipple, and Drea's pussy throbs against him.

She widens her legs, giving him a better look. "You see that, Thad? My pussy needs you." She whispers the last part, and Thad's dick becomes harder than that shit Wolverine's bones are made of.

He slowly pushes his dick inside of her as she grips him, inch by inch. "Oh, Drea." Thad sucks in a breath then slowly breathes as the sensation of Drea's tight pussy surges through every nerve in his dick. He pumps in and out of her. Drea feels too good to move fast, and going too slow, at the rate her pussy keep clenching, might just kill him.

"Ohhhh! Shit, Thad. Mmmm," Drea whimpers.

She holds his arms and looks down, watching his dick move in a forward and backward motion. "You like how that looks, Drea? You watching my dick inside you?"

"It's making me wetter."

"I know. I can feel it. You keep tightening around me too."

"Faster, Thad."

Thad thrusts as fast as he can. Drea wraps her leg around him and thrusts her hips up at the same speed as Thad.

"Hoooo! Drea, sshhittt! Baby, your pussy. Oh, God. Your pussy!"

"Fuck me, Thad. This pussy is yours. No other man is ever gonna have it."

And that's when Thad goes ballistic. He picks Drea up by her hips and fucks her until her words turn into a series of blubbering sounds. She keeps saying, "Thaaaa…, Thaaa…!" He assumes that's his name. "Yes, yes!" She squirts all over the bed.

That is all the permission he needed. "Argh, Drea!" he comes.

THE NEXT MORNING, HE AWAKENS TO THE SMELL OF breakfast and the sound of music. Bacon and Jazmine Sullivan, to be exact. He heads downstairs and sees Drea throwing down in the kitchen. She's stirring some grits while Jazmine sings to ole boy, telling him that she needs him bad. She looks up and turns down the music as he descends the last stair. "Good morning."

"Good morning, my cocoa king." Thad raises an

eyebrow. "I was thinking that can be your pet name. No good?" Drea shakes her head for emphasis.

"Let's put that in the *maybe* pile." He takes a seat at the kitchen island.

"That's just a nice way of saying *no*. If you don't like it, you can say so." She adds cheddar and jalapeño to the grits.

"I don't like it." He pours himself some orange juice.

"I can't believe you don't like it!" Drea whines.

"Don't be one of those people, I beg of you."

"Relax, I'm kidding. It sounded wrong the minute it left my mouth."

"What do we have going on here?"

"I told you I was going to make you breakfast."

"Indeed, you did. It smells amazing." He snatches a fried green tomato before Drea can stop him. She squints her eyes at him, and he blows her a kiss, resulting in a smile from her. While Drea cooks, Thad takes in the decor of her condo. It has a color scheme of white, cream and various browns. The spiral staircase leads to floor-to-ceiling windows, a small table with a desktop computer and a small bookcase at the top of the stairs. Downstairs is a living room with a brown corner sectional couch, built-in bookshelves on the white walls and windows that bring in a lot of natural light. Across from the living room is the kitchen with an island and matching cream-colored stools. In between the living room and kitchen is another small hallway that stores another bedroom, another bathroom and a closet. At the opening of the hallway is the front door. It's not super big, but it's enough room for one person. And it's nicely decorated, very Drea. Classy, not showy.

He turns his attention back to her. The house smells like his grandma Hattie's kitchen. Drea opens the oven and takes out some biscuits. The bacon give way to sausage patties, which are replaced by ham and rope sausage. Drea piles on the meat, grits and fried green tomatoes. No eggs. Thad hates eggs. She places the plate in front of Thad.

"Bon appétit," she says as she pours him another glass of orange juice.

He takes a bite, and *holy shit*! He sops up some grits with the biscuit. Drea giggles at him going to town on his plate. "Mmmm." Thad licks his lips. Drea sucks in a breath and bites her lip. Thad looks up from his plate. "Quit playing with me."

"What do you mean?" Drea grins.

"I mean, making me this amazing-ass breakfast while wearing that silk robe showing off those lovely thighs and those beautiful titties, and you have the nerve to bite your lip too?"

"You think my titties are beautiful?"

"Focus, woman," Thad jokes. "You're about to get yourself into trouble, and I have to head to work—and so do you."

"I'm working from home. Can you work from home, Thad?" Drea pokes out her lip.

He leans over and kisses it. "Sure."

"Can you work from home all week?" Drea asks.

"Sure." He smiles. He'll have to juggle some things, but it can be done. There's no way he was telling Drea *no*.

"So, tell me, you've been to plenty of Richardson family gatherings. Why did you only bring wine? How come we never got to experience what Ms. Olympia taught you?" He cuts up his friend green tomatoes and eats several pieces.

"At first, I wanted Latrice and Nadia to like me, so I didn't think showing off in front of my new sister-in-law would be the move. Then, after a long enough time, I offered to make something and bring it over. Momma Janet said no. She told me I was a guest and not to worry about bringing a thing but my appetite."

"Sounds like her."

"And whenever me and the ladies hang out, we usually go to a restaurant or get food delivered. So, I only cook for myself and my neighbors, but I do have something in mind for you. It's in the fridge." Drea bites her lip again. Thad can tell it's from nerves and not arousal. *Damn, it's so fucking sweet when she does that. Acting all nervous like she thinks I won't like what she wants to show me. She could open that refrigerator door and show me a severed sheep's head, talkin' about, "I'm going to cook this for you." And I'd eat every damn bite.*

Drea opens the fridge and takes out a Tupperware container of chicken legs swimming in a marinade. She lifts the top of the container, and Thad is swept away by the smell of his mother's home country, Haiti. Thad, Latrice and Nadia went there only twice, when they were kids, to see a great-aunt and their grandparents, respectively. He doesn't remember much. But he recalls sitting on his grandmother's knee and hearing stories about the various gods and goddesses within Haitian culture, and he distinctly remembers the food. His grandmother making poulet en sauce, to be exact. The same Haitian dish Drea has in that container. "You know how to make Haitian food?" Thad asks, inhaling the scent of his roots.

"Yep. I learned how to make it last year. I hired a chef to teach me."

"You learned how to make Haitian food for me?"

"Yes. Just in case anything ever happened between us."

"Drea, I don't know what to say."

"Say you'll fill me up with your come after you're done eating."

"That goes without saying, my love. And can I just say how much I love it when you talk dirty?"

"I know you do."

"Say something dirty again."

"Clitoris."

"I was thinking of something along the lines of how good you are at claiming my dick."

"Why? Don't you like the way I say *clitoris*?"

"You're right. That is hot."

Drea laughs.

"So, what's the plan for today?"

"Doing our nine-to-five duties and updating more paperwork before the wedding."

"So, nothing fun today." Thad smirks.

"Au contraire. I was also thinking, in between our adult duties, we could fuck each other's brains out. Sound good?"

"Yep."

And that's exactly what they did all day. Work and fuck. They also ate and took a quick nap. They're currently lying naked on Drea's bed. It's now seven o'clock at night. Drea's head is resting on his shoulder. They both breathe in rhythm. He palms her ass as he turns his head and kisses her. Drea made salmon salads for lunch, and they ate the poulet en sauce for dinner. It was amazing! Add "can cook her ass off" to the endless list of reasons Thad loves Drea. This is his forever. She is his forever.

4

DREA

It's the day of the wedding, and Drea is in one of eight bedrooms at Lance's house that has been transformed into a bridal suite. While she grew up around money and opulence, this is a whole other level. Lance's house is like MTV Cribs on steroids. It's an eight-bedroom, eleven-bathroom estate that boasts a gated driveway, a custom chef's kitchen, walk-in closets, a private patio in the primary bedroom, rooftop terrace, theater room, wine cellar, an indoor gym, a spa—the ladies made good use of that the day before—an oversized pool, an outdoor kitchen and a guest house. The ceremony will be in the two-and-a-half-acre backyard that includes a garden so beautiful, Lance and Jess should charge admission to see it.

Latrice is placing baby's breath in Drea's hair. Her braids are in a bun on top of her head with the rest down, and the baby's breath is wrapped around her bun. Her wedding gown is beautiful. Thin spaghetti straps flow into a gorgeous gown that ends at her ankles. There's a slit up the side showing much thigh. It's paired with white stiletto heels. With the weather still warm and sunny, they thought a summer garden party theme would be nice. Drea told Latrice and Nadia they could wear whatever they wanted, and they are dressed in light blue and pink summer dresses, respectively.

Latrice answers a knock at the door. A server enters seconds later with some hors d'oeuvres on a platter. "Courtesy of Mr. Greene. He wanted to make sure you had something to eat before the ceremony."

"Thank you," Drea says.

Lance's personal chef made tuna ceviche, spring lamb pan-fried dumplings, bacon and rosemary stuffed mushrooms and mini king crab frittatas just for the bride and her girls. Servers will offer guests a wholly different menu of hors d'oeuvres before and after the ceremony to be paired with their dinner. This was Drea's idea. She has attended far too many weddings where the couple scheduled the serving of food way too far into the reception.

Latrice finishes and looks at her work. "Nay Nay, what do you think?" she asks.

Nadia's looking at her phone, giggling, while Latrice and Drea stare at her. She finally glances up. "What are ya'll looking at?" Nadia's eyebrows are raised.

"I asked you what you think of Drea's hair."

"Oh." She puts her phone away. "It's nice. Looks good."

"Wow." Latrice laughs.

"What's so funny?" Nadia asks.

"How transparent you're being. You were obviously talking to a man," Drea says.

Rachel knocks on the door while opening it. "Oh, thank God! I knocked on like five doors. Why is Lance's house so damn big?"

"Because he's a retired NBA player," Nadia says, her tone dripping with sarcasm.

"It was a rhetorical question, smartass." Rachel takes a dumpling out of Nadia's hand and eats it, prompting Nadia to playfully smack her on the tush. Rachel yelps and everyone laughs. She heads over and hugs Drea. "Congratulations."

"Thanks, Rach."

"Of course."

"Nay Nay was grinning like a Cheshire cat and texting a guy," Latrice blurts. Nadia throws a pillow at her.

Rachel's eyes widen as she looks at Nadia, stunned. "Seriously?"

"Why are you all making a big deal of this? I have texted men before," she says with righteous indignation.

"Yeah, but never with a goofy grin on your face. Do you like this mystery man?" Drea asks.

"I like all the men I date," she snipes playfully.

"No, seriously. You know what I mean. Nadia, you date guys for a handful of weeks at most before you move on. We don't even know their names, and you most certainly don't giggle when you're talking to them. What's going on?" Latrice asks.

"Nunya business. And I'm sorry, but aren't we supposed to be focused on Drea? It's her and Thad's day after all."

"Oh, I don't mind." Drea bites into a dumpling.

"Well, I'm not saying shit." Nadia ends the conversation. "The baby's breath does look good, but I think hugging Rachel made it shift a bit. C'mon, I'll fix it, then we'll work on your makeup," she offers.

Drea goes over to her and looks around,

watching Rachel and Latrice chat. She feels at peace. She's here, about to marry the love of her life with the people she loves most surrounding her. *This is perfect.*

Momma Janet comes in and gives her a kiss. "You're about to become my daughter. You ready to be a Richardson?"

"Been ready." Drea smiles a mile wide.

<hr>

THAD

OUTSIDE IN THE GARDEN, THAD STANDS IN A WHITE button-down shirt, tan pants and brown loafers, ready to make Drea his wife. Lance and Quincy are by his side, while Nathan stands ready to officiate after volunteering to get ordained. As Thad's best man and venue host, Lance took care of everything like he said he would. Chairs, decorations, food. He really hooked them up. Thad feels lucky to have his brother by his side.

His dad approaches him. "You doing okay, son?"

"I'm great, Pop. I can't wait to marry Drea. I'm happy this day has finally come."

"Thad, it's only been three weeks since you proposed." Nathan chuckles.

"Okay, but if you count how long I've been in love with her—"

"No one is counting that. She didn't know, so it doesn't count," Lance chimes in.

"What? You think because you're letting us get married at your house and you paid for everything that you can say whatever you want?" Thad playfully furrows his brows.

"Yes, fool. That's exactly what that means." Lance shakes his head.

Earl pipes up, getting Thad's attention. "I'm glad to hear you're eager. Marriage is a lifelong journey. You cannot expect to be successful if you come half-hearted."

"Might have to have Poppa Earl officiate, Nathan, cause he's preaching today," Lance jokes.

Earl smiles, then continues, "You're about to become a husband, Thad. Do you know what that means?"

"Yes, sir. I do. It means I have to be ready to do anything for Drea, even lay down my life if necessary."

"That's it, son. No one is more important than the woman you love."

"You're right, no one is." Thad smiles and gives his father a hug.

"That's what's up," Lance agrees.

"You make sure you're that way with Jess too," Earl urges.

"Oh, no doubt, Poppa Earl. Jess is my everything."

"And I don't have to say anything to you. I've seen you around Latrice. You just continue worshipping my daughter," Earl says to Nathan.

"Yes, sir." Nathan laughs.

The wedding march music starts, and guests who were milling around the garden find their seats. Leticia comes out and drops rose petals on the ground, leading up to Thad.

"Uncle Thad, I forgot … What do I do now?" Leticia says.

"Just have a seat, sweetheart." Thad smiles.

"Okay." Lettie takes an empty seat in the front.

Next comes Jelani with the rings. He walks down the aisle, waving at everyone. He hands the rings to Lance just like they practiced. Lance gives him a high five. He smiles before taking a seat with his twin. Latrice and Nadia walk down the aisle next, taking their spot across from the groomsmen. The word for this affair is *minimal.* The guest list consists of Thad's employees from the barber shops; Ingrid, the sales associate at Mtindo; Leon, Amber, Shellie, Tyler and Momma Ernie, Tim, Eli and Rachel. Altogether, there's about fifty people in attendance. Funnily enough, most of the guests were just at Latrice and Nathan's wedding.

Finally, Drea comes down the aisle arm in arm with her brother. Mark hands Drea off to Thad. Thad and Drea smile as Mark picks up Lettie, takes a seat and places her on his lap. Jelani leans into him. He smiles back at his kids. He looks so relaxed and happy. All he had to do was lose that anchor he called a second wife, and the rigid, insecure asshole he used to be transformed into a kinder, calmer, happier person. Being the main cause of two failed marriages humbled the shit out of that brother.

Thad and Drea focus their attention on each other, and he takes her in. Drea looks like a vision in her white dress. The baby's breath in her hair makes her look regal. He takes her hands in his as Nathan speaks. "Dearly beloved, we are here to witness the union of Thaddeus Edmund Richardson and Andrea Michelle Johnson. We're skipping the 'forever hold your peace' part. If you have a problem with these two jumping the broom, take it up with someone who cares 'cause nobody here does."

"That's right," Momma Janet says.

Everyone laughs. It's cool to see Nathan come further out of his shell. When he offered to officiate, Thad was touched. He's pleased to see Nathan become part of the Richardson family so easily. He makes a great addition and is an amazing stepfather for Quincy.

"The couple has vows they would like to share. Thad, please go first," Nathan instructs.

"It was Quincy's fifth birthday." Thad turns around and smiles at his nephew. Quincy smiles back. "The theme was King Arthur. Quincy had just learned about knights and stuff. He was king of all the land, but he was unhappy the entire time because people kept pinching his cheeks." A few folks chuckle at the anecdote. "He'd had enough and proceeded to have an epic meltdown. I was all set to go into Uncle Thad mode and help Latrice out, but you came seemingly out of nowhere. And you picked up Quincy, and hugged him tightly and whispered something in his ear. He calmed down almost instantly. You stood and made a royal proclamation. You told everyone in attendance that they were not to pinch the cheeks of His Royal Highness King Quincy I. Everyone agreed, and Quincy enjoyed the rest of his birthday party. I tell that story, Drea, because that was the moment that I fell in love with you." Her eyes widen in surprise. "You probably don't remember this, but there was a moment when, after you calmed Quincy down, I approached you. And I know it sounds crazy, but I felt a—"

"Connection," Drea interjects. "I remember that was the first time we looked into each other's eyes. I know it sounds weird, but it felt like I could see into your soul. I felt warm, content, like I could—"

"Stay there forever." Thad finishes her thought.

Drea cries. "And it scared me. I had never felt anything that strongly for anyone."

"Me too. And it felt like it came out of nowhere."

Drea runs her fingers through Thad's beard.

She felt it too. Having her confirm it after four years makes Thad's eyes water. He had told nobody for fear that they would think he was crazy. *Hey, I felt this crazy connection to a woman I've known for years, and now I think I'm falling in love with her,* wouldn't have gone down as smoothly then as it does now. That moment was the first time Thad and Drea gazed into each other's eyes. It makes sense now why they kept getting lost in each other. Their souls bonded that day.

Thad wipes away Drea's tears. "Thad, you're too

good to be true. You're thoughtful, you're sweet, you're loving and smart. You're funny, and you have a magnetic energy that surrounds you. You're the person everyone immediately likes. And you're so unbelievably fine it's mind-boggling." Everyone laughs, and Thad grins. "I let the years go by, thinking there's no way I could be so lucky. When you told me you were in love with me, it was something out of a dream. That's why I told you I dreamed of you telling me that. I wasn't being hyperbolic. I have literally dreamed of this day and of you." Drea cries even harder. Thad takes a mini packet of Kleenex out of his pocket and hands her a couple. She dabs her eyes and takes a breath before continuing. Her voice breaks as she speaks. "Becoming your wife is a privilege and my greatest joy. I love you so much, Thad."

"I love you, too, baby." His eyes well up.

Nathan clears his throat. By this point, everyone is dabbing their tears away. "May we have the rings?" Lance hands the rings to Thad, who hands Drea his wedding band, and she slips it on his finger. He does the same with hers. It fits perfectly with her engagement ring. "With the power vested in me, I now pronounce you husband and wife. You may kiss the bride." Thad and Drea kiss and are met with hoots and hollers. "I present to you Mr. and Mrs. Thaddeus and Drea Richardson," Nathan announces. Everyone stands up and applauds.

THE RECEPTION IS IN FULL SWING, AND THE DJ PLAYS soothing music while everyone chats and eats. The guests are dining on the all-you-can-eat appetizers along with their choice of two dinners, prepared, again, by Lance's personal chef, Travis, and a group of culinary students. Those kids have bright futures ahead of them cause the food is immaculate: pecan-glazed fried chicken wings, roasted root veggie skewers, bacon-wrapped scallops and grilled shrimp in a white wine sauce. The dinner consists of a choice between a petite filet with a raspberry sauce, spring salad and roasted red skin potatoes, or roasted chicken, a pear and endive salad and buttery seasoned rice. Drea got the filet, and Thad chose the chicken.

Ras, one of Thad's newest employees, approaches them. He was recently paroled for grand theft auto. Thad works with an organization called Second Chances. He helps nonviolent offenders learn how to cut hair, and once they receive their license, he hires them at one of his shops. Working at We Cut Heads is a stepping stone for a lot of folks who end up working as a personal barber or opening their own shop. Thad's always looking for new and talented people to join his team. Ras may be his best hire yet. "Congratulations, Boss Man and Mrs. Boss Lady." Ras smiles.

"Thank you, Ras." Drea smiles back.

"Thanks, man. You having a good time?"

"Man, this is insane. I'm at Lance Greene's house. You really know how to hook your employees up."

"Just wait until Mel Sharp comes through. That's going to be a long day, but I know you'll be ready."

"Hell yes, I will. Thanks again for the opportunity, Thad."

"No thanks necessary. You earned it."

"Thanks, man. If you'll excuse me, I'm going to get some more of those pecan wings."

"Thank you for coming!" Drea calls out.

Ras gives her a nod of recognition.

THAD IS EATING HIS CHICKEN WHEN HE NOTICES DREA staring at him. "Yes, wife. How can I help you?"

"I love how you boost people up," Drea answers.

"I was just telling the truth. Ras is a skilled barber. I'll be sad to see him go when the time comes."

"You don't mind when your employees move on?"

"Not at all. I encourage it. Go out and find your way. If it doesn't work out, you have a chair and a station waiting for you. I don't believe in punishing people for wanting more."

She pulls him by his collar so they're face-to-face. She takes his fork and places it on the table. "You are so got damn sexy, Thad. Yes, you're handsome, and your body makes my coochie throb uncontrollably, but it's not just that. You're a leader. You're a brilliant businessman. You hire the best people to represent We Cut Heads. You take pride in what you do, and even though you're a kind boss, you make sure that what you built remains standing by not accepting any half stepping. Remember when we were all at the Park-Barrington ballroom for Momma Janet and Poppa Earl's anniversary party two years ago? I was in another room with Trice, Nadia and your mom. Your sisters hired someone to treat us all to mani-pedis. I was waiting on my turn, and I wandered out and found the room you and the other men were in. Admittedly, I left to get a quick peek at you, and you were running things. Your employees listened and respected your every word as they worked on your father and his friends. You were in charge, and it was incredibly fucking hot."

Thad stares at his wife wide-eyed and turned the fuck on. It's funny, Thad has been called fine and sexy by women pretty much since he hit puberty. Eventually, both words began to lose meaning. Some women weren't very creative when talking to him and the prettiest ones were usually the worst offenders. It was usually, *Damn, you're fine,* followed by them offering to go back to his place. Despite what some women think, men like to be wooed too, and a nice compliment can go a long way. Drea almost made Thad jizz in his pants.

"Hurry up and eat your food so we can sneak off to the guest house," he commands.

"You'll have to be quiet," Drea warns.

"I can be quiet," Thad asserts.

MINUTES LATER, THEY'RE IN LANCE'S GUEST HOUSE where they have been staying for the past two weeks. They put their respective houses on the market and placed their stuff in storage, a.k.a. one of

Lance's many guest rooms. They got to work the minute Drea accepted Thad's marriage proposal. Drea's condo already has a prospective buyer, and Thad's house is in the middle of a bidding war. They have their eyes on their dream house, and Charisse McGee, realtor to the stars, is in the middle of finalizing everything. The newly anointed Richardsons agreed they would rather have a house than a honeymoon. Lance got to work setting up a meeting between Thad, Drea and Charisse. She sold Lance and Jess their house and is sharp and stays on top of things. Thad and Drea are happy to be in such good hands.

Thad's pants and drawers are by his ankles as he holds up Drea. Her dress is around her waist and her thong in Thad's mouth to keep him quiet. She got the idea from the scene with Lem and Bird fucking in Big Momma's bathroom in the movie *Soul Food*.

"Uh, Thad. Fuck me harder," Drea whispers in his ear.

Thad pumps harder while groaning into her panties.

"How much time do we have before the cake cutting?"

"Two minutes." Thad gives a muffled response.

"You better make it count, husband."

He squeezes his hand between him and Drea, rubbing her clit while continuing to fuck her. Drea digs her nails into Thad's shoulder and breathes into his ear. The combination of her breath, nails and pussy are driving him crazy. She pulls the panties out of his mouth and kisses him. Every time he tastes her, it feels euphoric.

"Mmm..." Thad says, or at least he tries to since Drea's tongue is in his mouth.

Their kiss deepens. Thad communicates to her how much he loves her. Drea loves him right back because she sucks on his tongue in response. She breaks away. "Shit, Thad!" Hearing Drea scream his name is the best, but it's moments like this that Thad treasures the most. Hearing his wife quietly tell him how much he affects her simply by saying his name, that will always have him on cloud nine. She comes, whimpering and involuntarily shaking in his arms. Her pussy clenches and milks Thad. His come is captured inside of her, and they collapse onto the floor.

They get their clothes together, and as he's about to head back to their guests, she pulls on Thad's arm.

He turns around. "What's up, baby?"

"I just want to enjoy this moment with just me and you before we return to real life."

"Drea, as much as I'm loving this moment, too, there are millions more with just me and you awaiting us. Come on, let's start having them." He offers his hand. Her hand slides down his arm and wraps it around his. They interlock fingers and head to the next phase, together.

5

THAD

I t's the beginning of October and after staying at Lance and Jess' Thad is happy to be carrying the last box into his and Drea's new home. Charisse is a fucking wizard. She's *thee* realtor to the rich and famous and host of *Big Money Properties.* On the show, she gives tips on going to open houses and what to look for before you buy a home. She and her staff don't fuck around. Thad and Drea sweetened the pot after the initial introduction by Lance. They used their joint cachet with Mtindo and We Cut Heads and were set up with an appointment to meet with Charisse right away. Drea is gifting Charisse a discount on the latest creation by famed fashion designer Helena Dupar, and Thad has placed Charisse's husband in his coveted appointment book. This means only Thad will cut his hair, and Thad only cuts hair for a list of exclusive clientele, Lance being one of them. But it's worth it!

They told Charisse the type of house they were looking for and added that they wanted to stay in Thad's neighborhood. Drea liked the vibe of the area, and it's closer to her job and a lot of the family. Charisse came back two days later with the house of their dreams. Thad paid cash and denied Drea the opportunity to pay half. This house is his gift to his family, Drea and their future kids. He wanted to buy it himself.

And now they're moving their stuff in. A lot of stuff. Thad is looking around at the boxes and sees a huge sea of green dots. *Fuck!* He convinces himself the size of the house can more than make up for all the stuff they've respectively collected. The important part is they have a house. Thad glances around beyond the boxes and appreciates his new home. Natural light bathes the room, making the white oak floors appear to glow. He makes his way deeper into the living room and gazes up at the soaring ceilings before turning his attention to the floor-to-ceiling windows and a granite leather fireplace. The chef's kitchen is the house's crown jewel. As much as Thad and Drea love to cook, it will definitely be put to good use. He makes his way into the room and runs his fingers along the cabinets, also made of white oak. The screening room and game room are the noncooking crown jewels of the house. Thad cannot wait to host movie nights and play in the game room with the kids.

At the top of the floating staircase, there are five generous sized bedrooms with ensuite stone bathrooms. The way Drea's eyes lit up when she saw the bathroom in their main suite was what cinched it for Thad. He loved the house, but seeing how much she loved it made him put in a bid right away. Sliding open the glass doors that lead to the massive backyard, he looks at the manicured lawn, the saltwater pool and the spa. *Meditating out here is going to be amazing.* Thad and Drea have talked about taking over hosting from his parents when the time comes. The theater and the backyard did for Thad what the bathroom did for Drea. The thought of entertaining friends and family with barbecues, pool parties and movie nights fills him with pride. At thirty-five years old, he's been an adult for a while, but there's something about being a homeowner and a husband that—

"Thad!" Drea yells.

"Yes."

"Where are you?" she cries.

"I'm in the backyard. Are you okay?"

She makes her way to him, looking stressed. Her eyes are glassy, and her face is flushed. "No, I'm not okay. Thad, we have way too much stuff. We have to pare it down. All this clutter is giving me anxiety."

So, to no one's surprise, Drea's a bit of a neat freak. When Thad saw her condo, he figured her housekeeper must have been there that morning. Nope, her housekeeper hadn't been there in two weeks. Her condo was immaculate, and it's no shock that her old place sold quicker than his.

"Okay, well, let's just go through each box again and see what we need to keep and what we can donate. You wisely labeled each box's belongings, so it shouldn't take too long."

"Okay. Yeah, let's do that." Drea exhales. She looks calmer already.

She picks up one box and takes a seat on the floor. "Oh, these are my Birkins. They're not going anywhere." Drea delicately places the box where it was and picks up another one. "Shoes. I guess I could donate these. Hand me a yellow sticker."

Thad hands her a sheet of yellow stickers. He then finds some of his old appliances in a box. "I can donate this too."

"I thought we were keeping your appliances and donating mine."

"We can donate both. I was thinking about doing so anyway, and my parents gave us that money so we can use it on buying new kitchen gadgets."

"I thought we wanted to use that for furniture."

"We can spare to spend a little more. But the rest of it will go into a fund for our kids, just like we agreed."

"Okay. Jess was telling me about some of the stuff she and Lance registered for at Williams Sonoma."

"Cool."

"Honestly, that should make a pretty big dent in these boxes."

"You see, baby. There's always a solution."

Drea crawls over to Thad, who is now sitting on the floor, too, and wraps her arms around his shoulders. He stares into her beautiful eyes as she takes a seat on his lap and kisses him before running her tongue along the seam of his lips. "Alright, don't start nothing. You're the one who wanted these boxes out of the way," Thad says.

"Yeah, you're right."

Drea attempts to get up, but Thad grabs her by the waist and pulls her back. She falls on top of him, giggling. "Naw, woman, you ain't going nowhere."

"And who's going to stop me?"

"Oh, it's like that? You trying to challenge me?" Thad tickles Drea, then stands up while lifting her and twirls her around in a circle. Drea's laughter gets so loud, it fills the whole house.

Drea

After a month of marriage and living together, Drea's first official holiday as Thad's wife is today. Yeah, it's Halloween, but still, that counts. After spending a month combining their lives, they decided to forgo the harvest festival happening at Quincy's school tonight out of exhaustion. They plan to spend the evening watching movies and passing out candy.

Drea enters the kitchen to fix herself some coffee before she gets ready for the day. She looks at their living room, one of her favorite places in the house. She and Thad agreed on a coastal decor for the room, but loved it so much, they kept up the theme for the house. Bold aqua blue covers the walls. A bowl of seas shells is on the coffee table. Artwork of the beach and ocean from famed Black painter Lincoln Harewood adorn the walls. And pictures of Quincy, Jelani and Leticia are on the fireplace mantel. The whole room just gives off a relaxing vibe. That is, until Drea sees them. Three boxes.

One, two, three remaining boxes left in the corner of the living room, stacked like blocks. Three boxes of Thad's belongings that he has said he would take care of this week. It's been a month since they got married and moved in, and that's the last of either of their stuff. She wants to get whatever is in each box unpacked and put away, but Thad doesn't seem to be in as big a rush.

He enters the room from their bedroom, wearing a white undershirt and fitted jeans. *Mmmm, his muscular arms look—no, no, focus, D. Don't get all worked up over his body. His painfully incredible body. Just ask him why the boxes haven't been put away.* He smiles as he approaches Drea, picking her up and kissing her so hard she's dizzy when he's done. "What was that for?" she asks.

"I love you, no better reason than that."

"I love you too."

He kisses her again and again and again. Drea bites her lip. "Thad." She giggles shyly.

"I can't help it."

"So, what do you think if, after dinner tonight, we got the remaining boxes unpacked?"

"Baby, we've done a lot over the course of a month. I just want to relax for a minute. If you want, we can unpack everything this weekend."

Drea's not sure she'll survive over the weekend. Being around disorganization is no big deal to some people, but for her, it's chaos. Everything *needs* to be in its place.

Thad continues, "Relax. Now I'm going to make us crepes for breakfast." He does a really bad French accent, and Drea breaks her resolve and laughs. "That sound good, madam?"

She taps down her disappointment at being blown off. She just cannot fathom putting something off that you can do right now. But for Thad, putting away his stuff is no big deal. He'll get to it when he does. She plasters on a smile. The kind she used on dinner guests her mom insisting on introducing her to. She would never see most of them again, but no matter, *We must make the best impression,* her mother always said. And that shit stuck because the last thing she wants to do is annoy Thad, but she fears something worse than being blown off and that's having her feelings ignored. Drea shakes away that thought and instead says, "Sounds good."

6

DREA

It's early evening. Drea is at the boutique helping Tisha Moore pick out an outfit for the premiere for her film *Ice Storm* where she plays a meteorologist who has to save the world from a second Ice Age. It's one of those environmental action flicks like *San Andreas* or *2012*. Tisha has been dishing about the politics of Hollywood while Ingrid gets her measurements and Latrice and Drea show her various looks from different designers. Drea's phone buzzes and she quickly checks it. It's just the assistant to a client. Normally she wouldn't check her phone while helping another client but she was hoping it was her mother. Drea has sent numerous text messages and voicemails for a month telling her mother that she needed to talk to her and it was important. Drea wants to tell her parents about her and Thad but in person. And her mom not responding is making it remarkably hard.

Tisha's voice snaps Drea out of her thoughts. "The movie was supposed to come out in the summer, but the studio didn't think an action flick with a Black lead actress would sell. So, it was benched until February. I need to make sure whatever I wear on that red carpet stands out."

"Well, since the Ice Age is the theme, what about something with faux fur?" Ingrid suggests. Ingrid may work as a part-time associate, but the last thing Latrice and Drea wanted was for her to feel like she was *the help*. She's just as much as part of Mtindo's success as Latrice and Drea are, which is why they encourage her to give suggestions. "The fur can be connected to the coldness theme, and the faux part can be directed toward animal extinction, which is a huge issue related to climate change. You'll be seen as fashionable and aware."

"Ingrid, honey, I'm going to steal you from Trice and Drea, and you will be my new stylist," Tisha announces.

"As much as I would love that, I still have a whole year of school left, and I love my job," Ingrida replies. This isn't the first time someone has tried to poach her. She takes it in stride and gives the same answer. Latrice and Drea pay her an hourly wage she can live on, and she gets a commission for what she sells. And Ingrid can sell water to a drowning man. It also doesn't hurt that one perk of working at Mtindo is that she gets to attend events, premieres and parties as a representative of the boutique. Drea and Latrice have always been adamant that the store get all the attention, not them. Honestly, Trice, Drea, Nadia and Thad all have high-profile clients—they all should be more well-known than they are. But because they keep low profiles, they aren't splashed all over *TRNN—The Rich Nigga Network*. Drea still can't believe the company willingly calls themselves that. When Thad or Lance uses that word, the context is clear and they're typically roasting each other, but *TRNN* thrives on using it to get people to read their trashy yellow journalism about the Black wealthy and elite. Everyone, from celebrities to heiresses and socialites, are their targets. Drea wouldn't be surprised if the folks who run it weren't even Black.

"Well, in that case, how would you feel about attending the premiere as my special guest?" Tisha offers.

"That would be amazing! Thank you, Tisha."

They finish and get her premiere outfit ready. Her assistant will come pick it up after the alterations have been made. After Tisha leaves, the ladies pack up for the day since she was their last client.

"Well, I'm off to get Quincy ready for the festival before trick-or-treating. What's the plan for you two tonight, ladies?" Latrice asks.

"Thad and I are just handing out candy." Drea shrugs.

"And I'm going to head home and change. Me and some of my girlfriends are going to the WeHo Halloween Parade," Ingrid says.

"Be careful," Drea warns.

"We will be. No drinks from strangers, stay together and have fun. That's what my mom said this morning." Ingrid smiles.

"Oh, tell your mom I have the perfect dress for her and your dad's anniversary party."

"Thanks, Trice. She'll be so excited." Ingrid hugs her.

"How many years have your parents been married, Ingrid?" Drea asks.

"Twenty-five years. Just wait. Before you know it, you and Thad will be married that long."

"Hopefully, within those twenty-five years, I'll be

able to get him to finally unpack the last of his stuff," Drea jokes.

"As crazy about you as Thad is, all you have to do is wave that big ass of yours in his face and them ask him for whatever you want." Latrice chuckles.

"That's brilliant. I didn't think about doing that." Drea's eyes light up.

"Drea, I was kidding," Latrice says.

"Whatever, I'm desperate."

"You *have* to tell me how that goes." Latrice laughs.

"Yeah, me too." Ingrid grins.

"Will do." She nods in affirmation.

DREA ARRIVES HOME AND FINDS THAD ON THE PHONE as he sets up the candy to be handed out. He's wearing a "Thriller" T-shirt and some black sweats. He locs are held together with a hair tie. "Okay, Aunt Bebe. I'll talk to you soon. I love you too." *Aww. I love how much his family means to him. Stop it. Operation get rid of boxes, remember?* Thad gets off the phone, sees her and smiles. "Hey, baby. How was work?"

She looks at the three boxes and starts putting her plan into action. "It was good. Tisha Moore stopped by." While Mtindo doesn't go blathering about their celebrity clients, Drea figures telling her husband isn't a big deal. He cuts celebrities' hair too.

"Cool. I met her a few times. She's nice."

"Really? You met her?" Drea's voice goes up, something that happens when she's being nosy.

"Yeah, she even flirted with me a bit, but she's not my type."

"Is that so? So, Mr. Richardson, who is your type?"

"Well, *Mrs. Richardson,* I tend to like beautiful brown-skin honeys with small box braids, cute smiles and big booties." Thad smirks.

Don't give in to those charms, eyes on the prize. Time to get those boxes out of here.

"Speaking of which, wait here. Don't move."

"I'll be here."

Drea heads to their bedroom and changes out of her work clothes. She takes a shower and goes through her skincare routine before changing into a long-sleeve black lace bodysuit and nothing else. She lets her braids down. They look wavy after being in a big braid all day. She adds red lipstick, some black mascara and eye liner. Drea completes the look with a pair of black Louboutins.

She comes downstairs and finds Thad putting a

casserole dish with his baked pasta shells in the oven. He gets home at half-past four, while Drea typically gets home around six, so he's been getting dinner ready before she's home to not aggravate her controlling tendencies, but she cooks on weekends. *If only he could be this thoughtful with the boxes.* Thad stands up and sees her. His eyes look like they're about to fall out of his head. Drea heads over to the couch. Thad rushes over and sits next to her. She gets in his lap and turns around, shaking her ass in his face.

"Goddamn," Thad whispers.

Drea turns and smiles. "You ready to unpack those boxes now?"

"If that's a euphemism for sex, then, yes, let's unpack some boxes."

"What? No, Thad. The boxes that have taken over our living room."

"Wait, what? You shook your ass in my face to get me to unpack some stuff?"

"Yeah."

"Why?"

"Because, Thad, I can't live like this anymore."

"Drea, I told you we'll do it this weekend. I get it, baby, you like order, but—" There's a knock on the door. "I think it's our first trick or treater. You should put something else on."

"Oh, right." Drea runs to their bedroom and changes into some sweats before putting her hair in a messy bun and using makeup removal wipes on her face.

She hears a woman giggle, then Thad talking. "My name is Thad. I just moved in."

And what exactly does he mean by I *just moved in?*

"Oh, you're so close. I'm just down the street." Drea looks out and sees a young, attractive Black woman chatting him up. She has a young boy in a Ninja costume who looks to be close to Jelani's age with her.

"Cool. Nice to see more of our faces around here." Thad smiles.

"It certainly is." She eyes him as if he's a pork chop. *Okay, keep it in your pants, sweetie. I know my man is fine but have some decorum.* "You know I am famous for my blackberry cobbler. I'd be happy to make you some and bring it by to officially welcome you to the neighborhood." *Nope! Time to nip this shit in the bud.*

Drea takes her place next to Thad and says, "That sounds delicious."

"Oh, hi!" Ms. Thang's voice goes up a whole octave.

"Hi, I'm Drea. Thad's wife." She offers her a friendly tone along with her hand.

Ms. Neighbor Lady shakes it with her eyes looking like slits. "Nice to meet you," she says with no warmth.

"You as well."

She looks at the young boy. "Jarreau, thank Mr. Thad for the candy."

"Thank you," the little brown cutie says.

"You're welcome, little man. Happy Halloween."

"Happy Halloween, and welcome to the neigh-borhood…both of you."

"Thank you, Iona," Thad replies.

Thad

Thad closes the door and head to the kitchen. He opens the oven and checks on the shells. When he closes it, Drea is right in front of him. *How the fuck did she get from the door to here so quickly?* She must have been fueled by anger because that is exactly how she looks.

"Okay, Drea, if this is about the boxes, we can unpack them—"

"*I* just moved here," Drea interjects.

"What?" Thad asks, his brows furrowed in confusion.

"That's what you said, Thad. You said *I* just moved here. I was literally standing right behind you and you said 'I.'" Her eyes get glassy, and her lip quivers. *Shit.* "I'm going to lay down in one of the guest rooms. Please do not disturb me." Drea walks to the guest rooms. After a few seconds, Thad hears the door close.

Fuck. Fuck. Fuck! He feels like the biggest moron on the planet. Yes, Drea is a neat freak, and he should have known keeping the boxes in the living room would annoy her. He wants to go through the items in the boxes to determine what he should keep and what he'll send to his family in Kentucky. Thad, Latrice and Nadia have a loving relationship with their mother's side of the family, but everyone is so spread out it makes staying in touch difficult. But their dad's family is all in Kentucky, so they've always been closer to Earl's side. Thad has some WWII memorabilia from his grandfather. When he died, he left it all to Thad, and he's kept it pristine condition all this time. Now he wants to send some of it to his relatives. His Aunt Bebe wants to donate some to a museum opening in Lexington that's dedicated to Black WWII vets.

He's okay with donating to such a worthy cause. He just needs to figure out what he wants to keep. This is something he intended to do this week, but the shops have been packed. He's also been so busy. When the shops are full, he likes to stop by and meet the customers, and he holds weekly meetings with his staff at each location. He had to hold the meeting via Zoom for the OC and San Diego locations today while working from his flagship shop in Inglewood. In other words, he's tired, which is why he suggested the weekend. He wanted to surprise Drea by showing her what was in the boxes and why it was so important for him to go through them, but now she's pissed. And Iona's appearance didn't help. She asked him not to disturb her, but Thad has to do something. He pulls out his phone and calls his dad just as the doorbell rings.

He opens the door and greets a trick or treater and their mom. She looks Thad up and down, and he simply smiles and bids them goodnight. *Lady, please. I'm in enough trouble.* "Dad, are you there?" Thad asks.

"Yes, son. I'm here."

"Cool. Sorry, I had a trick or treater stop by."

"No problem. What's up?"

"Just checking in." He doesn't want to immediately tell him he screwed up. He'd rather work his way up to that. Unfortunately, his father knows him way too well.

"Son, you've only been married five weeks, what the hell did you do to piss that woman off already?"

"How did you know?"

"I can hear it in your voice. It's faint, but it's there."

"What is?"

"Heartache."

Thad fesses up. "I messed up, Pop. I told Drea I would finish unpacking this week, and I didn't because things were so crazy at work. And just now, a woman and her son came to the door, and I told her that *I* had just moved into the neighborhood. And I did it with Drea in the room."

"Drea is a neat freak, so I can imagine she's not pleased living with unpacked boxes. And hearing you not even acknowledge her to a new *female* neighbor couldn't have helped."

"Ouch, thanks, Dad."

"You're welcome."

"She wants to not be disturbed, but I want—"

"Then leave her alone."

"But—"

"Thaddeus, leave her alone," Earl repeats in an authoritative tone.

"Okay."

"I'm serious."

"I know. I hear you." Thad and his sisters know that when Earl uses that tone, he means business. They never push back.

"Good. When she's ready, she'll come to you. When she does, apologize, and explain yourself. Don't go getting defensive. Keep it simple. Apologize and explain. That's it."

"I will."

"Alright."

"Thanks, Pop."

"You're welcome. Good luck."

Thad ends the call, and the oven timer goes off. Just as he's taking the shells out of the oven, the guest room door opens, and Drea comes and takes a seat at the kitchen island. He honestly didn't expect her to come out this soon. She's only been gone for twenty minutes.

"Hey," Thad says.

"Hey."

He makes her a plate, then slides it to her. "I wasn't expecting you to come out so soon."

"Just because I'm upset doesn't mean I shouldn't eat. Besides, that smells really good."

"Thank you. I stuffed the shells with crab meat

and *scrimps*. I know how much you love them scrimps," Thad jokes. Calling shrimps *scrimps* with a goofy exaggerated Southern accent has been an inside joke between them for years. Drea fights hard not to smile. "You want to laugh, Drea. I can see it on that beautiful face."

"Shut up. I'm mad at you!" Drea whines.

"I'm sorry. For real. I know how much you like order, and I know I said I'd take care of the boxes this week. But work has been insane."

"Oh, my God! Thad, why didn't you tell me? I wouldn't have nagged you."

"Because I'm a man who doesn't like burdening his woman with small shit."

"You having a hectic life is not small shit."

"I guess. As for the boxes, they're filled with WWII memorabilia that I inherited from my grand-father. My Aunt Bebe wants me to send some of it to her because a Black WWII veteran museum is opening in Lexington, and she wants to donate some things. I wanted to look through the boxes before deciding what to send. That's why I haven't put anything away yet."

Drea drops her fork in frustration. "Thad!"

"What?" Thad replies, looking surprised at her annoyance.

"You can't keep stuff like that from me, either. Now I feel like a bitch for even saying anything."

"Drea don't feel bad. I'll take the boxes to the garage, and I'll sort through them later."

"Can I help you sort through them?"

"Sure. And about me saying 'I just moved in,' baby. I misspoke. I have been living alone for years. Saying *I* or *me* was just out of habit. It had nothing to do with you or us."

"I know. It still stung since she was so shamelessly flirting with you."

"I mean, she was just being nice." Thad opens the refrigerator and pours himself and Drea some blueberry-pomegranate juice.

"Um…no, she was flirting. Thad, that woman offered to bake you a whole-ass cobbler. New neighbors usually bring brownies or cookies. They don't offer to bake *whole-ass cobblers*. She was picturing you as Jarreau's new stepdaddy," Drea explains.

Thad chuckles. "Little man is a cute kid, but that was not going to happen. We're finally together. Not only that, but we're married." Thad shakes his head. "There's no breaking that."

"You're right, there isn't. We should work on making sure it remains that way."

"I'm listening."

"If we're bothered by each other's words or behavior we express how we feel and don't let it build up."

"Agreed."

"Also, weekly check-ins. Every Friday after work. We'll check in with each other, see how our week has been going. How does that sound?"

"Sounds like a plan."

"Good." Drea puts another shell on her plate and heads to the couch. "You coming? I thought we were going to watch a movie."

Thad smiles. "*The Blackening* or *Vampire in Brooklyn?*"

"*The Blackening*, please."

"Coming right up."

7

DREA

Drea squirms, her hips involuntarily rising from the couch to give Thad more access to her pussy. His tongue moves in a circular motion inside of her. "Mmmm. Fuck." Drea spreads her legs wider. "Thad. God, I love you so much."

It's been a couple of weeks since Halloween and their weekly check ins have been going really well. So, well that Thad now has her spread eagle in their living room right as they were heading out to dinner.

"I love you, too, baby." He licks her folds. "You taste so fucking good. I'm addicted to eating your pussy, you know that, right?"

"Well, since we were about to leave when you

lifted me up and carried me to the couch, I'd have to agree. You are very addicted."

Thad sniffs her coochie. "Smells so fucking good." He keeps sucking her folds before he starts fucking her with his tongue. Her inner walls clench around his tongue. He pushes inside deeper.

"Wooo! Fuck, Thad. That feels so fucking good, baby."

He pulls his head away and stands before unbuckling his belt and pushing down his pants and boxers. He thrusts his dick inside her slick opening and lets out a cry, "Ahh! Fuck, Drea. So. Fucking. Tight." Drea thinks he's about to pass out when he pounds her like he's challenging the IUD to do its job.

"So good!" Drea cries out.

"Careful, baby. You know what complimenting me does."

Drea gets a call on FaceTime. She picks up her phone and is about to silence it when she sees who's calling. Vivian Johnson. Her mother. "Oh, shit."

"I know, baby." Thad groans.

"No, Thad. I mean, yes, this feels unreal." Drea pulls Thad so he's pressed down on top of her. "Oh, fuck. Thad, make me come." He winds his hips as he sinks deeper inside of her, just like she likes it. "Yes,

yes. Just like that. Keeping fucking me like that." He keeps going. "Oooo, fuck. You're trying to get me pregnant. You said, *fuck that IUD*."

"It's not me, baby. It's your pussy. That shit's so good it turns me into a fucking animal."

Drea's phone buzzes again. "Of course she's calling right now."

"Who?"

"My mom."

"Do you want me to stop?"

"Not until I get what's mine. Keep going," Drea demands.

Thad fucks the living shit out of her. He wasn't kidding about that whole animal thing. Drea doesn't even remember how they got into this position, but somehow, Thad got her on all fours and is currently fucking her from the back and spanking her ass too. "Ahhh! Drea, your pussy is too good."

"Oh, Thad! Thaaad!" Drea comes all over his dick. He pulls out and comes all over her ass. That's the last thing Drea remembers before falling asleep.

After a thirty-minute nap, they are cleaned up. She has a bowl of peach sorbet in her hands as she and Thad sit beside each other and call her mom back. He changed their dinner reservation to delivery. They're waiting for the food, but Drea couldn't wait and needed something in her stomach to cool her off. That's what fucking Thad does to a sister. It depletes her calories while making her sweat. It's like a sexy version of HIIT except you have a massive, euphoric orgasm at the end.

"It's certainly about time you called me back" is the first thing out of Vivian Johnson's mouth. *Seriously? I've been sending you message after message with no response, but you have to wait thirty minutes and—ugh! Calm down, don't let her get to you.*

Her mother looks ravishing as usual, her hair perfectly coiffed. The side part is impeccable, not at all crooked, and no hair is out of place. She's wearing a bold red Chanel blouse with, no doubt, a black wrap skirt. Drea can only see her mother's upper body, but she knows Vivian's taste. Her mother's makeup is light but impactful. She always said, *Makeup is meant to enhance God-given beauty, not make it trashy.* A red lip, mascara and eyeliner are all it takes to enhance Vivian's beauty. It always baffles Drea why her father would ever cheat. It wasn't until she was older that she understood, in their social circle, the men cheated. That is just the way it is. Husbands and fathers make gobs of money and financially support their families, with the whole family understanding he won't be faithful.

Ms. Olympia made no disrespectful comments about Drea's parents, but she said something that stuck with Drea. It was probably the thing that most made her reject the life her mother tried to force on her. She took Drea to get ice cream one day after her etiquette class, and Drea asked her if she thought taking the classes would get her a husband.

Ms. Olympia smiled as she said, "I suppose they couldn't hurt, but no man worth your time is going to care about your posture, Drea. He'll care about what's in your heart. He'll recognize how blessed he is to have you and won't want you to get away." Ms. Olympia was married to a man named Mr. Jerry. That's what Drea called him. And he was the opposite of her father. Whereas her parents never showed affection, that's all Mr. Jerry and Ms. Olympia did. He constantly gave her kisses and hugged her. Nothing inappropriate, of course, just embraces to show her she was loved. While both her mother and Ms. Olympia have had a tremendous impact on how Drea looks at relationships, only one is sitting in front of her, waiting for a response.

"Sorry, Mother. I couldn't answer right away," Drea explains. "Wait, are you in a car?"

Drea looks at the scenery in the background and it looks familiar. *Shit, she's right down the street from us.*

Vivian ignores Drea's question. "There I was, enjoying a lovely lunch with Bernadette St. Charles. You remember her, don't you, darling?"

"Yes, Mother."

"Well, I was a having a delicious seafood risotto when Bitzy and I were interrupted by that harpy Alexis Stevenson. She came by under the guise of checking in on the upcoming fundraiser, and as she was leaving, she said, 'Oh, and by the way, Vivian, I hear congratulations are in order. My grand-daughter worked under Chef Travis Beacon at an event a month ago. Imagine my surprise when I found out it was your daughter's wedding.'"

Fuck, fuck, fuck! Out of all the people to tell her mother, it had to be her mom's arch-frienemy, Alexis. This woman and her mother have a rivalry that has existed for so long, it bled out into the next generation. While Drea and Alexis's daughter Bianca are not on friendly terms, the most that happens between them is shit-talking. Either way, their mothers are both fabulously wealthy, so they need to bury this beef. It's been going on for far too long. Drea planned on inviting her parents to dinner at the house. Then she was going to tell them in person. Her nuptials aren't something Vivian would be shocked by, annoyed but not shocked, but not finding out from Drea herself? That is a grievous sin.

There's a knock on the door. *Double fuck!* Drea opens it and sees her mother's longtime driver, Sid.

"Hello, Sid."

"Hello, Andrea." Sid bows his head and looks at Thad, giving him the same greeting. "Hello, Andrea's husband." Thad waves. "Your mother is in the car and would like to know if it's okay for her to come in."

"Of course it is."

"She thought you might say that and has the following reply: 'Are you sure, Andrea? I would hate to go where I'm not wanted. For instance, your new home or your wedding, apparently.'"

"She is more than welcome in our home." Drea fights the urge to roll her eyes. Her mom knows why Drea married so quickly. Hell, Drea's been threatening to get married behind her mother's back since she was sixteen. Her mother isn't hurt because she wasn't there. She's pissed because she wasn't there to control everything. But theatrics are Vivian Johnson's go-to when she's been slighted in any way. She has a permanent discount at one of LA's most expensive restaurants all because a hostess lost her reservation.

Sid walks over to her car that's parked outside their house and opens her door, while Thad and Drea stand on the porch and wait for her to make her entrance. If she had to describe her mother, she'd use the following description: One part Emily Gilmore from *Gilmore Girls*, two parts Big Dee Dee from *Half & Half*, and a whole heaping of Marian Gilbert—Whitley's mom—played by the incomparable Diahann Carroll on *A Different World* and a pinch of every Lynn Whitfield character.

Vivian exits the car right as a young man on his bike rides by. He's so busy staring at Drea's mom that he almost swerves into traffic. That is the pull of Vivian. Though she and her mother aren't super close, Drea is not immune to it. She finds herself wanting her mother's approval even though their values couldn't be more different. Vivian Johnson, quite simply, is a diva. Full tilt. Vivian completely ignores the scene behind her and walks up the stone walkway, approaching them. She's at the edge of the stairs when she looks to her left and sees Dr. Foster, Thad and Drea's next-door neighbor. He stares at

Vivian with an open mouth, mesmerized. She turns her head back toward them.

"Andrea."

Drea clears her throat. *Don't be nervous. Stand firm.* "Mother."

"Shall we go inside?" Vivian asks, without acknowledging Thad…yet.

They all walk inside, and Vivian immediately gets to work giving her two cents. "Your home's decor seems to have a coastal theme."

"Well, Thad and I both like the water, and we wanted our home to have a relaxing tone."

"Andrea, have I taught you nothing? Coastal themes are passé and they only work for vacation homes, not your main house."

"Speaking of which, Mom, how did you know where we live?"

"Another secret you kept from me." *Do not fall for her guilt trip.*

"It wasn't a secret, Mother—"

"Then please explain why I had to get your address from your brother?"

Oh, crap. I should check on Mark. God knows what she did to make him give her my address. "Mom, I called you and sent you text messages numerous times, and you didn't return them. I wanted to invite you and dad over for dinner so I could reintroduce you both to Thad and you could see our home."

"Reintroduce," Vivian repeats. She looks over at Thad. He smiles at her. "You do look familiar."

"It's nice seeing you again, Mrs. Johnson," Thad says, looking charismatic as hell. His smile is warm, and his voice is jubilant, but not overly so. Classic Thad. Charming to no end.

"Remind me of how we know each other." Vivian says, seemly unaffected, but Drea can tell a tiny bit of Vivian is impressed by him. Thad has a way about him that makes most people drop their guard. His looks certainly don't hurt.

"Yes, I'm Thaddeus Richardson, Latrice's brother."

"Oh, yes! Of course. The barber." Vivian takes a good look at Thad before speaking. "I suppose I should have had a second son so your other sister could marry one of my kids too. Seems to be a sibling tradition with you Richardsons." Vivian offers Thad a smile. It's bright and sweet, but underneath, it's cunning. Drea has to admit, no one can cut you down and look so kind doing it like her mother. It's like witnessing art. Too bad for her, Thad won't fall for it.

"I suppose it is. I guess that's a positive testament on how well you raised them."

"It is, isn't it? It's unfortunate that things didn't work out between Markus and Latrice."

While her mother is not a fan of divorce, she holds no ill will against Latrice. Drea always thought that, in her own way, Vivian admired Latrice's bravery. The good news is, now that Mark is a better father, her parents will get to see Quincy more.

"It is, but Latrice is happy, and Mark seems to be too," Thad answers.

"Yes, I hear she married a *younger* teacher. If that's not love, I'm sure I don't know what is."

"Yes, I guess that's true," Thad replies. Drea can see him realizing in real time that his mother-in-law is a lot to handle.

Vivian makes her way into the backyard. "Thaddeus, darling, is this an outdoor gym?"

"Yeah. I do weight training and yoga."

"My friend, Cathryn Dubose, just had the most incredible indoor gym built in her home. I'll have her send you the info."

"That's not necessary, Mrs. Johnson—"

"Thaddeus, please, I'm your mother-in-law. You can call me Ms. Vivian."

"Right, well, Ms. Vivian, I am perfectly fine with my outdoor setup."

Vivian re-enters the house. "Nonsense. Now, how many rooms does this love nest have?"

"Five. A main bedroom and four others," Thad answers.

"Why so little?"

"We think five bedrooms is plenty. Drea and I have a room. We're planning on having two kids. And Drea can have her own office—"

"But that only leaves you with one room. You have to build the gym there, so what about your guest rooms?"

"We thought one guest room would be enough."

Vivian lets out a disappointed sigh. "I don't know why you kids want to make things so much harder for yourselves. What's through here?" She walks through the entryway that leads to the home theater. She looks around and even tests the seats.

Thad turns to Drea and lowers his voice. "Is she going to go through the whole house pointing out stuff?"

"Yep, what she approves of and what she thinks needs to be fixed."

"She doesn't seem to be approving of anything."

"Exactly."

"You know, kids, if you're going to have a private theater, you might want to expand and add more seats. Philip Ashton just had a private party for his grandson, Ethan. They had a private screening of one of those comic book films. His theater seats fifty. How much does this seat?" Vivian asks knowing full well there isn't anything close to fifty seats in here.

"Ten." Thad replies.

"Oh, no. That won't do," Vivian says. She gets up and makes her way into the kitchen. She looks through the cabinets and the fridge.

"Mrs.…uh Vivian, can I get you something to drink?"

"I was wondering when you were going to offer, Thaddeus. Yes, I'll have something cold to drink, please," Vivian answers as she inspects the oven. "Your father and I just got a new oven. Multiple burners, a gas range and only twelve thousand. I can send you the info."

"That's not necessary, Mom, but thank you." *That actually sounds really awesome, but I can't let her know that. She'll make a whole production about how she was right.*

Thad hands her a glass of iced tea. He stands back as she sips it. "It's a recipe I found online. It's white tea with a touch of peach and a hint of strawberry. I hope you like it, and my apologies for not offering sooner. Your sudden visit threw me off. I assure you I have much better manners than that." Thad grins.

"I remember Janet and Earl, so I have no doubt." Vivian turns to Drea, looking more impressed…but only slightly.

God, I love this man. Keep charming her, baby.

Thad continues, "And as Drea mentioned, we would love to have you and Dr. Johnson over for dinner."

"Well, since you two decided to jump the broom, I wasn't able to throw any parties leading up to the nuptials. Nor was I able to give any input on the ceremony." Vivian's eyes are clearly on Drea.

"Honestly, mother, we didn't want to be a bother. Thad and I preferred something more intimate and small."

"I see, and this intimate setting couldn't have included your mother's input?"

"Mom—"

"No, no, Andrea, I'm sure Lance Greene's back-yard is just as opulent as the ballroom at the Park-Barrington in Beverly Hills."

"Mom, Thad and I wanted our own unique ceremony. Everybody gets married at the Park-Barrington."

"Not everybody. You know Sussy Van Horne wasn't able to get her daughter, Chenelle, in."

"Mom, stop gossiping… Wait, seriously? No, that's not important. Mother, Thad and I got married the way we wanted, and we knew that you wouldn't be open to that."

"So that's why I wasn't involved? Because we would have disagreed. Drea, we disagree on everything. That doesn't excuse you from excluding me." Vivian's eyes are downcast as she looks…hurt. *Shit. Well played, Vivian. Well played.*

"Okay, Mom. You're right. Thad and I are sorry we hurt you," Drea says with sincerity.

Vivian's eyes light up, and she smiles brightly. "Splendid. I'll be throwing you a newlywed party."

I should have known. I should have seen this coming. Why the fuck didn't I see this coming?

"Sounds great," Drea says, voice strained.

"Fabulous. I'll be in touch with the details. Thaddeus, the tea was delicious. Thank you."

"You're welcome."

Thad and Drea walk her to the door, where she's met with the delivery man with their dinner order. "You two ordered Vincente's for delivery? The ambiance is part of the dining experience." Drea takes their food and thanks the delivery man. "So long, children. I'll be in touch. Let's go, Sid."

Vivian gets in the car. Sid waves before he drives off.

"Why do I feel like we just got played?" Thad asks.

"Because we did." *Well played, indeed.*

8

DREA

It's Thanksgiving. Thad and Drea are on the road on their way to Momma Janet and Poppa Earl's house. Drea feels like a boxer on her way to the fight that could make or break her career. A few days ago, Momma Janet said the words Drea has been dreaming to hear, "Drea, you want to join us in the kitchen?" Drea put Momma Janet on hold and did a happy dance that made Thad look at her like she'd lost her mind. But she didn't care. She was joining the ranks of Richardson women, and she was going to the big show. Drea had to admit, she was surprised by Momma Janet's call, but then, she figured Thad must have said something. The weekends when she cooks have turned into his favorite time of the week. He is always gushing about how much he loves her cooking. And she is ready. There are grocery bags full of fixins in the back of the car.

Drea goes over her menu and calculates how long it will take Latrice, her, Nadia and Momma J to use the oven for each dish. "If the mac and cheese goes in by three, we should be fine. I can put the ham in while Latrice's dressing is cooking. The ham can be at the bottom of the oven and the dressing on the upper rack. Nadia's going to need the oven for her roast, so I should…" Drea looks over at Thad, who is trying not to laugh. "Shut up, Thad!" Drea throws a croissant at him. He catches it and takes a bite while continuing to laugh. They stopped to get coffee and breakfast for everyone.

"I'm sorry, baby, but I love it when you go full on super nerd. You start crunching numbers and shit. I love it! It's sexy as hell."

"So what? You want me to dress up like a sexy accountant and—"

"Dear God, yes!" Thad eyes Drea, taking in all of her at a red light.

"Thad, chill. We're almost at your parents' house."

"Hey, you're the one who put that image in my head."

"Do you want me to carry a ruler, Thaddeus?" Drea purrs.

"Stop that, Drea."

"You want me to tap you gently on the balls when you're being naughty," Drea says in a breathy voice, channeling her inner Marilyn.

"Wait, why do you have a ruler if you're an accountant?"

Drea switches back to her normal voice. "I don't know, just go with it." She goes back to her Marilyn voice. "So, how about it? Do you want your balls tapped, daddy?"

"Drea, don't make me pull over."

"Why? What are you going to do? Spank me? Is that what you want, baby? To get your hands on all this ass?" Drea licks her lips.

Thad hits the brakes, then pulls over into a mostly empty parking lot. "Get in the backseat," he orders.

She lets out an excited squeal as she follows his orders. He rewards her with a smack on her ass, making her squeal some more.

Twenty minutes later, Thad knocks on the door. Latrice answers, eating some grapes. She takes one look at them and shakes her head, laughing. "Drea, your shirt is on inside out, and, Thad, your fly is open." She chuckles. They both quickly adjust themselves. "Disgraceful. There is a child inside the house, you two," Latrice playfully chides as she lets them in.

"Please, you know Quincy's asleep," Thad says.

According to Thad, every year on Thanksgiving morning, while dinner is getting prepared by the adults, Quincy very happily goes to Thad's old room and goes back to sleep. Latrice doesn't even take the baby out of his pajamas. She brings a change of clothes so he can shower and dress once dinner is ready. Drea cracked up when Thad told her that. If it's one thing Quincy's going to do when there's no school, it's sleep in.

"Can you two go five seconds without fucking?" Latrice asks.

"Listen, we have time to make up for being scared and ignorant. Plus, we're newlyweds. And you've been doing stuff too. That's why you got that bun in the oven," Thad says.

Latrice rolls her eyes and heads to the kitchen. Thad and Drea follow. They find Nay Nay, Poppa Earl, Nathan and Momma Janet. "You pregnant yet?" Momma Janet looks at Drea like she's trying to spy a baby bump.

"Not yet, Momma Janet." Drea smiles. She looks at Thad, who gives her a smirk that says, *I told you so.*

The breakfast and coffee are disbursed. And

grocery bags are placed on the counter. Latrice and Nadia share a curious look. Maybe Thad told them about her cooking too. Her poulet en sauce has become one of his favorite meals. Drea's planning on making another Haitian dish today, griot. Along with mac and cheese, bacon-and-onion green beans and a ham. Nathan and Earl retreat to the den to enjoy their breakfast while the meal is prepared.

Momma Janet looks at Thad. "Well, go on, Thad. Go join your daddy and Nathan."

"But, Mom, I always help in the kitchen." Thad furrows his brows.

"Well, yeah, that was before, and now Drea is going to join us." Momma Janet gestures to Drea, making her smile.

"You're bumping me for my wife? But I'm your son." He looks pitiful.

"Yes, and thanks to you, Drea's now my daughter." Momma Janet turns to Drea. "Drea, baby, I even got you your own apron." Momma Janet picks up a folded apron and unfurls it. In perfect calligraphy, it reads, Mrs. Drea Richardson. Drea's mouth is agape, and she has tears in her eyes. She pushes Thad out of the way and hugs Momma Janet.

"Oh, my God! Momma Janet, this is so beautiful!" Drea cries.

"That is cold. Ya'll are some cold-blooded women." Thad snatches an extra croissant before he leaves. "If you'll excuse me, since I'm not wanted here, I will drown my sorrows in French pastries." The women all look at him, unimpressed by his attempt to gain sympathy.

"Where did you get this made?" Drea turns to Momma Janet, ignoring Thad.

"Cold-blooded! All of you, and, Drea…did you seriously push me? I'm your husband. What kind of nonsense is this?"

"Thad, stop your bitching, and go to the den," Momma Janet says. Thad shakes his head and leaves as Drea, Latrice and Nadia giggle. "Okay, so, Drea, we know you aren't that equipped in the kitchen, so we're going to start you off with something easy, dinner rolls. You can work your way up next year."

So much for Thad telling them I can cook. "Well, Momma Janet, I actually brought some stuff for me to make while you all work on your dishes."

"Oh, sweetie. That must have been Thad's for when he thought he was cooking. It's fine, we'll just make it." Momma Janet looks in the bag at the ingredients. "Thad was ambitious, wasn't he?"

"Actually, all of the ingredients are mine. I plan

on making mac and cheese, ham, green beans and griot."

Latrice, Nadia and Momma Janet all look at her. Their eyebrows are raised, their eyes wide in surprise. "Since when can you cook?" Latrice asks.

"Since I was eleven years old. You remember Ms. Olympia. I told ya'll about her."

"Your nanny?" Nadia asks.

"Yeah, she taught me how to cook. Gave me lessons for years."

"Okay, then, Drea, let's see what you're working with," Momma Janet teases.

"Yeah, rich girl. The daughter of Dr. Greyson Johnson who grew up with nannies, and designer clothes and ponies. Let's see you handle a couple of real cookin' ass bitches." Nadia talks smack before realizing she cursed in front of her mother. "Sorry, Momma." She smiles sheepishly.

Momma Janet rolls her eyes. "This would make for an interesting holiday. I say the three of you each make a side dish with the same vegetable, and we'll ask the fellas to decide whose is best."

"That works for me," Drea says.

"Cool," Nadia agrees.

"Let's do it," Latrice adds.

They decide on potatoes. Drea will make scalloped potatoes, Nadia will make roasted red skin potatoes, and Latrice will make garlic mashed potatoes. Now that Drea has one more side dish to make, she gets started on the ham.

"Check this out, rich girl. What you know about this here?" Nadia shit-talks while gesturing to the beef roast she's cooking.

"She don't know nothing about that," Latrice jumps in.

"Trice, are you two serious? Enough with the rich girl stuff. What has gotten into you both?" Drea asks.

"You're in the Terradome now, Ms. Drea. Me and Trice take this cooking thang seriously, and we intend to win," Nadia explains.

"But you're also competing against each other," Drea argues.

"Yeah, but for now, it's us against you." Latrice smiles. Both of them sound playful but serious. *Fine, if it's a little competition you want, let's do this.*

"Okay, may the best Richardson woman win," Drea declares.

"Oh, don't worry. I will," Nadia says, making Latrice shoot a squinty-eyed glare at her before Nadia's phone buzzes. She quickly takes it out and reads the message, smiling the whole time. She glances up and sees everyone looking at her. "Stop looking at me," she says, before returning her attention to her roast. Momma Janet, Drea and Latrice all snicker at Nadia's little girly moment.

The day goes swimmingly as the women find a rhythm as they move around the kitchen. Drea adds more water to her green beans as they cook on the stove. She adds more glaze on the ham before moving on to check on the pork shoulder for the griot in the dutch oven. It's almost ready to move to the parchment paper and be placed under the broiler. Drea places her potato slices in a circular pattern. It's a good thing she brought extra cheese. She moves around with purpose, completely shutting out everything around her. Cooking makes her feel at peace. Maybe it's because of how much love she puts into it. She has ear buds in and is going at her own pace when Thad walks in. Drea discreetly pauses her music when she sees Latrice pointing at her and looking like she's chastising Thad.

"Seriously, Thad! You could have told us Drea knew how to cook." Latrice smacks Thad's arm with a potholder.

Nadia chimes in. "Yeah! We're in here thinking we got her beat, and she's just gliding around the kitchen making dish after dish like it's second nature. You knew we'd get competitive. Why didn't you warn us?"

"Because it's funnier this way." Thad shrugs. Drea almost chuckles but doesn't want them to know she's listening. "Why are there so many potatoes?" he asks.

"We're competing for the best potato side dish," Latrice answers.

"Interesting. It's either going to be a tie or Trice will win."

"How do you figure?" Latrice asks.

"I'm going to vote for Drea's because of course I am. Nate and Quince will vote for you, and dad will vote for Nay Nay. The determining vote will be mom's," Thad explains.

That's right. If Momma Janet votes for me or Nay Nay, it will be a tie between either of us and Latrice, but if Momma Janet votes for Latrice, she wins.

Latrice has a look of determination on her face. She looks at Nadia and Drea, then mouths, *You're toast.* It was on! The kitchen turned into *Master Chef: Richardson Edition.* The ladies are shouting warnings to each other, "On your left, Trice."

"I need the oven!"

"Behind you!"

When the meal is finally done, the women have

created a feast fit for royalty. Turkey, collard greens, and baked yams courtesy of Momma Janet. A beef roast with roasted red skin potatoes and honey glazed carrots courtesy of Nadia. Garlic mashed potatoes, lemon pepper chicken wings and creamed kale with breadcrumbs courtesy of Latrice. And finally, ham, mac and cheese, griot, scalloped potatoes and green beans with onion and bacon courtesy of Drea.

After the ladies finish placing the food on the table. Momma Janet walks toward the den but stops short of entering it. "Alright, ya'll. Brace yourselves," she says to her daughters. "Fellas, the food is ready." She rushes back over to the girls just as the guys—including Quincy—enter the room. They all look at the dinner table and smile. "The ladies are having a special competition for best potatoes so don't be shy."

"My plate is about to be stacked." Thad grins.

"Okay, let's have a seat," Momma Janet says. "Earl, please say grace."

Everyone sits, and Poppa Earl leads them in a prayer. "Dear Lord, it's your faithful servant, Earl Richardson. I come to you again, Lord, with thanks. Thanks for my lovely family, which includes a new son and daughter and soon-to-be a new grandchild—"

"Or two." Momma Janet looks over at Thad and Drea, who give her a shy grin.

"C'mon now, baby, I'm talking to the Lord." Poppa Earl kisses Momma Janet's hand and she giggles. "We thank you for the bountiful meal we're about to enjoy and humbly ask, Lord, that you keep us united as a family for the rest of our days. In Jesus's name, amen."

"Amen," everyone replies.

Thad stacks his plate with everything Drea made because, of course, he does. She giggles at her silly husband and his sweet devotion to her. She stacks her plate too. Meal plans don't exist on holidays. When everyone is satisfied with the amount of food chosen, they eat in silence…almost. Thad makes "Mmmmm" sounds every other bite.

"Thad, we get it. You like your wife's cooking."

"I *love* my wife's cooking, Trice. Seriously though, you did your thing with these potatoes, baby. They are good." Thad grins at her.

"Thank you," Drea simpers.

"I like these green beans, Auntie Drea," Quincy chimes in.

"Thank you, baby." Drea beams at him.

"I have to admit, this ham is good," Nadia says with reluctance.

"I know how hard that must have been for you, Nay Nay," Drea jokes.

"Oh, my God!" Momma Janet blurts out. She looks at her plate and then up at Drea. "Drea, this griot… It reminds me of my mother's." Momma Janet places her hand on her mouth and holds back tears.

"Oh, Momma Janet. I don't know what to say." Drea's eyes water.

"Auntie Drea, you *Ratatouille'd* Gran Gran." Quincy smiles.

Drea turns to Thad with a huge grin. "Oh, my God! Q's right. I *Ratatouille'd* your mom."

"Okay, I think that cinches it. Drea's the winner," Poppa Earl announces.

"What? Wait, but the competition was for potatoes, Dad," Latrice points out.

"Tricey, everyone is praising her food, and your mother just unlocked a childhood memory after taking a bite. Potatoes or no, she wins," Poppa Earl explains.

"Fine, you win this round, Andrea, but just know that I'm coming for you," Latrice says, before taking a bite of what turns out to be Drea's potatoes.

Latrice closes her eyes. "Mmm. Mmmm!" When she opens them, she realizes what she's eating and looks up to see Drea, Thad and Nay Nay looking at her and snickering. "Oh, shut up! All of you." Latrice gets up from the table and stalks off, making everyone burst out laughing.

"Trice. Come back!" Drea calls out.

"Forget you, Drea!"—Latrice shouts back—"with your extra creamy, delicious potatoes."

Everyone laughs.

"If you're not going to finish your plate, Trice. I'm taking it," Thad warns.

Latrice immediately comes back and sits down. "No, you aren't. I'm pregnant, but I will fight you to protect this plate."

***

HOURS HAVE PASSED SINCE DINNER, AND EVERYONE IS asleep with full bellies. Drea wakes up from sleeping in the den with Thad. She's in his arms as he continues to slumber. They're lying on the foldout couch. Drea scoots out of Thad's hold and tiptoes to the kitchen. Momma Janet and Poppa Earl are in their room. Nathan and Latrice are cuddled on the couch, and Nadia's in her old room, probably texting her mystery man. And Quincy is back in Thad's old room. Drea opens the fridge and takes out two of the pies her in-laws got from Carver's Bakery. She carefully cuts a slice of chocolate pudding pie and a slice of peach pie.

She places them on one plate, then puts the pies back before grabbing a couple of forks and walking carefully back into the den, where she finds Thad awake. He looks over at her and smiles. "I was wondering where you went."

"Went to score some dessert. Which one do you want to try first?"

"Peach," Thad says. Drea hands him a fork. "I think that works as a pet name?"

"Peach? Really? You don't strike me as a peach."

"Naw, baby. For you. It works as a pet name for you."

"Because of my booty," Drea jokes.

"Yes, and because it's your favorite fruit."

"That's true."

Drea takes a bite of peach pie, then Thad does. They go back and forth between the chocolate and the peach. "How about I name you Chocolate—"

"No," Thad replies. "C'mon, Drea. I'm a dark skin brother and you love chocolate. That's too easy."

Drea thinks it over. "I'll think of something."

"I know you will. Drea?"

"Yes."

"You went in that kitchen with the odds against you, and you did your thing, woman. I cannot praise you enough."

"Thank you, Thad, but the happy noises and the dancing in your chair said enough." Drea laughs.

"I can't help it, baby. The gauntlet was thrown down, and my wife showed up ready and won."

Drea giggles. "Thad, stop."

"No. I will never stop giving you your flowers, you hear me?"

"Yes, I hear you." Drea smiles, biting her lip. The two snuggle after finishing their dessert. She rests her head on Thad's shoulder.

"Drea, when was the last time you saw Ms. Olympia?"

"I haven't seen her since I was eighteen. The last time we spoke, I was twenty. She moved to Tennessee to take care of her mother, and we lost touch. I tried finding her on social media, but that was a bust. Even Nay Nay couldn't help. I hope she's happy, healthy and doing well."

Thad nods.

"Thad." Drea exhales.

"Yes, my love."

"Nothing. I wanted to hear your name on my tongue."

"I like how it sounds. Say it again?"

"Thaadd," Drea says in a seductive tone directly in his ear.

He turns his head, looking her right in the eye. He rubs his nose against hers. "Drea," he whispers.

She plays with his beard, then kisses him. Again and again. And again….

9

THAD

Thad and Drea have their belongings on their bed as navigate around their bedroom to each pack a bag for the weekend. "Why are we doing this again?" Thad asks.

"Because your sister insisted that I should get a bachelorette weekend."

It's true, Nadia floated the idea of having a makeup bachelorette weekend. She made arrangements for the ladies to spend a weekend at the Park-Barrington resort and spa. The ladies include herself, Latrice, Nadia, Rachel, Amber and Jess. But this is an *all-girls* weekend, so Leticia; Amber's daughter, Shellie; Nathan's mother, Momma Ernie and Momma Janet will be with them. Nathan suggested the fellas do something too. So now, Thad is going camping with Nathan; Leon; Rachel's husband, Tim; Mark; Lance and the kids—Quincy, Jelani, Quincy's best friend and Tim's stepson, Eli; and Leon's son, Tyler. And while Thad loves every single one of these people, he was hoping to spend the weekend butt naked with his wife.

"You're thinking about naked weekend again, aren't you?" Drea says.

"Yes," Thad says with a guilt-ridden expression. "This just would have been the perfect weekend for it."

"Any weekend would be the perfect weekend for it. We rarely work on Saturdays and Sundays and when we do, it's always remote."

"Yeah, I know, but still."

Drea slides her arms around his midsection from behind. "I know this isn't what you wanted to do this weekend, but c'mon, you love camping. Remember how much fun you had last year with Quincy in Joshua Tree?"

"Yeah, that was fun."

"And now you're going to stay in cabins in Idyllwild. That really does sound fun, and I'm not just saying that to get you hyped."

"It actually is a nice town. Okay, I'll admit I am looking forward to going."

"That's the spirit. We need to finish getting packed. Both our rides will be here soon."

"Okay."

Thirty minutes later, Lance pulls up in the luxury van he rented, ready to pick up Thad. Thad doesn't move an inch. Drea raises a brow at him. "I thought you said you were looking forward to going."

"I am."

"Then why aren't you going? Your ride is here."

"Yes, but yours isn't."

"Thad, it's fine. You can go. Latrice sent me a text. She said they're three minutes away," Drea contests.

"Then I'll only be standing here with you for the next three minutes." He grins. "We can check in while we wait. How are you feeling?"

"Excited, but I am going to miss you. How do you feel?"

"Same. I won't be able to stop thinking about you."

"Me too." Drea smirks, looking down at the ground, her face flushing.

"It's so fucking cute when you do that."

Her face flushes more. She always does this whenever he does or says something thoughtful. Thad truly believes it's the little things that matter most. He would go to the ends of the earth for this woman, but he always sends a small gesture to show her just how much he loves her.

Nadia arrives in a party bus. "Drea, grab your shit and let's roll."

"I'm coming." Drea picks up her two carry-on bags while Thad carries her rolling duffel. They get her luggage in the van, and she turns to Thad. "I'm going to miss you."

"I'm going to miss you too, peach."

"You two are sick. It's only a damn weekend." Nadia rolls her eyes.

"Hush up, Nay Nay." Thad frowns, making Nadia roll her eyes again.

"Come here." Thad pulls Drea against him and leans down. He makes sure none of the kids are watching. It's early, so they're all still asleep. With the coast clear, he kisses her. Soon, they're making out in front of their family and friends. It's like that scene in *House Party* where Kid and Sydney make out while Play and Bilal watch in shock. Thad's tongue snakes around Drea's. He's lost in her, held captive by her warm tongue and soft lips. Just as he thinks he'll stay lost forever, a horn honks.

"If ya'll don't stop this lovey-dovey stuff, we're going to be late," Nadia announces.

Drea kisses Thad once more before boarding the

van. He turns and joins the fellas. As he takes his seat, he notices that all the guys are staring at him. "Thad, I got a personal question for you," Nathan says.

"What's up?"

"Did you and Drea have sex last night?" he asks.

"Is this question really necessary?" Mark asks.

"Sorry, Mark. Put some noise canceling headphones on," Nathan replies.

Mark does so.

Thad chuckles, then answers Nathan's question. "No, we spent the night watching a baking show. Why?"

"You're pent-up," Tim says.

"Why do you say that?" Thad asks.

"That kiss said it all," Tim responds.

"Yeah, T. If you know you're going to be going on a boys' trip or going out of town, you have to fuck before you go," Lance says from the passenger seat. He hired a driver to take them to the cabin. Nay Nay did the same thing for the ladies. "Now, for the whole weekend, you're going to be thinking about how much you miss Drea, and you're going to be counting down the days until you see her."

"Pffftt!" Thad blows a raspberry. "That shows what you know. I would've been doing that anyway."

"Yeah, but you're going to be doing it even more now," Nathan adds.

"Can I take these off, or are you still talking about Thad porking my sister?" Mark asks.

Thad nods, and Mark takes off the headphones. "Sir, did you say 'porking'? You can tell your ass grew up in a white neighborhood," Lance jokes.

"I don't know. I have never used that word before, nor have I heard any other white guys use it," Tim teases.

"Yeah, Amber's got uncles and cousins, and I have never heard them say that shit, either," Leon piles on.

"It's official Mark, you talk whiter than white folks." Thad chuckles.

"Fuck each and every single one of you." Mark smiles, flipping everyone off.

The gentlemen laugh.

Three hours later, the kids are now awake. They hop out of the back seat and run around the grounds. The fellas rented a ten-bedroom cabin with state-of-the-art appliances and a fully stocked kitchen, a playroom with pool tables, a jacuzzi on the patio, Wi-Fi, flat screens and a front desk available 24/7. Every bedroom has an amazing view of the mountains. This place is excellent. Thad relaxes. *It's fine. I'll see Drea again in approximately sixty hours.*

I can handle it. I'll be fine. As long as I stay busy, I can do this. He claps his hands. "Okay, gentlemen, let's unload the van." The rest of the men chuckle. "What's all the giggling about fellas?"

"You're taking charge so you can keep yourself busy and keep your mind off your woman," Lance answers.

"Yes, I am. So, get your asses outside and let's unload the van," Thad says, his voice tense.

"I hear tension in your voice, Thaddeus," Lance teases.

"I'm fine!" Thad argues.

"Alright, if you say so," Lance teases.

Don't listen to Lance's big head having ass. You are fine and will continue to be fine.

Later in the day, Thad's on the grill cooking burgers for lunch, when Mark approaches. "Thad, I have a favor to ask."

"What's up?"

"I have a recipe for a sauce I want to try out, and I thought we could have it on the burgers."

"Okay, let me taste it first before we try it out with everyone else."

"That's fair. Thanks!" Mark goes back into the cabin and heads to the kitchen.

Thad is flipping the burgers when he spots Tyler,

looking frustrated. He recognizes that look. Brows furrowed, nostrils flared and the constant, aggravated sighing. It's got to be about a girl. It isn't surprising, seeing as how Tyler is the eldest of the kids at age eleven, and he started junior high this year.

"Hey, Leon," Thad calls. Leon's enjoying a beer and chatting with Lance and Nathan. Tim's currently showing Quincy and Eli how to properly start a fire in a fire pit while Jelani watches. Tyler is supposed to be paying attention too, but he is, of course, preoccupied.

Leon approaches Thad. "Hey, Thad, what's up?"

"Does Tyler have a girlfriend?" Thad asks.

"You know, I shouldn't say anything, but I could use some help. No, he doesn't have a girlfriend, but he wants to have one. He likes a girl in his class, Cynthia Saucedo. They got partnered up on science project, and turns out, they have a lot in common," Leon explains.

"He looks like he could use some help too."

"Yeah, I wanted to stay out of it, you know. Let him figure it out. He's already pretty embarrassed that Amber and I know. He called himself discreet, but he's eleven. So, it didn't take long before we figured out what was going on."

"Shellie told you, didn't she?"

"She did and had the nerve to bribe us too."

Thad and Leon laugh. Leon looks over at his son and shakes his head. "I hate to see him struggle like this."

"We'll all help. It takes a village."

"Thanks. I was going to just ask Nate, but I think getting the perspective from all of us will make him listen more," Leon agrees. "Hey, Tyler, come here."

Tyler walks up to his father. "Yeah, Dad?"

"How would you feel if we shared your dilemma with the fellas and got their opinions on it?" Leon asks.

"I don't know. It's pretty embarrassing." Tyler looks down at his phone.

"Tyler, we've all been eleven, and we all are happily married men who have dated before finding our wives. We can help," Leon says.

"What about Uncle Mark?" Tyler asks.

"He's learned from his mistakes, so the next time he finds someone, he'll know what not to do. So even he can help you," Thad explains.

Tyler looks at them like he's considering their words. "Okay. I guess that couldn't hurt."

"Cool," Leon says. "Hey, fellas, Tyler here has a question for us," he announces.

All the men turn their attention to Tyler. Mark comes out of the kitchen, stirring something in a bowl, and Tim calls a timeout on fire safety. Tyler lets out a breath. "There's this girl, Cynthia, and I really like her. Cynthia and I have become friends since we share a science class, and she flirts with me a lot. But I don't know what to do now. What's my next move?"

All the men smile and give each other the same look. A look that communicates that they've all been where Tyler is now.

"Ask her out," Lance says.

"And take her where?"

"Take her to a park. That's free," Tim replies.

"Our school is right next to a park, and most of the kids go there to eat their lunch. I don't think she's going to be very impressed by a park. I need something that's going to excite her like a Birkin bag."

"And that's the problem with you youngins'. It's not about the amount of money, son. It's the thought that counts," Leon says. "Women see effort more than they see dollar signs."

"Leon's coming in hot, preaching on this Friday afternoon," Thad jokes. The fellas laugh.

"Didn't she kiss you on the cheek yesterday?" Quincy chimes in.

"What?" all the men say at the same time.

"Q!" Tyler looks at Quincy, horrified.

"Tyler, you buried the lede," Tim remarks. "Dude, you are in."

"I am?" Tyler replies.

"Yes, boy, if you don't ask that girl out…" Leon nudges his son's shoulder.

"Okay, but should I wait until Monday and do it face-to-face? Or I should just text her now? My friends said I should wait for her to come to me," Tyler replies.

"First, stop listening to your friends," Nathan says.

"Amen." Lance chuckles.

"And second, ask her out now," Nathan adds.

"I won't seem desperate?"

"No, you won't," Thad assures him. "Tyler, I started falling in love with my wife four years ago. It took seeing my sister being brave before I said something—but I did. And now look. You won't regret saying something. What you will regret is being wishy-washy and staying silent. She's giving you the green light. Take it."

"Okay. Thanks, everyone." Tyler goes into the house for privacy.

A timer goes off. "It's ready." Mark jumps up.

"What is?" Tim asks.

"My sauce for the burgers. Wait until you guys taste this." Mark scoops up some with a spoon and hands it to Thad. He puts the spoon in his mouth. Tears form in his eyes as his mouth burns within seconds. *Holy fucking shit!* His mouth is on fire. Normally, he loves spicy food, but this isn't spicy, it's nuclear. There's no fucking way he's feeding this shit to anyone, especially not the kids. No living creature should eat this. Thad's head feels like it's on fire. His throat is melting, and he can't stop the tears. His vision is so blurred he doesn't see Nathan hand him a bottle of water. Instead, he sees a brown blur with squiggly glasses hand him something clear. Thad takes the bottle and practically swallows the whole thing.

"Uncle Thad, are you okay?" Quincy asks.

Thad wants to reply, but he can't. His vocal cords have disintegrated. Nathan hands him another water. He finishes it just as fast as he did the first bottle. He takes some breaths and swallows. It hurts like hell. Thad turns to Mark, who looks alarmed.

His eyebrows have shot up, and his eyes are wide. Thad approaches him with his fist clenched, and Mark's eyes widen even more. Thad calms himself. *Relax, he didn't mean to do it. Calm down. You can't murder your wife's brother. Drea will be pissed.* Thad's heartbeat—which minutes ago was going so fast he thought his heart would burst from his chest—has slowed. Everyone is gathered around him. He can hear Mark explaining the ingredients of the sauce. Thad hears "chili peppers" and "I added a few more."

An hour later, after drinking gallons of water and taking a cold shower since his whole body felt like the Human Torch's, Thad is lying in bed. He wanted to keep busy this weekend so he wouldn't think so much about Drea. Tyler's girl problems did make her pass through his mind, but concentrating on giving Tyler guidance and focusing on the grill helped. Nathan has taken over making dinner. Thad hears all of them downstairs eating, laughing and talking.

There's a knock at the door. "Come in," Thad says, his voice still scratchy. *What the fuck kind of chilis did Mark put in that sauce?*

Lance opens the door. "You doing alright, bruh?"

"I guess," Thad answers. Thad is shirtless, with only drawers on under the covers. His stomach is hurting, in addition to his mouth and throat. He's in the type of pain where even wearing clothes hurts.

"I'm sorry, T."

"What do you mean?"

"You were going to keep yourself busy this weekend so you wouldn't be thinking about Drea the whole time, and Mark's sauce took you out."

"Thanks, L. I appreciate it." A thought occurs to Thad. "None of the kids ate that shit, did they?"

"No, Tim actually used it to start the fire."

"And it worked?"

"Yep. That shit was one hell of an accelerant."

"What the fuck did that nigga put in that shit?"

"Way more peppers than necessary. He said the peppers were supposed to give it a smoky flavor, and so he added more."

"You cannot kill your wife's brother," Thad mutters to himself. Lance laughs. There's another knock on the door. "Come in," Thad croaks.

Mark pokes his head in. Thad tries not to scowl, but it must not be working because Mark approaches him as if he's a growling dog, with a bowl of ice cream in one hand and an iPad in the other. "Again, I am sorry, Thad. I come with a peace offering." Mark hands him the bowl.

Thad takes the ice cream. "Thank you." Mark hands him the iPad. "Is this so I can kill time?"

"No, not really. I sent Drea a text asking her to call you. Told her not to freak out and that everything was fine, but that you needed to talk to her. She's at lunch with the ladies and said she'd call you when she gets back to their suite. I figured talking to her would make you feel better."

"Thanks, Mark. This almost makes up for you destroying my esophagus." Thad gives him a half smile.

"I also asked Drea to help me learn how to cook, and she recommended the chef who taught her Haitian cuisine."

"Stay the hell away from the food of my people, Mark," Thad warns.

"No, I'm not diving into anything like that. Apparently, she teaches beginners, and I'm starting with eggs."

"Good." Thad eats another spoonful of ice cream.

"Alright, I'll let you get some rest. If you need anything, let me know," Mark says. Thad nods in agreement, and Mark exits.

"I'm going to let you get some rest too." Lance heads out. "And don't trip, it's only fifty-four more hours until we see our women, cause I know you've been counting down."

"Fuck you." Thad grins.

Lance laughs again and heads back down.

Thad looks at the iPad and wills Drea to call.

DREA

The ladies head into the suite, talking over each other. They had an amazing lunch at LW Calabasas. They were treated to a preview tasting menu of entrées that Langston Walker is thinking of unveiling next year. The fact that he still is so hands on with his restaurants is impressive, considering how busy he is. Besides being a restaurateur, he's also a former chef, a food scientist—Drea didn't even realize that was a thing until she watched his show—and host of *Have Food? Will Travel*. Right after lunch came shopping, then a private tour at Rossmore Winery, where the kids were given grape juice and chilled at a nearby garden. Shellie taught Lettie how to make bracelets from flowers. After wine came dinner, and now a nightcap. The day really got away from her, but Mark said Thad was fine. And she sent him pics of the places they went, and he replied…kind of. Drea sent Thad pictures of her lunch, the winery gardens, the wine she enjoyed, her dinner and some of the stuff she bought. Thad usually would have responded with something funny or flirtatious. And he would have asked her what her thoughts were on the food. Instead, he simply responded to each one with a happy face emoji. Couple this with Mark saying Thad was fine about five times, and now she's a little worried. *That's not too many times, right?* Drea rushes to her room. While all the ladies and girls share the suite, everyone has their own room.

Drea puts down her shopping bags and picks up her iPad. She sits on the bed and calls Thad on Face-Time. *It's almost nine at night. Hopefully, he's not—* "Drea?" he says in a sleepy voice—*asleep.*

"I'm sorry, Thad. Go back to sleep."

"No, it's okay. How was your day?"

"It was amazing! We had lunch at LW here in Calabasas. It was divine. We tried a tasting menu of all the new entrées Langston wants to try. Did you see my pictures?"

"I did. Why are you saying *Langston* like that?" Thad playfully frowns.

Drea loves it when he plays jealous. She eggs him on. "Like what?"

"Like you personally know him. We watch his show. You don't have to put so much extra on it." His frown deepens.

Drea giggles. "Thad, are you jealous?"

"It's hard not to be when you told me you had a crush on the guy."

"It's just a crush. It doesn't mean anything."

"Sure it doesn't," Thad teases. "I got all your pictures, baby."

"Then why didn't you respond? And why does your voice sound so hoarse? Does it have anything to do with Mark's text? He kept saying you were fine. What happened?"

"I made the mistake of letting your brother make a sauce that was supposed to go with the burgers I was making. I tasted his sauce before anyone else to make sure it was good. I know Mark doesn't have a lot of experience in the kitchen, so I figured I'd try his sauce and offer him my thoughts. If it didn't come out okay, we'd figure out how to improve it."

"I'm scared for you to continue."

"Drea, I don't know what kind of peppers or chilis that man used, but my whole body is on fire. My throat is killing me, which is why I sound like this, and my stomach is fucked up. And there's the added bonus of a numb mouth, a pounding head and the peppers making me high. You know how Robert Emerson was on *Hot Ones* by the time he got to the fifth wing?"

"Yep, Sean Evans looked really concerned."

"Yeah, well, I think I'm where he was at by the eighth wing."

"Oh, Thad." Drea looks at him with soft, sympathetic eyes. She's glad it's not worse, but that sounds awful.

"I'm actually a little hungry too. All I've had since it happened is ice cream and water. But I'm scared to eat anything."

"Send Mark to the store and ask him to get you white rice, bananas, yogurt and apple sauce. I'm going to send you a list of safe foods for you to eat. Has anyone been checking on you?"

"Thank you, baby and don't worry. The fellas have been texting me and Lance and Mark have been checking in on me."

"Thad, I feel terrible. I pushed you to go on the trip, and this happens. We should have just done naked weekend."

"While I would never argue against naked weekend, I have to disagree with you. Drea, you had a great day with your friends. I love you, and I love us being together. But having a life outside of each other is important too. I'm glad you had fun, and I hope you continue having fun this weekend. I want to hear all about it."

"Thad, baby, I need you to tone down the thoughtfulness. It's too sexy. You're at a ten, and I need you to be at a four, a five at the most. I am wet as hell right now, and need I remind you that your mother is on this trip? I don't want to be turned on in front of my mother-in-law." Drea squirms.

"Are you squirming to get some friction on your clit?" Thad asks. His husky voice is even huskier with his burning throat.

"Fuck, Thad. Please don't say *clit* like that." She puts a pillow between her legs.

"I wish I could watch you fuck that pillow, Drea. I'd love to see that pretty pussy come all over it. Wet it up." *Wow, he is high.* Thad does dirty talk well, but he's always careful of what he says. He's so high right now that his filter is gone. He keeps going. "I want to watch while you wet up that pillow, my love. Then I want to smell it before I bury my tongue in your pussy. I'mma suck on your pussy lips, then on that clit. Your pussy is so sweet. I could eat that joint all day. I'mma eat you off the bone, baby. You make my dick so fucking hard. Just thinking about you. Just a mere thought and I brick up. You're so sexy. You're so beautiful. I want to feast on you."

He growls. "Your titties, your ass and that pussy. You drive me crazy. Look at you. So got damn fine. Look at what you do to me." Thad lowers the tablet so the camera is on his dick. Drea's eye widen as she feels the drool pooling in her mouth. His dick is hard as hell. The veins are popping out. Shit, it even looks thicker and longer. Drea's pussy throbs uncontrollably. It's like it has a mind of its own and is begging for his dick. Thad grabs his dick and jerks it. "I need to be balls deep in you. I'm gonna fuck you just how you like it when we get home."

"Go faster," Drea says, her voice above a whisper.

Thad jerks his dick faster. "Gonna come in your pussy, in your ass, on your titties, on that pretty face and down your throat." Drea whimpers. She grabs another pillow and bites down before humping the pillow between her legs. She angles the tablet so the camera is on the lower half of her body and Thad can see what she is doing. "Yes, Drea, baby, hump the shit out that pillow. Rub that pussy on it. Uhhh!" Thad pumps his dick into his hand faster.

"Fuck, Thad. Give me that dick."

"I'mma give it to you, baby. I should have fucked

you before I left. I'm pent-up, Drea. I need your pussy."

She turns around so her ass is on camera as she humps the pillow until she can feel the buildup toward completion. "Thad, I'm about to come."

"Push the camera in more. I don't want to miss anything."

She does as he says, before biting down on the pillow in her mouth, then she squeezes the hell out of the one between her legs. She can feel wetness sliding onto the pillow. The sensations are building and building until… "Thaaa!" Drea cries into the pillow as she grabs it and sinks her fingers in deep.

When her pussy is finished throbbing, she removes both pillows and looks at the one she humped. It's soaked.

"Thad?" Drea looks at the camera, which is now on Thad's face. He has an intense grimace.

"Show me the pillow," he commands.

Drea picks up the pillow she humped and shows him how wet it is.

"Argh! Drea, shit."

He lowers the camera to his dick, which erupts with streams of come that land on his chest and stomach. He lifts the tablet so the camera is back on his face. His eyes are heavy. Drea knows she doesn't have much time before he goes to sleep.

"Good night, Thad. I love you."

"Good night, baby. I love you too."

Drea ends the call and gets a laundry bag. She stuffs the pillow into it before she sneaks out of her room and goes to the laundry room in the suite. She throws laundry detergent and the pillow into the washer.

"Drea!" Nadia yells from the front room, startling her. Drea jumps and yelps.

"Yeah," she responds.

"Get out here. We're getting ready to play 'Never Have I Ever.'"

With your mom and Latrice's mother-in-law?

Drea turns the washer on and heads into the front room. She's surprised by what she sees. Drea has been around Momma Janet and Momma Ernie, but she's only really seen them as mothers. Right now, both women are holding drinks in their hands and are uproariously laughing.

"How was your talk with Thad?" Amber teases.

Drea's speechless. *Shit! Did they hear us?*

Latrice reads her best friend's mind. "Relax, Drea, we didn't hear you, but you spent most of the day with us. So, it's safe to assume you just called to check in with your husband. I just checked in with mine. Is Thad okay?"

"What happened to my son?" Momma Janet asks.

"Mark happened." Drea explains Mark's culinary faux pas.

"Aw, poor Thad," Rachel says.

"What the hell made Mark's bougie ass think he could make anything edible?" Nadia refills Momma Ernie's Scotch.

"I have no idea. I was going to chill on asking him to attend mom's party, but sense he basically poisoned my husband, he's going."

"I have to admit, I do kind of miss your parents' parties. The food was always really good," Latrice says.

"Thad said we should take Ziplock bags and sneak some food home," Drea jokes.

"I would pay money to see the look on your mother's face if you did that," Latrice says.

Drea laughs. "Okay, but speaking of mothers or mothers-in-law, you two are playing 'Never Have I Ever'?" Drea addresses Momma Ernie and Momma Janet.

"Hell yes. We're here to have fun, too, and both Lettie and Shellie are asleep. And don't you all go easy on us because we're older. Ernestine and I are women, and we have had some experiences. Don't go treating us like 'momma' anybody." Mom—Janet says, before turning to Nadia. "Give me a refill, Nay Nay."

Nadia refills her mother's glass of rum punch. "Okay, but the minute you start talking about some of the nasty stuff you've done—"

"Especially with our dad," Latrice chimes in.

"Exactly. The minute you start that, I'm out." Nadia makes herself a margarita and takes a seat, shooting off a text before they get started. Momma Janet playfully rolls her eyes at her daughter.

Drea pours herself a glass of Moscato and sits as well. Amber's drinking rum punch like Momma Janet. Rachel's drinking a vodka cranberry, Latrice is drinking just cranberry juice and Jess is having a Tom Collins.

"Okay, let's do this. Never have I ever…slept with a married man," Rachel says.

"Oooo, Rach!" Nadia teases. "You're starting off scandalous, aren't you?"

Rachel smiles and shrugs.

"Drea, you took a sip!" Momma Janet looks at her with shock.

"What? Your son is married." Drea gives an impish smile.

"Drea, c'mon, you know that's not what Rachel meant." Jess laughs.

"Well, it that case, no. Considering my parents, there's no way I would do that."

"So, we're all just going to ignore that Momma Ernie took a sip?" Rachel says.

The ladies look at her in shock. Momma Ernie is a devout Catholic who never misses Mass. She is the epitome of the phrase "spirit filled and righteous."

"Oh, close your mouths. He became my husband, but he did start off as someone else's. They were married for a hot second. She was a spoiled rich girl who lived in a wealthy neighboring county. He thought they were star-crossed lovers, but it turns out, she just wanted to piss off her parents by marrying someone poor cause they insisted on marrying her off to some rich guy's son. Rumor had it, the rich guy was her father's boss. Charlie, that was my husband, he worked on the janitorial staff. Her parents found out and went to their team of lawyers to end the marriage. It took some time, and as they were getting everything finalized, he and I met and fell in love. He fell for me despite being newly dumped and heartbroken. He never took what she did out on me." Momma Ernie treats herself to more Scotch. "I was married to him for ten years before he passed. A few years later, I realized I had too much love in me not to share it, and the Good Lord led me to becoming a mother. I miss that man every day."

"Momma, you never thought about getting remarried? Not once?" Amber asks.

"No, baby, not at all. My Charlie was the best there was. There was no replacing him. I'm talking kind, gentle, filled with love and passion. And don't get me wrong, Charlie grew up in the sticks. He was tough as nails when he needed to be, and he did not play about me."

"Now, that's it!" Momma Janet raises her glass. "Too many women settle for not being alone when they can have a man who loves them and looks out for them. I know for a fact that my Earl would give his life up for me. And that's all we want, to feel safe, respected and loved."

"Exactly, Janet! And that is how Charlie made me feel. Safe, respected and loved. I remember this one time, we went to a bar and grill for a date night, and I'm pretty well endowed"—Momma Ernie gestures toward her breasts. That is an understatement. This is in no way meant to be disrespectful, but Momma Ernie could feed a whole maternity ward—"and Gelbert Simpson, the town drunk and pervert"—she continues—"was even drunker than usual. He came up to me, and he insisted that I go home with him. He was making some rather disgusting comments about what he wanted to do to my body. Charlie was in the men's room, but just as Gelbert reached out and snatched my arm, Charlie came up behind him, turned him around and grabbed him by his collar. Charlie said, 'Get your motherfucking hand off my wife or I will break your arm.' Gelbert's drunk ass tried to swing on Charlie." By now, all the women are hanging on Momma Ernie's every word. "Charlie ducked out the way and punched him right in the eye, then slammed his head down on the table and made him apologize to me. It was a small town, and Charlie was well-liked. He was known for always lending a helping hand, so no cops got involved."

"Go, Charlie!" Rachel cheers.

"Go, Charlie, indeed," Momma Ernie agrees. She closes her eyes. "I can still remember the smell of his cologne. Now that was a man. Took real good care of me. Like it was his duty. I raised both my boys to grow up into men like him. He would have been an amazing father to them. The world needs more men like Charlie. Men who love their women out loud and aren't going around worrying about what some fool says. Calling him soft or a simp and whatnot.

The type of man who ignores all the noise and loves his woman even harder."

"That is a tough act to follow," Latrice says.

"Yes, he was. I never even dated after he passed. I didn't see the point. I miss so many things about him. His hugs. How he would whisper sweet things in my ear. How he would buy me 'just because' presents, insisted on fixing things around the house right away so it was one less thing I had to worry about…and the sex! Wooo, Lord Jesus." Momma Ernie raises her hand like she's testifying. "That man knew his way around a coochie." She fans herself.

Drea does a spit take. "Momma Ernie!" Latrice says.

"Baby, it's like Janet said, we're women, not just somebody's momma." Momma Ernie pats Drea on the back. Drea responds by thanking her and giving her a squeeze.

"I know. I just did not see that coming," Latrice replies.

"Wine is not going to get it. I think I'll have some of that rum punch." Drea gets up and pours herself a glass.

"Let me preface this by saying that the following statement refers to the loving relationship that Momma Ernie and Charlie shared, not other stuff."

The women giggle. "But Charlie reminds me a lot of my grandpa," Rachel says. "He loved my bubbe so much."

"How long were they married?" Jess asks.

"Seventy-seven years. And I never saw them fight once," Rachel answers.

"Wow, they must have been so young when they got married," Latrice comments.

"Yep, they were both nineteen. When the war ended, they both moved to New York with their respective families. She got a job as a seamstress. He worked at a bakery. One day, she walked in for a loaf of rye, and three weeks later, they were married."

"Wait, they met one day and three weeks later, they were married?" Nadia asks. Latrice is sitting on the couch with Nadia kneeling on the couch cushion, putting Latrice's hair into twists.

"Yep. My grandfather said it was love at first sight. He said my bubbe was his bashert. That's Yiddish for 'destiny.' They both died when they were ninety-six. She died first, and he only lasted two months without her. He gathered the family—three generations—to say goodbye. The last thing he said to us was, 'So long, kids. I'm going to go check in on my best girl.' He closed his eyes, and the next morning, he was gone."

"That's so romantic." Amber swoons. "Leon better be lost without me after I die."

"I told Earl he wasn't allowed to get remarried, or I'd haunt him," Momma Janet said. The ladies laugh. "Ya'll are laughing, but I'm serious."

The ladies continue to laugh and drink as Drea thinks about Momma Ernie's and Rachel's tales of love. Drea is sipping her second rum punch when she feels a sudden sense of dread. The idea of losing Thad, no matter how old, scares the shit out of her. She loves him so much, there's no way she'd be able to live without him.

Without thinking, Drea pulls out her phone and calls him. She gets up and wanders to her room and looks out the window. The moon is full, and the stars are twinkling. Thad's phone stops ringing and goes to his voicemail. Drea leaves a message after the beep. "Hi, Thad, you don't have to call me back. I..." Drea lets out a humorless chuckle. "I don't even know why I called you, but Momma Ernie and Rachel just told us the most romantic stories. Momma Ernie was married before she adopted Leon and Nate. His name was Charlie, and she *misses* than man, Thad. She described him, and he was so protective of her. He beat a drunk guy's ass for grabbing her." Drea giggles. The rum is definitely getting to her. "She said that Charlie was the type of man who loved his woman out loud and didn't worry about some asshole calling him soft or a simp. The type of man who ignores all the noise and loves his woman even harder. And Rachel, her grandparents were married for seventy-seven years. Can you believe that, husband? They got married when they were nineteen! I'm looking out the window right now at the moon and stars, and I'm thinking of us. I love you so much."

Drea's voice cracks. "I don't think I can live without you, Thad. It would be too painful. I have to die first. Rachel's grandfather only lasted two months without his wife. Two months without you would be too long. I'd have to go right after you. I would miss you so much. I'd miss you holding me at night right before we fall asleep, your voice, your laugh, your cooking…" Tears stream down Drea's face at the very thought of saying goodbye to him. "…watching you work out, watching and quoting our favorite shows together, the intimacy we share, and not just the sex, even though I really, really love the sex. I cannot emphasize that enough. I love everything about you, Thad. You can't die. You are not allowed to leave me." Drea hears footsteps. "I have to go. Someone's coming. I love you." She ends the call. There's a knock at the door. "It's open," she responds. Rachel enters.

"Hey, Drea, is everything okay?" Rachel hands her a mug of hot cocoa.

"Thank you, and yeah, I'm fine." Rachel quirks her eyebrow, clearly not buying it. Drea confesses. "I may have left Thad a voicemail professing my undying love for him and telling him that he's not allowed to die. And before you say anything, yes, I am aware of how cheesy that sounds."

"I wasn't going to call it cheesy. As a matter of fact, it's right on brand for you two."

"What do you mean?" Drea puts the mug on a nearby nightstand.

"You two are each other's bashert, Drea."

"You think Thad and I are each other's destiny?"

"Yeah, you don't?"

"No, I definitely believe that we're meant for each other, it's just that I didn't realize other people thought so too. Hell, I'm still wrapping my brain around Thad believing it."

Rachel approaches her and puts her hands on her shoulder, giving her a warm smile. "I have great instincts about this type of stuff, and the simple fact is, you and Thad are soulmates." Rachel chuckles. "Wow, talk about cheesy."

"I know. I didn't want to say anything but… yikes." Drea playfully cringes.

"Shut up, you know what I mean."

"No, I do. It's like we've been sold on the idea of that special, perfect someone, and it never occurred to us that we'd have to kiss so many frogs—"

"So many frogs. Too many frogs." Rachel rolls her eyes. No doubt she's thinking about her ex-husband, Mitch. Drea only met him once, and she's been friends with Rachel for five years. That's how long her son, Eli, and Quincy have been best friends. Drea, having only met him once, truly shows how often he comes around. Because if he were an active father, he'd be part of the crew just like Rachel's husband, Tim, is.

Drea chuckles. "And with each frog, our belief in the special, perfect someone diminished. So, when we finally meet them, we don't believe that they're real. We even go so far as to deny our feelings. I convinced myself that I only saw Thad as a friend for years before I was honest with myself, and even then, I kept my mouth shut. I think on some level, I was still in disbelief."

"Oh, I understand. Remember how reluctant I was to go out with Tim, even though you all kept nagging me to?"

"Yep. You were determined not to catch feelings for that man." Drea smiles.

Rachel lets out a sigh. "The harder I fought, the deeper I fell, and that's when I realized that Tim was my bashert and I needed to stop fighting." Rachel smiles at Drea. "I'm really glad you stopped fighting, Drea."

"Me too."

The two friends hug.

THAD

IT'S SUNDAY MORNING, AND THAD, ELI AND QUINCY are chasing Jelani around in a snow-covered clearing by the cabin. Thad adds the lack of snow until the very last minute to the list of reasons he's relieved they're leaving early. Being sick and lying in bed most of the weekend is definitely a close number two. The surprise diarrhea he had yesterday got the number one spot for why this weekend sucked. After drinking some ginger tea, taking some anti-diarrheal pills and sleeping most of Saturday, he's feeling a little better. He barely got to play with the kids. He didn't get to cook or really hang out with the fellas, and the Wi-Fi reception situation has been shitty, to say the least. And finally, since it's almost two weeks before Christmas, they were all excited to see snow, but it didn't decide to show up until now. When they're leaving. At this point, he just wants to go home to Drea. He saw she left him a voice message, but couldn't listen to it due to the spotty Wi-Fi and reception. It's a two-minute-long message so it couldn't have been an emergency. Besides, Tim's phone is working better than anyone's. If something had happened, Rachel would have called by now.

"Uncle Thad, do you want to hear a joke?" Eli asks.

"E, can we get a break?" Qunicy asks.

"No, I told you, Quince. This is never going to end," Eli remarks.

These two crack Thad up. Eli is definitely the comedian to Quincy's straight man.

"Sure, E. Hit me," Thad says, tickling a squirming and giggling Jelani.

"Why did the scarecrow get a pay rise?" Eli beams while Quincy shakes his head.

"I don't know, Eli. Why?"

"Because he was outstanding in his field."

Thad nods. "I like that one. It makes you think."

"It took Tim three minutes to figure it out." Eli smiles.

Thad laughs.

"Hey, ya'll! We got everything packed up, and we're heading out." Nathan calls out.

Thad picks up Jelani and places him on his shoulders. Quincy and Eli follow behind. Thad heads over to the van and gets Jelani strapped into his car seat before letting Quincy and Eli in the van, then taking his own seat. Thad looks around, and the men all look exhausted. Without Wi-Fi, keeping the kids entertained proved to be a challenge. Thad's not sure what that says about society's reliance on videos and streaming for kids, but he knows that keeping four kids occupied without the aid of a screen isn't as easy as it once was. Yesterday was so jam-packed it's no wonder the crew are fighting to keep their eyes open. They took the kids on a morning hike—Thad tried to participate, and by participate, he got out of bed before promptly laying on the floor—then into town to see the new Pixar movie, then to lunch, a walk around some of the shops around town— resulting in the kids each buying something for their moms that their dads, of course, paid for—and finally, dinner around the fireplace and bed. Meanwhile, Thad's day was filled with shitting and trying not to shit. He's so ready to go home, and he can tell the fellas are too.

The driver heads out. After thirty minutes of driving, Lance asks, "So, kids, did you have fun?" When nobody responses, he turns around and looks at them. Quincy, Jelani and Eli are asleep, and Tyler is texting his new girlfriend. Lance shakes his head and laughs.

———

"THAD." THAD OPENS HIS EYES AND SEES LANCE looking at him.

"What's going on?"

"You're home. We're in front of your house."

Thad gets out of the van and grabs his bags before addressing everyone. "Kids, I wish I could have spent more time with you. I'll take you all out somewhere soon."

"Feel better, Uncle Thad," Quincy says.

"Thank you, Quince." Thad smiles.

"Bye-bye, Uncle Thad."

"Bye-bye, Jelani. I'll see you on Christmas."

"Okay," the adorable little one says.

"Tyler, congratulations on you and Cynthia, and remember—"

"Small gestures go a long way. Got it, Uncle Thad."

Thad nods. "Gentlemen, always a pleasure." Tim salutes Thad, while Nathan and Leon wave goodbye. "And Mark…" Mark looks at Thad. "…while Christmas is an exception, it's going to be a minute before we can hang out like this again." Thad playfully frowns.

Mark smiles. "Understood."

He waves and heads up the walkway to the house. Now he just needs his woman to come home. The van drives away as he enters the house. He punches the code for the security alarm before dropping his luggage by the front door, telling himself to pick it up before Drea gets home. He quickly pulls out his phone and listens to Drea's voicemail. By the time the kids woke up, everyone was talking, joking and laughing, so he couldn't listen while in the car. He hears her voice and damn near melts into a puddle on the floor. *That woman!* She doesn't even know the half of it. The power she has over his heart is insane.

He listens to her describe Momma Ernie's husband.

His name was Charlie, and she misses than man, Thad. She described him, and he was so protective of her. He beat a drunk guy's ass for grabbing her.

Drea's giggle at the end makes Thad smile.

"Go head, Charlie. Rest in peace, brother." Thad looks up to Heaven. "Though, personally, I would have thrown the nigga out the window." Thad knew about Charlie from some stories Nathan told him while they were having beers one night. Nate described him as "the man who should have been my father." He sounded like one hell of a guy. Drea's message continues,

She said that Charlie was the type of man who loved his woman out loud and didn't worry about some asshole calling him soft or a simp.

"I heard that!" Thad agrees.

The type of man who ignores all the noise and loves his woman even harder. And Rachel, her grandparents were married for seventy-seven years. Can you believe that, husband?

"No, I cannot, wife." Thad responds like Drea is

in the room with him as he washes his hands and makes himself a sandwich to test out his stomach. He's been living on apple sauce and rice with butter for the past two days and is starving. He doesn't fault the crew, but having to smell the food they were cooking and grilling had been torture. "Seventy-seven years." Thad lets out a low whistle. "Shit, they had to be seventeen or eighteen when they married."

"They were nineteen," Drea says.

Thad looks up and sees Drea. He stares like she's a mirage. As goofy as it sounds, seeing her in the flesh makes him miss her more. He approaches her and reaches out to touch her like she's not real. "Baby, I missed you so much."

"Prove it and kiss me like you missed me," Drea orders.

"Shhiiiiit!"

Thad kisses his wife like it's nobody's business. When he's done, she collapses against his chest and takes in his scent. "Mmm." *God, I love it when she does that.* "Momma Ernie said she can still sometimes smell Charlie's cologne. Wait, were you listening to my voicemail for the first time?"

"Yes."

"Oh! You don't have to listen to the rest." Drea grabs Thad's phone.

"Give me back my phone, woman." He chases her around the kitchen island. When he catches her, he gives her a tickle. She giggles again, and that feeling of warmth and hardness down below appears.

"Thad, it's embarrassing. I had a little too much to drink, and I got vulnerable and mushy."

"I like vulnerable and mushy." Thad holds the phone to his ear and listens to the rest of the message.

I'm looking out the window right now at the moon and stars, and I'm thinking of us. I love you so much. I don't think I can live without you, Thad. It would be too painful. I have to die first. Rachel's grandfather only lasted two months without his wife. Two months without you would be too long. I'd have to go right after you. I would miss you so much. I'd miss you holding me at night right before we fall asleep, your voice, your laugh, your cooking, watching you work out, watching and quoting our favorite shows and movies together, the intimacy we share, and not just the sex, even though I really, really love the sex. I cannot emphasize that enough.

Thad looks up at Drea and smiles. "I'm afraid to ask which part you're on," Drea says.

"I really, really love the sex, too, peach," Thad answers.

Drea covers her flushed face in embarrassment, making Thad laugh.

Her message continues.

I love everything about you, Thad. You can't die. You are not allowed to leave me. I have to go. Someone's coming. I love you.

Thad looks up after he's done listening and gives her a teary-eyed smile. He has never felt more loved by a woman than he does now. *This woman wants to die first so she doesn't have to experience the pain of missing me.* He quickly goes through each woman he's has ever had a serious relationship with, and none of them have ever come close to saying anything that heartfelt. The closest one came was claiming his dick as hers. In the end, it always boiled down to sex. The women Thad dated wanted access to his money and access to his dick, but not much else. *Drea loves me, all of me. So much so that she doesn't ever want to be without me. That type of shit makes a man feel like a king.* "Baby, that was beautiful. For real. You have nothing to be embarrassed by. Letting me know how much I mean to you is always welcome."

"What if I say something mushy in front of your friends?"

"You mean all my *married* friends?"

"Is Mark not your friend?" she teases.

"Too soon, baby. Too soon, and as of right now, he has been bumped down to an acquaintance," Thad answers.

"Okay, but what if I accidentally say something mushy in front of your employees?"

"My employees already know how much I love you. They were at our wedding."

"Okay, I'll keep the mush coming."

"Please do. Oh, and there's no way in hell you're dying before me."

"Excuse me, sir—"

"No, no, Drea. You are not leaving me first. No way. Rachel's grandfather is a strong man cause two months is a lifetime compared to how long I'd last without you. I'd be like Lance in *The Best Man Holiday* during Mia's funeral. People would have to check on me daily."

"Okay, how about this? We agree to die at the same time," Drea suggests.

"Like in *The Notebook*?"

"Exactly."

"Cool, that works."

"What are you doing?"

"Making a sammich and hoping it doesn't aggravate my diarrhea."

Drea's silent for a while before she says, "What the fuck did he put in that sauce?"

"That is what I have been asking myself all weekend, peach! He said they were just chili peppers, but what kind of chilis slowly kill a person, one bodily function at a time?"

Drea chuckles. "Go sit down. I'll make your sammich."

"Baby, I can—"

"Thaddeus, it's still the weekend, and I make the food on the weekends, remember?"

"Right. Thank you, peach."

"You're always welcome, my king." Drea reorganizes all the sandwich fixings.

"I like that!" Thad grins.

"My king? As your pet name?"

"Yeah. I was just thinking that your love makes me feel like one."

"My king it is, then."

"I feel like I should upgrade yours."

"Don't you dare. I love *peach*. Who knows, maybe I'll get a tattoo on my ass of a peach or Princess Peach or both." She purrs.

"You stop trying to get me going." Thad playfully frowns. "My stomach still ain't right. Or at least let a brother eat first."

"Okay, coming right up." Drea laughs.

Twenty minutes later, she comes to the couch and hands Thad a plate with his sandwich. Turkey, aioli, tomato and provolone pressed into a panini. His stomach grumbles. He is going to destroy this sandwich and its maker. Drea takes a seat next to him with her own panini. Thad takes a bite of his. *Fuck, that's good!* The melted cheese and tomato under a crispy, perfectly toasted sourdough is enough to make Thad wish he could taste it for the first time for all eternity. And the turkey makes the perfect addition. *Drea's ability to put together the perfect amount of ingredients in the perfect combo should be studied by food scientists. Just not Langston Walker.*

"Baby, this is amazing," Thad gushes.

"Thank you. I hope it doesn't upset your stomach."

"It's worth it if it does. What kind you eating?"

"Prosciutto, pesto mayo, provolone and sundried

tomato." He gives her half of his sandwich, and she gives him half of hers.

Thad grabs the remote from the coffee table. "Let's watch the episode of *The Gordons* where Grandma Phyllis dies and the family gets high at her funeral."

"Okay, here we go. Season three, episode nine," Drea says.

"You know the season and episode number."

"Leave me alone, Thad!" Drea playfully whines.

"Listen, if there's ever a game show where you need to know random pop culture shit, you are definitely being my partner."

"I would have been your partner anyway." Drea grins.

"Um, how do I put this? I love you, Drea, but if there's something like three million dollars on the line and I need someone who knows about a subject you know nothing about, there's no way in hell I'm giving up three million dollars as some test of my loyalty."

"Yeah, babe, I was kidding. If you ever picked me to be your partner for a game show where you knew we'd fail and missed out on three million dollars, I'd divorce you."

"And rightfully so too," Thad agrees.

They high five each other before snuggling together and finishing their paninis while they watch the Gordon family get high at a funeral.

11

DREA

Drea and Thad are in the Range Rover. Drea sings, repeating the line, "We're going to the farmers' market." Next, she does a little happy shimmy in the passenger seat. Thad looks over and laughs at her. She looks back at him and smiles. "Don't act like you're not excited too."

"You're right. I am."

They look at each other at a red light. "We're going to the farmers' market!" The couple sings and shimmies together.

Drea and Thad *love* the farmers' market. And today's visit is extra special. Momma Janet recently surprised everyone and announced she wanted to take a break from hosting the holidays. Thad and his sisters immediately called her to check in on her. After assuring her kids that she was fine, she told them that Thanksgiving is going to be her only hosting and cooking holiday. And barbecues don't count since they're mainly Earl's thing. She told the kids to decide among Thad and Nay Nay who would host. Latrice and Nate are exempt. Her being six months along isn't ideal to host a big dinner. Drea immediately volunteered for herself and Thad as host. That was two days ago, and Christmas was in five days.

The house has been cleaned, a tree has been selected and trimmed. All that is left is the food for Christmas dinner, and the newlyweds plan to put out a feast. The menu includes prime rib roasts, Cornish game hens, yeast rolls, herb mashed potatoes, mushroom and garlic green beans, roasted Brussel sprouts with tons of bacon and brown butter and maple-glazed turnips. For dessert, chocolate chip cannoli cheesecake, lemon and raspberry cake and vanilla custard pie topped with strawberries. Their guests—Latrice, Nathan, Quincy, Mark, the twins, Nadia, Momma Janet and Poppa Earl—have been told not to bring a thing but their appetites.

They pull the ticket out of the parking kiosk. The

bar raises, allowing them entry into heaven on earth. Thad quickly parks, and they head out, ready to tackle the shopping list. First stop is to the coffee vendor. After they're fully caffeinated, it's time to get down to business.

"Fig and goat cheese crostini as an appetizer," Drea suggests as they approach Greta, the goat cheese lady. She always brings her goat, Gertie.

"Merry Christmas, kids!" Greta greets them.

"Merry Christmas, Greta," they both reply.

"What can I do you for?"

"We'll take a container of the soft cheese, please?"

"Flavored or plain?"

"Plain. We're going to pair it with fig jam and sliced and toasted baguettes."

"That sounds delicious. Well, I hate to burst your bubble, kids, but Trudy's not here. Came down with a nasty flu." *Shit, shit, shit!* Drea is more than a little excited to take over hosting and cooking duties this Christmas. Make no mistake, despite them disagreeing on just about everything, Drea learned a great deal from her mother. Especially when it comes to hosting. Vivian can dazzle a crowd with the best of them. Drea has studied and is ready to finally use what she's learned in her own home.

Having the best of everything—the appetizers, the meal, the libations and the dessert—plays a huge role in being a great host, and Trudy's fig jam is the only jam worth making the appetizer for. Greta must see the annoyance on Drea's face. "Don't fret. There's always Sheila."

"Yeah, baby. I know you love Trudy's jams, but Sheila's are good too." Thad smiles.

Sheila. Her jams are...fine... Okay, they're freaking amazing. Drea just isn't a fan of Sheila. She guises her flirtation with Thad as small talk or urging him to purchase something more, but it's definitely flirting. It's her way of trying to get him to stay longer. Her jams are good as hell, and Drea is always down to support Black business, especially a Black woman, but she's close to losing two customers. The funny part? She really thinks Drea can't tell what she's doing. Iona, their neighbor from Halloween, had more shame. She at least had the self-respect to not actually bring over a cobbler, and she's been overly nice to Drea for the past two months. It was obvious that, once she saw Drea, her hopes had been dashed. A few other single women in the neighborhood have tried and failed to get Thad's attention as well. It's been happening a lot less lately. Iona, or somebody, must have put the word out that Thad is off limits. In the environment Drea grew up in, a man being off limits quite simply meant he wasn't a cheater. These men were rare, but they existed. These were the men who were so disinterested in cheating on their partners that anyone seen flirting with them was persona non grata. Drea hopes that's the case with the single ladies in the neighborhood cause it sure isn't with Sheila.

They thank Greta for the cheese and make a quick stop to purchase a couple of baguettes before they head to Sheila's booth. "Thank you! Please come back next week," Sheila says. If Drea were insecure, she'd be scared because Sheila is gorgeous. Like Thad, she has locs. They're thin, brown with highlights and wavy. She has smooth brown skin and is curvy, like Coke bottle curvy, and she has thickness everywhere. Thighs, titties and ass. Though Drea's ass is still rounder and fuller. "Hello, Thaddeus. Hi, Drea." Sheila smiles, except when she greeted Drea, it didn't reach her eyes. *Hi, Drea* could not have sounded more obligatory if she tried. The subtext of *I have to be nice to you because you're buying my product* couldn't be louder.

"Hi, Sheila," Thad replies. "We're looking for some fig jam."

"I see the baguettes and goat cheese. Are you making an appetizer?" Sheila flutters her eyelashes. *Let's see if I can count the number of times Thad ignores her.*

"We are. Having family over for the holiday. It's our first time hosting," Thad informs her before looking around. *Number one.*

"Hopefully, it will be permanent," Drea chimes in.

"Like I said, baby, you did your thing on Thanksgiving. I'm sure everyone will be happy with what we come up with." Thad rubs Drea's lower back. *Mmmm, tingly.* Thad now tickles her back and her left side, causing Drea to crumple in a fit of giggles.

Sheila clears her throat. "We have regular fig jam, balsamic fig jam, grand mariner and fig and honey. Which do you have a taste for?" she asks only Thad, leaning against her counter.

Thad immediately turns to Drea. "I don't know. What do you think, peach?" Thad asks. *And that's number two.*

"Why don't you try some?" Sheila washes her hands and puts on some gloves before grabbing a small sample spoon. She takes a bit of the balsamic fig jam and holds it to Thad's mouth. *Wow, really?* Without missing a beat, Thad takes the spoon from Sheila and tastes it.

"I like it." He smiles at Drea before turning to Sheila. "Could you please give a sample to my wife?" *That's three strikes! Too bad Sheila doesn't know she's out. I'm almost embarrassed for her. Almost.*

Sheila hands Drea a small spoon of the jam. She turns to Thad and smiles. "So, what else will you be serving?"

"We're serving prime rib, Cornish hens, mashed potatoes, roasted turnips, rolls, green beans and Brussel sprouts," Thad replies.

"That sounds yummy. I might have to stop by for a plate," she jokes. *Pffft, you wish.*

"Let's get the balsamic, Thad," Drea says, sensing his discomfort.

"Okay." Thad grins at Drea. "Can we get two jars, please?" he says to Sheila without taking his eyes off Drea.

"Perfect," Sheila answers. *Numero cuatro.* She rings up the two jars and takes Thad's credit card before trying one last time. "Have a Merry Christmas, and if I don't see you before, Happy New Year's. Maybe you can come back, and I can show you some of the new jams I'll have in stock," she purrs.

"I don't think so," Thad says. "You enjoy your holiday, Sheila. Come on, peach. We got a lot more booths to check out." *Numbuh five!*

"Coming." Drea smiles. They hold hands and walk away from Sheila's booth.

"I'm checking in with you," Thad says as they walk away.

"You are?" Drea asks.

"Yeah, it's not Friday but I know how much you hate it when women flirt with me. You play it cool and don't get worked up, but I know you hate it, Drea. Are you okay?"

"Yes, Thad. I'm okay. Thank you. Are you?"

"I'm good, peach." He smiles and shows those dimples she loves. She sticks a finger in one and smiles back. He takes her hand and grasps it as they continue to the next vendor.

<hr>

It's Christmas Day! And the Richardson's house is merry and bright. Their tree is huge, without being ostentatious, and filled with decorations. There are presents ready to be unwrapped under the tree. And the rest of the house's decor is straight out of a winter wonderland. There are snowflakes etched onto the windows and removable snowflake decals on the walls. The seashells have been replaced with figurines of Santa, the elves and his reindeer, with Rudolph in the front. And there are stockings for Thad, Drea and each guest hung up on the fireplace.

Dinner is in approximately four hours. Everyone has been told to be here at six on the dot, and so far, Thad and Drea are making great time. She snaps green beans while Thad peels potatoes. When he's done, he takes the turnips and washes and peels them before cutting them into cubes and placing them in the fridge. They're getting the sides and some apps prepped before putting them in the oven. The main event will be the hens and the prime rib. Thad rubs mustard, Worcestershire sauce and garlic all over the meat. Drea looks up and peeks at him while wrapping marinated shrimp in prosciutto. Thad's brows are furrowed in concentration, and Drea chuckles.

"What's so funny?" Thad asks.

"You. The way you're rubbing that meat."

Thad smirks, then licks his lips. "That's cause I know how much you like to eat my meat," he says, low and husky.

"Indeed I do, but I'm more focused on how you're *rubbing* it."

Thad playfully lets out a sigh. "Drea, you know

not to get me started. We got a dinner to fix. I'mma need you to chill."

"I'm not doing anything." Drea twerks.

"Drea…"

"I mean, I could see if I was going out of my way to distract you, but I'm not." Drea smacks her ass cheeks.

"Drea…" Thad's voice gets lower.

She rubs her ass against his groin. "Am I displeasing you, my king?" She turns and gives him a doe-eyed, innocent look.

Thad takes off his mustard covered gloves and slams them on the counter like he's really mad. "Get in the bedroom."

"Yay!" Drea cheers.

A HALF HOUR LATER…

"Dang it, Drea." Thad rushes out the bedroom, pulling his sweatpants up over his ass. Drea tilts her head and takes a good look. *Gray sweatpants were made for men like him.* She licks her lips, then looks up to see Thad staring at her, looking fake scared. She bites her lip and slowly approaches.

"Drea, no," Thad says, looking like a whole meal with those sweats and a painted-on white T-shirt. His locs are tied back, and his beard is freshly trimmed. This draws her attention to his lips. So succulent.

"I'm gonna eat you," she whispers.

"No, Drea. You're not allowed to eat me." Thad grins trying desperately to sound authoritative.

"I'm gonna eat you." She wiggles her tongue, following him into the kitchen.

"Drea." Thad picks up a pair of tongs and snaps them in Drea's direction. "Back! Get back, woman. I have to put this meat in the smoker."

"I'm gonna eat you." She squeezes her breasts together.

Thad licks his lips.

That's right. You want to lick these titties, don't you?

Thad washes his hands and grabs the meat like a baby and rushes past Drea, who watches him carefully. Thad puts the meat on the preheated smoker and closes the lid. Drea waits as he walks back inside the door. "Andrea. We have sides to make and appetizers to finish. Get your fine ass in that kitchen."

Yes! Tell me what to do, daddy. Drea bites her lip. She takes her hand and slides it down her shorts, rubbing her clit. She maintains eye contact with

Thad. "That feels so good, Thad. Don't you want to play with my clit?"

"Baby, what is going on? I thought this dinner was really important to you."

"It is, but fuck if you don't make me wet," Drea moans.

"Drea…" His voice goes up an octave. Thad clears his throat and keeps his eyes on the floor.

"Mmm. Yes, Thad."

Thad grabs his dick in a feeble attempt to hide his erection. Drea giggles at the sight of him gripping his big, heavy dick. "Drea, stop playing with yourself…fuck! That was the most difficult sentence I've ever had to say…and wash your hands. We're going to finish this dinner. You hear me, woman?" Thad tries so hard not to sound turned out.

Drea gets close and sniffs him. She takes her fingers out of her shorts and places them on Thad's lips. He licks them clean. Drea stares up at Thad before answering. "Whatever you say, my king," she says softly.

Thad looks like he's about to cry. Just like Drea wants him.

Minutes later, Drea stuffs the hens, whose innards have been removed, with chopped up Granny Smith apples. She ties their legs together before brushing on the glaze, made with butter, honey, brown sugar and ground clove. She puts them in the oven at three hundred and fifty degrees for twenty minutes. Thad is mashing the potatoes. Drea takes the prosciutto wrapped shrimp and places them on a serving dish. She gets up to place them on the coffee table when Thad gets her attention.

"Say there, wife?" Thad says with a country accent.

Drea turns around. "Well, howdy, husband! What can I do you for?" she says in her Dolly Parton impression.

"It's getting better," Thad compliments.

"Thank you. What's up?"

"Nothing, I just thought I'd bring up the fact that you haven't complained once about us cooking together. You haven't said anything about me being in your space. And you haven't tried to take over. I think you may like me."

Drea shrugs. "A smidge." She smiles. He smiles back.

THAD ANSWERS THE DOORBELL. LATRICE, QUINCY, Nate, Nadia and Momma Janet and Poppa Earl are all at the door.

"Did you all come together?" Thad asks, hugging them one at a time and letting them into the house. They each take off their shoes and put them in a cubby. This is something Drea implemented recently after reading an article on an uptick in germs.

"No, we just all showed up at six, like you told us to," Nadia says. "Now let's eat. I can smell the food, and it's making me lightheaded."

"That was from skipping lunch," Latrice replies.

"I wanted to have room for this feast Thad and Drea promised," Nadia says.

Drea arrives in the living room and goes around giving everyone a hug. After she hugs Momma Janet, her mother-in-law looks at her face and asks, "You pregnant yet?"

"No, Momma Janet." Drea smiles.

"Okay, so why are we not being taken into the dining room and eating?" Nadia asks.

"We need twenty more minutes, Nay Nay," Drea says.

"Yeah, but ya'll told us to be here at six," Nadia replies.

"Nadia, relax and have an appetizer."

"I can't. Latrice's hungry self won't let anybody get any."

"I said I'm sorry, Nay Nay," Latrice pleads, looking contrite.

"You literally slapped my hand when I tried to get a shrimp!" Nadia argues.

"I'm sorry, but my appetite has been out of control lately." Latrice gives her a sheepish smile.

"She's not lying. I woke up at three in the morning to find her ordering herself a meatball sub," Nathan says.

"Dang, Trice. A three a.m. meatball sub craving?" Nadia jokes.

"I had a taste for one." She laughs.

Mark knocks on the door as he opens it. "Merry Christmas, everyone." He enters looking stressed. He has creases in his forehead, and his jaw is tight. There's a young woman behind him. Each twin holds one of her hands. She smiles sheepishly at Drea.

"Merry Christmas," everyone replies. Quincy gives his dad and siblings a hug. The twins talk over each other, trying to talk to Quincy.

"Hey, Quincy, could you and the twins go play in the game room?" Drea asks.

"Sure, Auntie Drea." Quincy takes the kids into

the other room.

"I'll go with them," Momma Janet volunteers.

"I'll go with you, baby," Poppa Earl says.

"Hello." Drea offers the young woman a greeting.

"Hi, I'm Suchi," she answers.

"Yes, of course. My apologies. Thad, Drea, this is Suchi. She's a child psychologist who has been working with the twins. She uses music to help them open up about their feelings of abandonment."

"Wow, that's really cool," Drea comments.

"Her progress with the twins has been amazing. Suchi has been with us on a probationary period that ended a week ago. She's going to work with Jelani and Lettie three times a week for the next year." Mark replies.

"Congratulations on the new job, and it's a pleasure to meet you, Suchi," Thad says. He stands up from bending to get another tray of shrimp out of the oven. He turns around and smiles at Suchi. Her mouth is agape and her eyes wide.

"Wow, you're gorgeous. Like, male model gorgeous. Why are you so handsome?"

Thad chuckles and gives her a big bright smile. "Thank you, and my parents. Those are my sisters." Thad points to Latrice and Nadia. Latrice waves while Nadia looks up from her phone and smiles at Suchi.

"You have a ridiculously good-looking family," Suchi says.

"I like her." Nadia says to Latrice who chuckles.

"Thank you. I tend to overshare. It's a thing I'm working on. I meant no disrespect." Suchi says the last part to Drea.

"You're good." Drea smiles.

Suchi smiles back and looks relieved. "Great. Thank you."

"So does that mean she can stay for dinner?" Mark asks. "Suchi's plans for the holiday fell through at the last minute so I invited her to join us. Is that okay?"

"Of course," Thad answers.

"Thanks, I would've asked sooner, but something happened. I don't want to bring anyone down with the details—"

"Mr. Johnson, I think you should tell your family," Suchi says.

Mark looks at her and takes a deep breath.

"Mark, what's going on?" Drea asks.

He looks around and sees Latrice, Nadia and Nathan looking at him. And they all look concerned.

"Mark, remember when I told you, you have a village?" Latrice asks.

"Yeah." Mark gives a weak smile. "It's about the twins. All day today, Jelani has been waiting for Acacia to come back home. He asked Santa when I took them to the Grove if he could 'bring mommy back.' Acacia's in Paris now, and God knows where she'll be by New Year's. It's impossible to get ahold of her. Anyway, in lieu of a phone call with her children on Christmas, she sent me this." Mark hands Drea his phone.

Drea reads the text message.

ACACIA

Tell the kids I said Merry Christmas and I'm sending them something from Paris.

Drea reads it to herself again. "That's it? It's their first Christmas without her, and this is all she does?"

"Yes. I, now, have to tell my five-year-old son, whose only wish was for his mother to come back, that she couldn't even bother calling." Mark retrieves his phone.

Fuck you, Acacia!

"Nadia," Drea says.

"Yeah."

"I'm going to need a defense attorney when I see that woman again. If you get my drift."

"I do, and I'll make sure whatever charges you get are dropped," Nadia says.

"Thank you."

Drea hates Acacia. She always has. This is the bitch her best friend walked in on Mark screwing. When Drea slapped Mark for cheating on Latrice, she drew on energy from the ancestors. That's how disgusted she was by her brother's actions, and to cheat on Latrice with Acacia, of all people. She was nothing but a hanger-on who was always around the wealthy to weasel her way in. She was destined to be a side chick, and Mark's dumbass had to go and marry her. And worst of all, two innocent kids got dragged into this mess. Mark is at least trying to make amends to all that he wronged. What's this bitch doing? Hopping around Europe, probably trying to find her next meal ticket. Since Latrice is way past all this stuff, Drea takes it upon herself to hate Acacia for her.

"Go get the kids, Mark. We'll all be here," Drea says. "We can help."

Mark goes and gets the twins. Drea offers Suchi some mulled wine. She shakes her head. "I know I'm not technically on the clock, but still, I'd rather not, just to be safe. I will take some cider though. Thank you."

Drea makes her a mug of cider when she hears crying. "But I asked Santa, and I've been really good!" Jelani cries.

Mark carries a crying Jelani into the room, and Lettie holds Mark's free hand. Poppa Earl, Momma Janet and Quincy follow. Thad and Drea rush over to join the others in comforting the twins.

"I'm sorry, buddy," Mark says.

"This is your fault, Lettie," Jelani accuses.

"Jelani, baby. This isn't Lettie's fault," Momma Janet says.

"But it is, Grammy Janet," Jelani says.

"No, it's not." Lettie defends herself.

"You said you were glad mommy's gone, and Santa heard you," Jelani says.

"That's not true, sweetheart," Latrice says.

"Then why isn't mommy home?" Jelani sobs as Latrice hugs him.

Fuck you, Acacia!

Lettie has tears in her eyes. "I am glad mommy's gone."

"Lettie, don't say that!" Jelani begs.

"But I am. Daddy's not mad anymore, J. And there's no more yelling."

"Kids don't blame each other. Your mother left because she wanted to, not because of anything either of you did," Drea says.

"That's true," Suchi says. She kneels in front of Jelani, who is now sitting on Nathan's lap while Latrice rubs his back. "Jelani, it's okay to miss your mommy, but don't forget you have a sister, a brother and a daddy who love you very much. Not to mention all these other nice people. They all love you, and I know you love them too."

"I do. I love Quincy, Lettie, daddy, and my aunties, and Uncle Thad and Uncle Nathan. And I love Grammy Janet and Grampy Earl," Jelani says.

Aw, this sweet baby! Seriously, fuck you, Acacia.

"I know you do, sweetie. You can love your mommy. Just remember, you have people who love you right here." Suchi looks at Lettie. "And as for you, Little Miss. It's okay for you to be mad, and it's okay to be hurt. But just like they love your brother, everyone in this room loves you, too, and if you need to talk to someone, you have plenty of people in your corner. Always remember that." Suchi smiles.

"Thanks, Sushi." Lettie hugs her.

"Yeah, thank you, Sushi." Jelani hugs her too.

Suchi hugs them back.

"After such an emotional moment, it feels weird to say this, but dinner is ready," Thad offers.

"How about it? Do you two want to get some food?" Suchi asks.

The twins nod their heads. This new phase in their little lives is far from over. This hurdle has been cleared, but there will be plenty more in the future. But Suchi is right. The twins have a lot of people in their corner.

Later that night, everyone's bellies are full and appreciatively satisfied. Folks went home with plenty of leftovers—except Mark and the twins— they were staying in the guest rooms. Drea comes out of the bathroom in pjs with her hair wrapped. She wanders to the front door, where a light got left on, only to find Thad sitting on the floor next to the tree. He's wearing pjs and a head wrap. "I have another present for you, peach."

"The new dutch oven and Gucci Jackie O bag were enough." Drea smiles.

"In the great words of Luther, it's never too much. Not when it comes to you, my love."

Drea simpers, "Thank you."

"Come here." He pats the floor, and Drea sits beside him. "Close your eyes," he whispers in her ear. Drea does as he says, her every nerve ending tingling with anticipation. He places something in her hands. A box. And it's wrapped. "Open your eyes and open your gift."

Drea opens her eyes and sees an impeccably wrapped gift. She tears it open like a little kid making Thad laugh. She cannot believe her eyes and looks back at Thad, who smiles at her. It's an original Ava Love doll! These dolls were the Cabbage Patch Kids and Tickle Me Elmo's of the early aughts. They were made by a Black woman named Mitzy Carter in Springfield, Illinois. Mitzy wanted to make a fashion doll with proud Black features and an authentic Black fashion aesthetic. She has made Avas from around the country and, eventually, the globe. Mitzy's still alive and living well off the royalties from the Ava Doll, the TV series, the animated movies, the lunch boxes, etc. The first Ava Love doll was controversial. It was taken off the market and reworked. She was supposed to be nineteen, and her derriere was seen as *too authentic*. Mitzy was trying to get Black girls to be proud of their shape, something she struggled with as a girl who developed early. And folks got in a tizzy, saying the doll was being used to sexualize kids. So, they took the dolls off the shelves and made her behind smaller. Drea loved the doll and begged her mom to get it for her.

Even though she said it was too expensive, Drea always suspected that Vivian was a parent who disapproved of it. Having developed early herself, Drea felt seen thanks to Mitzy and Ava.

Drea grabs Thad and kisses him. With each kiss, she intends to send a message to him. She intends to let him know how much he means to her, and not to toot her own horn, but this kiss blows the previous ones out of the water. Thad seems to agree because five minutes pass before they stop. "Merry Christmas, Drea. I love you."

"Merry Christmas, Thad. I love you too."

12

DREA

"I'm Thaddeus Richardson, and this is Andrea Richardson, my wife," Thad tells the valet. Drea always gets a tingle when he calls her his wife.

"Ah, yes. You're the guests of honor. Mrs. Johnson asked that you park in a special, designated spot. Allow me." Thad and Drea exit the car, and the valet slowly and carefully parks the Range Rover between two other large cars, making it impossible to fully get in or out without one of the other cars leaving first. *Sigh, of course. Make it so we can't leave and have no choice but to stay until everyone leaves. I must say, I can always count on her lack of subtlety to make a point.* The valet driver literally climbs over the back row of seats and arrives in the trunk, where he taps the back window. Thad approaches and opens the trunk for him. Both Drea and Thad look at him as if they can't believe what they just witnessed.

"How much is my mom paying you to make sure we don't leave?" Drea asks. The valet avoids eye contact, making her chuckle. "You can relax, we won't say anything," she tells him.

He looks up at Drea and relaxes. Clearly, he sees that they aren't like the uptight guests he's, no doubt, encountered tonight. "An obscene amount of money, and not just me, the other valets too." Drea looks at the other valets, who all nod in agreement.

"Jesus, Vivian. She's being so extra, even for her," Drea complains.

Thad tips the valet anyway and takes her hand as they head to the front door. "That may be, but you and Mark were coming up with code words for when you're ready to leave."

"She didn't know that," Drea grouses.

They get to the door and there's a note:

Welcome to our New Year, New Love Party to celebrate the New Year and the union of our daughter, Andrea Michelle Johnson, to one, Thaddeus Edmund Richardson. People, let yourself inside, and have a libation...or two. This is a festive occasion. Have fun!

"I have to admit, that made me feel all warm inside. It's very welcoming. I forgot how good your mom is at this. She had me not wanting to leave Latrice and Mark's engagement party even though people kept asking me snooty questions pertaining to my status and money."

"Yeah, that's going to happen again tonight. But a million times more because now we're the focus, and trust me, extra focus will be on your being a barber while ignoring the businessman part entirely."

"Why?" Thad looks confused as fuck. It's kind of adorable how clueless he is to these types of folks, especially considering his proximity to them. That just shows how little real interaction he has with them. It's always work-related, and he is affable to everyone who comes into his shops. But he leaves it at that. You're a client, and he's your barber. That's it. Plenty of folks have tried to get Thad to come to *this* party or fly out to *that* country, and he's politely declined, to where he doesn't get asked much anymore, which is how he prefers it. His lack of exposure to this lifestyle, even after Latrice and

Mark were married, has left him woefully unprepared for tonight's festivities.

"Because, my darling, these people don't see you unless you're a CEO, a CFO, a doctor or a lawyer. You need to have an MD or esquire behind your name for you to even register with them." Drea playfully shivers at the thought, as if it made her skin crawl.

Thad laughs, shaking his head. "By the way, did I tell you how beautiful you look tonight?"

"Yes, you did. I believe this is your sixth time."

"Let's make it seven. You are fine as hell. I'mma give you those slow strokes when we get home."

"Thad! Please focus." Drea flushes and simpers. Thad smirks, and Drea clears her throat and continues, "The folks we are about to encounter thrive on the competition, and we're not competition in their eyes. So, they're just here for the spectacle. Most of them are probably going to be surprised we even showed up."

"Why? The party is for us."

"Yes, but you see, husband, they think that my mother threw this party to save face from not attending our wedding. They're here on the off chance that a family squabble ensues. When the simple truth is, she added us to this already existing party so she can have something to control. She couldn't control our wedding, so she's settling for this."

"So, what's the plan?"

"Fuck it. We go in and enjoy ourselves," Drea says.

"I like that plan." Thad smiles.

They loop arms and walk in. The chatter and talking comes to a standstill when the couple of the hour walks in the house. Vivian is at the top of the stairs. She looks ravishing. She has on a black Vivian Westwood off-shoulder satin gown, with a gorgeous black pearl necklace. Her hair is radiant and styled like she's an old Hollywood actress. She always loved the glamour of forties and fifties Hollywood and used to show Drea old movies when she was little. She makes her way down the stairs and greets Thad and Drea. "Welcome, kids. Allow me to introduce you."

"Vivian, I must say you look absolutely stunning. You and Drea are definitely the two most beautiful women here." Thad smiles.

"Why, thank you, Thaddeus." Vivian grins. She looks at Drea, and for a second, her face registers approval. It doesn't last long. Soon, she's greeting the guests. "Hello and welcome, everyone! I see the guests of honor have arrived. Happy New Year, and Happy New Love. In a few hours, we will be ringing in the new year, and what better way to celebrate new beginnings than to celebrate the new love of my daughter, Andrea, and her husband, Thaddeus? Please don't be shy, congratulate them on their nuptials."

Everyone smiles and applauds like a bunch of seals. But Drea sees it in their eyes. Whether it's envy, superiority or outright contempt. The envy comes in hard from the women who are checking out Thad and asking themselves some serious questions about their own marriage. Next, she spots the superiority in a lot of the men. They think they make more than Thad and, therefore, believe they're better. And last is contempt, and, unfortunately, the women are the ones holding that down too. She knows that a lot of the women here went along with whatever their parents forced on them. Drea attended school with them, she participated in charm school with them and had a mother similar to their own. One who foisted marriage on them from the time they were teenagers.

But unlike Drea, they did what mommy and daddy said, and now, they're in unfulfilled, miserable marriages with kids they probably didn't even want.

Truth is, Drea isn't throwing shade at any of these women. She's simply seen this for far too many years not to recognize it. She's sure they do as well. Drea honestly feels sorry for every person who fits into each category, but not enough to let them disrespect her or Thad. And that's why, instead of tolerating this shindig, Drea thought she and Thad should enjoy themselves and forget anything else. If people want to come at them sideways, let 'em. She and Thad can handle themselves. Drea will deal with the fallout from her mom later.

Here comes a practitioner of envy and contempt, Simone Fincher, with her husband, Theodore. "Drea!" Simone gushes.

"Hi, Simone. Hello, Theodore. This is my husband, Thad," Drea introduces them.

"A pleasure to meet you. So, Vivian tells us you're a *barber*." Simone says the word *barber* like it's a contagious disease and not an honorable profession.

"Yes,"—Thad smiles—"I am."

"Well, good for you. I'm sure you're very popular and have a slew of customers," Simone condescends.

Thad looks at Drea like, *Let me tell her.* Drea shakes her head. Simone isn't worth making them look foolish. She's the type who doesn't understand the concept of shame. Each year, she makes Theo buy her something extravagant whenever their neighbor buys anything nice for his wife. She's forced Theo to express his love by purchasing her things. Drea doesn't regularly speak with these people, but when she and her mom do talk, it's 50 percent gossip, 50 percent overbearing and critical. All 100 percent is Vivian.

"Thank you, I'll keep my finger crossed," Thad says in a smartass tone, making Drea chuckle.

Simone looks at them both like she smells something foul. She quickly course corrects and brags about her husband. "Theo here just became the head of cardio at the hospital. They're going to hang his portrait on the hospital wall near the entrance."

Theo smiles. "Maybe I should get my hair cut before they paint me. Think you could fit me in?" he asks Thad. "I'd be happy to become a client, even if it's only to help boost sales for a bit."

Drea can see Thad biting the inside of his cheek to not laugh. "My shop does have a wait list—"

"Wow, now that's impressive. Good for you. I can add my name, if you'd like. How many people are ahead of me?"

"As of now"—Thad looks at his phone—"about a hundred and fifty people are ahead of you." He looks up and smiles. The look on Simone's and Theo's faces makes Drea wish she could relive hearing Thad's answer again and again. "But I'll tell you what. The next time you go see your man about a cut, ask him not to get so distracted. Your hairline is slightly askew," Thad says, and Drea now has to hold in a laugh. Simone and Theo mumble congratulations and walk away. Thad turns to Drea. "You're right, peach. This is fun."

A server comes by and offers them each a glass of champagne. They take it as Mark walks over. "I know I burned up your husband's mouth, but—"

"Tut, tut. You are staying, Markus," Drea interrupts.

"Drea, please, if mom introduces me to one more single woman, I will scream."

"I'd actually pay to see that," Thad says.

Another two servers approach. One offers Mark champagne, and the other offers each of them a mini slider. Mark takes the drink, while Thad and Drea take the food.

"You should eat, Mark. It's going to be a long night," Drea says.

"I will."

Vivian approaches. "Markus, there you are. I need to introduce you to Diane Kempler's niece, Melanie. She's newly divorced." Vivian looks at

Drea. "Straighten your back and shoulders square, Andrea, and smile." Drea straightens her posture and smiles. Pleased, Vivian smiles back.

"Sybil Lewis," Thad says.

"Excuse me?" Vivian asks.

"That's who you remind me of tonight. Sorry, she was a Black actress—" Thad begins.

"I know who Sybil Lewis was, Thaddeus. I'm surprised that you do." Vivian looks impressed.

"I used to watch old Black indie movies with my grandfather growing up. He was a WWII vet, you know," Thad says.

"Really?" Vivian literally clutches her pearls. "That's quite impressive, Thaddeus, and something I wish I knew sooner. When I invited our dear friends, the only thing I could tell them about you was that you're a barber. Is there anything else you're hiding about this man, Andrea? Does he save orphans in his spare time?"

"Not anymore. He's training Quincy to take over," Drea replies.

"Speaking of my grandson, you will be bringing Quincy over more now, won't you, Markus?"

"Yes, Mom."

"Good, now don't dawdle. Come along." Vivian takes Mark's arm and leads him away.

Mark turns around and mouths, *Help me.* Drea and Thad both just shrug.

"She likes me." Thad grins.

"She does. I must say I am impressed too, husband."

Thad does some pop locking. "That ain't nuthin', wife. By the time I'm done, your momma's going to love me more than Mark."

"You're well on your way." Drea laughs.

"Hell, I'm even dealing with more nonsense than Mark is too. He has to be introduced to beautiful women, boo-hoo. At least he doesn't have to sit back and wait for people to come over and mock his profession."

"Or straighten his posture," Drea says, making Thad chuckle. "Speaking of which, here comes another couple. It's Naomi and Tucker Hampton. Both are super shallow. This will be fun."

Naomi gives Drea a hug. "Drea, how long has it been?"

"A few years. I haven't seen you since Mark and Latrice's wedding," Drea answers.

"Of course, so sad how that ended. I heard she bounced back with a younger man." Naomi says. "And a teacher. I guess we know who's the bread-winner in that house."

"More and more women are jumping ship and getting themselves men who aren't providers," Tucker says, looking at Thad. "It's really sad."

"I guess that depends on what these men are providing. If their wives wanted nothing more than a walking ATM, and that's all they have to offer, then I suppose that's fine. But if they're looking for a man who will love, honor, cherish and respect them, that's probably worth a lot more to these ladies," Thad replies.

"You're so dreamy," Drea tells her husband.

"Thank you, baby."

Thad leans down and kisses Drea's shoulder, sending a surge of tingles down her body. She shivers, then giggles. Thad smiles at her, and they get lost in each other's souls. By the time they realize they've been staring, they chuckle and look up, only for Naomi and Tucker to be staring at them like they're insane.

"Our apologies. It's hard not to get captivated by her," Thad explains.

"That's so beautiful," Naomi says.

"Not nearly as beautiful as my Drea is," Thad adds.

Naomi actually fucking swoons. "Wow." She turns to her husband. "How come you never talk to me or about me like that?" She stands there, waiting for an explanation.

Tucker fumbles his words. "I…uh….you never mentioned—"

"I shouldn't have to tell my husband to compliment me, Tucker." Naomi rushes off.

Tucker gives Thad and Drea a cutting look, and Thad shrugs and smiles as Tucker follows his wife.

"I have a feeling we're going to start a bunch of fights tonight," Thad says.

"You think?"

"If me showing you affection and speaking highly of you just made that happen, then yes, these men are cooked."

Over the course of the next hour, Thad and Drea greet people, Thad's profession gets mocked and he ends each interaction by praising Drea. With everyone here waiting to see a spectacle, Thad has made sure that they won't get one, at least not with him and Drea. Each couple has walked away dumbfounded that these two actually love and *like* each other. They all thought there was going to be something gossip worthy, only to walk away confused.

There are murmurs in the crowd, and soon, Drea sees why. Her father, Greyson, has made his appearance. Whenever her parents throw a party,

Vivian does all the detailed work, while her dad simply makes an appearance, charms some people and joins the festivities as her mom runs everything.

Greyson approaches them. "Andrea, hello. This must be my new son-in-law. I'm Dr. Greyson Johnson." Her father offers Thad his hand.

"Thaddeus Richardson, a pleasure to meet you again, sir," Thad says.

"Have we met?" Greyson asks.

"Yes, I'm Latrice's brother," Thad answers.

"Of course, of course. Shame about her and Mark. I really thought they would make it," Greyson replies.

Thad looks at Drea, and they have a conversation through facial expressions. Thad's mouth is puckered like he just ate a lemon, but Drea can tell he's amused and trying to hide it. He's asking his wife, *Is he serious?*

Drea smiles and nods. *Yes, he is.*

"So, a lovely night for a party, isn't it? The skies are clear. That'll make the fireworks at midnight more noticeable," Greyson offers in way of small talk.

Thad's eyes widen. *He's literally talking about the weather, peach.*

Drea smirks and snorts out a small laugh. *I know, just smile and nod.*

Thad smiles and nods. Greyson looks around and sees someone. "Ah, there's the crab cake girl. If you two will excuse me." He walks away.

"And that is the last we'll be seeing of him," Drea comments.

"Really?" Thad asks.

"Yeah, I told you, he and I don't talk much."

"I can't believe he actually talked about the weather. And didn't ask shit about me."

"Of course not."

Greyson catches up to the server and is soon surrounded by admirers. He works the crowd like a seasoned politician. He can manipulate them with his good looks and charm. Folks might be jealous of her parents, but they also strive to be them. Hence why they never miss a party and folks die to be invited to one. They'll stay in Greyson's face for the opportunity to kiss the brass ring. That's a big part of the reason Drea and her father aren't close. She would never fall for that.

Drea sees her mother go over to the DJ. She takes the microphone to make an announcement. "Alright, everyone, let's have the first dance be with the happy couple of the evening."

Thad and Drea make their way to the middle of the room and dance. The DJ plays "Giving You the Best That I've Got" by Anita Baker, and they are transported to another world. The people in the room disappear, and it's just them. They dance on air as Anita turns into Keith Sweat and Jacci McGhee telling them to make it last forever. Soon another Keith—Washington—is on deck, crooning about kissing and loving his woman all through the night. Thad rubs his hands up and down Drea's back. He holds her close. Drea clings to his broad shoulders. Thad passionately lip syncs the part where Mr. Washington tells his love that tonight is the night they will share. He orders her to turn off the lights and get close to him. When he gets to Keith's long note, Thad gets on his knees and begs Drea, making her laugh out loud. The song changes to "Fire and Desire" by Rick James and Teena Marie. Thad and Drea look at each other and know they have to do Martin and Gina's interpretation of the song. They know they look silly, but who cares? They survived being grilled by her mother's intolerable guests. Besides, the goal tonight was to have fun. It is their party, after all. Thad sings along when Rick sings, "LOOOVVE them and leave them."

"Sing, my king!" Drea cheers.

Mark shakes his head and laughs at them. Pretty soon, it starts a domino effect, and more people laugh and join in the fun. A few men take their ladies' hands and dance with them. A few even sing along with Thad and Drea. "I gotta say, I am surprised by the music choices your mom made," Thad says.

"Don't let the bougie fool you. Vivian Johnson listens to old school R&B. Her and my dad would go see an Atlantic Starr concert as quickly as they'll see a production of Bizet's *Carmen*," Drea replies.

"I'm going to get you a drink." Thad kisses Drea's hand. She smiles and squeezes his hand before turning around, only to find Bianca Stevenson, Alexis's daughter, standing before her with her hive.

Drea could not be less pressed. If this grown-ass thirty-something woman wants to hang on to a twenty-year-old beef, then she's welcome to, but Drea will not partake.

"Hello, Drea," Bianca offers.

"Bianca," is all Drea's offers.

Thad returns. Drea feels his lips on her bare shoulder blade and smiles. He kisses his way up until he's kissing her shoulder and then moves on to her neck. He hands her the drink. "Here," he says.

She turns and looks at his handsome face and

says, "Thank you." He kisses her lips like a soldier coming home from war. "Mmmm," Drea sighs. He backs away and rubs his nose against hers.

"That was quite a show you two put on." Bianca gets the attention of the happy couple. She wears a smile similar to Sheila's. It doesn't reach her eyes. Her hive offers shallow smiles of their own. *Jesus, why do women like this always have a team of followers?* Bianca, that horny mom from Quincy's school…? Hell, even Drea herself has a crew, but they aren't mindless drones who do what she says and let her be the leader.

"Why, thank you," Drea says. "Bianca, ladies, this is my husband, Thad."

The ladies examine him like he's a piece of raw meat. By now, Drea is sure Thad is used to the stares. Still, he keeps himself composed as ever and smiles. "A pleasure to make your acquaintance, ladies." Thad smiles. *Those dimples.* Drea can see in real time the ladies sizing him up. One is truly doing the most, shoving her way in front so Thad can shake her hand. He does her one better and offers her one of those Thad smiles that feels like a warm coat on a winter's day. She smiles widely and giggles. Knowing these ladies' husbands, that's probably the most attention she's gotten all week.

"So, you're the *barber*?" Bianca says, sounding somehow even more condescending than Simone did earlier.

Thad readies himself for more of the same. He stands his ground and nods while not taking his eyes from Bianca. "I am. Does your man need a cut?"

"No, thank you." Bianca waves at her husband, Anthony Thomas. Drea went to school with him too. He's basically Mark if her brother had stayed on the path he was on. His relationship with Bianca can best be described as birds of a feather. Anthony barely acknowledges his wife and turns back to talking to the other guests he was conversing with. "My Anthony has a personal barber who comes to our house. Do you do home visits, Thad? Or can you not afford to leave your little shop?" Bianca asks this like she really wants to know.

"Wow, they really aren't hiding the rudeness anymore, are they, peach?" Thad turns to Drea and smirks.

"In her defense, Bianca is always like this." Drea sips her drink.

"I just asked a simple question, Drea. It's not my fault you're both so sensitive." Bianca sneers.

"I'm not trying to have any back-and-forth with you, Bianca," Drea clarifies.

"Neither am I." Drea's about to walk away with Thad, when Bianca decides that the option of shutting the fuck up just won't do. "Though, I can't say that I'm shocked by your choice in a husband." She looks down at her own wedding band. "We all held out hope that your mom could find you a doctor—like my Anthony—or a CFO, like your brother. But a barber? And apparently, you didn't have to look that far to find him. He's Mark's ex's brother, I think. The well must be dry as hell."

Take the high road, take the high road and ignore her. She's going low, so I should go high, just like Michelle Obama said. I know this. I do. To be petty is to sink to her level. Drea looks at Thad. The look he gives her tells her he has her back, no matter what. "I'm about to be petty as hell." Drea finishes her drink.

"Knock yourself out." Thad kisses her on the forehead. "I'll get you a refill." He heads back to the bar.

Drea smiles as he walks away. She turns her attention to Bianca, and her smile fades. "The well is dry, Bianca. That much is true."

"Didn't that feel good to admit?" Bianca taps Drea's shoulder.

"It did, but it didn't feel nearly as good as how much my husband satisfies me in *every. Single. Aspect* of my life. I am very lucky, Bianca. I wake up with a smile on my face 'cause I love my husband and he loves me. But most importantly, we like, trust, and respect each other. And that shit feels amazing. Otherworldly. I never knew it could be this good, and I'm mad at myself for not finding him sooner. That man loves me down. And let me tell you a little something else about him. Thaddeus isn't a businessman, he is a *business* man. You want to visit my husband's shop, you have to add your name to a waitlist a mile long. So not only does he make money moves, but he's compassionate, loving, kind, hilarious, sexy, fine as frog hair, and I know you all noticed. Thaddeus lives to keep a smile on my face. Does Anthony—or any of your husbands—do that for you?" No one responds. "That's what I thought."

"Are you through, Andrea?" Vivian asks.

Drea turns around. "How long have you—?"

"Your entire speech. A word, please?"

Bianca and her hive chuckle. Drea looks at them like they have the combined IQ of a raisin. "What are you smirking at? I'm thirty-three. What do you think she's going to do? Send me to my room without dinner?"

Drea turns and heads to the study and opens the door. Vivian hands her a finger of Scotch. Drea takes it and drinks it, despite hating Scotch. Vivian is quiet, eerily quiet. She stands in front of the fireplace with a roaring fire going and just stares at it. Drea gets closer and is soon standing next to her mother. "Mom, I'm sorry, but the whole party was *barber* this and *barber* that. I'm proud of my husband and his accomplishments."

"It must have felt good to tell Bianca off like that. You must have enjoyed making them all look foolish. You, of course, get your ability to look down on those who challenge you from me. I just wish I wasn't one of the people you looked down upon."

"Mom—"

Vivian turns to face her. "Have a seat." Drea sits down and listens to her mother. "My life has been spent making men look good. First, my father, by being the perfect daughter, then my husband, by being the perfect wife, and even my son. I have been a lot to a lot of people, and it's been some of the best years of my life. I have worked hard to make Dr. Greyson Johnson look like a God. The way those people laugh at his every word, the way they stand at attention when he enters a room, and how he responds was all manufactured by me. I took a Black man who had nothing but a name and I made him into an esteemed doctor who has performed historical surgeries. I told him he could go out and play, but that he'd better not bring any nonsense to my doorstep. When he had a pregnancy scare with some nurse, I put an end to his playtime. Your father hasn't cheated since. I earned that. I gave him my loyalty and my support. I built him up and made him into what I believed him to be. I never wavered when he questioned his greatness. I told him that he deserved it and whoever doubts him would soon eat their words. I made that man who he is, and he knows it. I built this family. I built us from the ground up. And I am proud. Do my children drive me crazy? You, with your hard head and Mark, who can't seem to keep a woman?"

Drea quietly chuckles.

"Yes, but despite that, I am proud of my children. Your brother, the CFO of Enerex and you the co-owner and finance manager at Mtindo."

"You know what my title is?" Drea asks.

"Of course I do, Andrea. I'm your mother."

"It's just that you always made my job seem so inconsequential to you." Drea scoots closer to her.

"It wasn't that, Andrea. Your choosing a career was like a slap in the face. It was like a slight to all the hard work I put in making generational wealth for my family," Vivian explains.

"Mom, forget the family for a minute. What did you want? I did what I wanted, and it was never meant to hurt you, by the way. I wanted to live my life on my own terms, not what our social circle deemed acceptable, and I could not be happier. But building a legacy for your family can't be all that you wanted."

"Sweetheart, we are Black. And quite a few of the people out there are white. And yet, they clamor to be invited to one of my soirees. I am the queen B to them, and yes, they are cunning, conniving and manipulative, but damn it, so am I. I built our family," she says again, this time more assertively. "I got us to the top. And I am not letting any one of those families who think that just because they're white, they're more deserving of the top spot. I did my job, and I did it well. And for that, I am happy. This is what I wanted."

"Mom, that's amazing, but that can't be all there is. What about love?"

"What about it? I love your father, and he loves me."

"But not in a way where your heart skips a beat when he enters the room. Where he makes you feel like he would stop the world for you. Like he can't breathe without hearing your voice. Was it worth it to sacrifice that, Mom?"

"Yes. Andrea, there was stiff competition for your father, but I got him and I knew what that meant for our future. And now, after all that I sacrificed, people fight to become your father's intern. He has won awards and saved so many lives. That is what I came to love. The man I made. And he loves the woman who made him."

"Mom, all you did was rattle off some of Dad's accomplishments. That can't be all that you love about him. What about romance? Affection? Teasing, sex—?"

Vivian holds up her hand. "That's enough, Andrea. Look, you're a romantic, and that's something I have come to realize. I don't understand it, but I know it's how you see things. I just see them in a more practical manner. As long as my family beyond my generation continues to rise, then I don't need romance. I am happy with my life choices. Trust me."

"Okay, Mom. I respect your decision. I don't get it, but I respect it. And for the record, I know we don't always see eye to eye, but I have always held a great deal of respect for you."

"Of course you have." Vivian smirks. "And for the

record, child of mine, I am happy for you. I'm glad that my sacrifice meant that you were able to find love. I just wanted you to be financially well-off too. Is that a crime?"

"I suppose not."

"And I do like Thad. He's very charming."

Drea laughs. "He's going to love that you said that. I love you, Mom."

"I love you too, sweetheart." They hug. "And why am I just now finding out that my son-in-law is an entrepreneur?"

"Mom, I tried to tell you when you stopped by."

"Oh, well, try harder next time. A grandfather who was a World War II vet, a vast knowledge of film, and there's a waitlist for his shops. Oh, I cannot wait to throw this in Alexis's face."

Drea laughs. She sees her love and reunites with him.

"Where did you disappear to?" he asks.

"My mom and I had a talk. The countdown is about to start. I'll tell you what happened later. Come on, let's go."

A crowd has gathered outside. Drea sees Bianca, who cuts her eyes at Drea before watching her and Thad. Drea sees sadness there. Their marriage may not be conventional, but at least her mom is happy with the results. Can women like Bianca say the same? Vivian took charge and made Greyson into the man she's proud to call her husband. She sacrificed the warm, gooey, lovey-dovey stuff because making a name for her family was more important. But these poor women can't even say they built their families a legacy like Drea's mother. They're with men who don't even see them. Drea watches as the countdown from ten begins. She's grateful to have Thad, a man who not only sees her, but who recognizes that he didn't always, and who has gone above and beyond to absolve himself from making what he sees as a foolish mistake. *Nine. Eight. Seven. Six. Five. Four. Three. Two. One. Happy New Year!* The fireworks are an impressive array of colors. Unfortunately, they're also really loud. Drea feels sorry for anyone with a pet or PTSD right now. This is beautiful, but insensitive as hell. Thad turns her toward him and looks at her. Sees her. He lays a kiss on her so disrespectfully delicious, by the time they are done, folks are staring. They smile and gaze at each other.

Happy New Year! Thad mouths.

Happy New Year, she mouths back.

13

THAD

Thad waits with Lance and Jess as Drea finishes getting ready. He hates to say he told her so, *but* he told her so. She agreed they would have dinner together after work on Friday. Thad sent Drea reminders to set out what she was going to wear. She does this all the time with her outfits, but she's been working late getting things ready for Uncle Sam, so she forgot. And now Jess, Lance and Thad are waiting for her to come out so they can make their reservation.

"Thad!" Drea calls out.

"Yeah."

"Where are my black strappy shoes?"

"They're in your walk-in closet on the left-hand side."

"No, those are my Manolo's. I'm talking about—"

"You're Loubous, I know. They're on the left-hand side, peach."

"I don't see them," she whines.

"They're there."

"Thad, I'm telling you, I don't see them."

"Baby, and I'm telling you, they are there."

"Come find them for me, please," Drea begs.

He lets out a sigh and gets up from the couch to help her find the shoes that are probably right in front of her face. He walks into the closet, and yep, they are right in front of her face. Thad takes them off the display stand, where she put them so she would remember where they were, and hands them to her.

"I thought you meant that they were in one of the drawers on the left-hand side. You didn't say display," Drea teases.

Thad kneels and taps his knee, telling Drea to place her foot there. "Come on, Cinderella. Let's get these shoes on." Minutes later, they come out to Lance and Jess grinning like fools at them. "Why are ya'll looking at us like that?"

"You knew which shoes she was talking about without her having to tell you, and you knew exactly where they were. And she knew you'd find them.

Ya'll are married!" Jess says, playfully wiping away imaginary tears.

"Yep, if my eyes were closed, you two could be Poppa Earl and Momma Janet." Lance agrees with his wife.

Thad and Drea smile at their friends' observations. Marrying Drea has to be the easiest decision that he has ever made. It's like winning the lottery every day. It's wonderful to hear their love is evident by those around them, especially when so many are happy couples themselves.

A half hour later, the foursome is sitting at the table and waiting for their server. They made it with five minutes to spare.

"All I'm saying is you can't blame me for not seeing the shoes," Drea laments.

"According to Thad, they were right in front of you," Lance says.

"Of course you're going to take up for him," Drea complains.

Thad and Lance look at her like, *Nice try*.

"No, but seriously. Why can't you ladies ever find anything?" Lance asks.

"Thank you. Questions that need answers," Thad agrees.

"Excuse me, does this sound familiar?" Drea

stands up and pats herself down. *"Drea! Hey, peach, you seen my keys?"* Drea says, doing her best Thad impression. Jess and Lance laugh loudly. Jess even goes so far as to point *and* laugh at Thad.

"Okay, it's like that. Well, how about this—?"

"You cannot use what happened tonight as an example, Thaddeus," Drea sits, cutting him off.

"Fine." Thad clears his throat. *"Thad, where did you put the paprika? I can't find it."* Thad imitates Drea. "It's where it always is, Drea." Thad scrunches up his nose. *"No, it's not. Come find it for me."* He smirks at Drea. "I find it and hand it to you. I don't know why you can't see things that are right in front of you."

"Whatever." Drea pouts.

"And why do ya'll always do that?" Lance asks.

The server comes and gets their drink orders. She instructs them on how to use the QR code to order their entrée before going to retrieve their drinks.

"Jesus, what ever happened to ordering from a menu?" Thad asks.

"You sound like an old man who's two seconds away from saying, *Back in my day...*" Jess teases.

"Look, the old heads are right sometimes. I want to look at a menu, then tell a human person what I want to eat. Is that too much to ask?" Thad inquires.

Jess chuckles at Thad before turning to Lance. "Why do we do what?" she asks.

Lance continues, "Use sex as a weapon. Drea just gave Thad the pouty face. Ya'll know what that does to us."

"On God. The pouty face, the sad face, the doe eyes, which this one reigns supreme." Thad points at Drea, who then blows him a kiss. He catches it and winks at her, making her giggle. "And that too! That fucking giggle. You know what gets us riled up, and you use it against us. And don't let them combine the giggle with the breathy voice. Diabolical," Thad states.

"Yeah, so?" Drea says while Jess shrugs.

"Just evil temptresses, and happy to be evil temptresses too. Let me tell you about this one." Lance points at Jess. "We got into a debate, and she turned out to be wrong. And instead of saying, 'My bad, L. You were right,' Ms. Jesslyn decides that rubbing her ass against my groin was sufficient enough."

Jess does a little shimmy and laughs before sipping her wine. "That's because I know how much you love this ass."

"I know that feeling. Thad uses my butt as a pillow when we lay on the couch." Lance and Jess laugh. "One day, I'm going to surprise him and eat a bunch of beans." Drea chuckles.

Thad raises a single eyebrow, looking at her with suspicion. Drea laughs. Having achieved his goal of making her smile, he turns his attention to Lance and Jess. "What was your debate about?"

"What Kyle's job was on *Living Single,*" Lance answers.

"He was a stockbroker," Thad and Drea answer at the same time.

"Yep, this one thought he was a…what did you call it, baby? Uh, yes, 'a financial something or other.'" Lance points at Jess. She playfully smacks his arm. "But the initial discussion was about Kyle and Overton, specifically. Most dudes fancy themselves to be a 'Kyle,' but they don't have Kyle's charisma, just his sexist way of thinking, and they consider being an 'Overton' soft."

"Well, fuck that. I'm definitely an Overton. Back in the day, women would see me and think I was a Kyle, and quite a few of them were disappointed when they discovered I was not."

"Those women don't know what they're missing," Drea says. "Don't get me wrong, I like Kyle, and I love him and Max together, but I love being married to an Overton. I always thought Synclaire was the one to be, out of the four of them," Drea says, looping her arm with Thad's.

"Seriously? You wanted to be Synclaire over Khadijah?" Jess asks.

"In terms of romantic relationships, yes. In terms of my hustle and business acumen, I'm definitely a Khadijah, but I'm way better at owning and running a company. I'm sorry, but my girl almost lost Flavor like a million times," Drea replies. They all laugh. "No, but seriously, in terms of romance, Synclaire beat the other ladies by more than a mile. It took Khadijah and Max the entire damn run of the show before Scooter and Kyle got their shit together, respectively. Synclaire had her man by the end of season one. Now let's compare that to the vanilla version of *Living Single*."

Jess laughs and shakes her head while Lance chuckles as he takes a sip of his beer.

Drea continues, "On vanilla *Living Single*, it took Ross and Rachel from season two until the last damn episode. Synclaire and Overton wiped the floor with everyone in terms of recognizing their soulmate and handling their business. The only couple that comes close in comparison are Ben and Leslie on *Parks and Rec*." Drea and Thad quickly look at each other and say, "I love you, and I like you," simultaneously. They burst out laughing, and Drea lays her forehead on Thad's shaking shoulder.

"What the fuck was that?" Jess asks.

"We made a pact that any time *Parks and Rec* gets mentioned, we'll say that to each other," Drea explains.

"Yeah, like Ben and Leslie. And whoever says it the quickest wins," Thad adds.

"Wins what?" Lance asks.

"Nothing. They just win until we come up with another game," Thad replies.

"You don't win anything. That's stupid. What's the point?" Lance derides them.

"For real. Ya'll are corny as hell. I bet you two are one of those couples that says, *You hang up first. No, you hang up first,*" Jess chides.

"That only happened once," Thad mumbles.

Lance and Jess lean against each other and laugh at them.

"Don't act like ya'll don't get cheesy too," Drea accuses.

"Yeah, but we don't display it like you two." Jess smiles.

"Hey, we love our love, and we are proud of how much we love our love," Thad says. Drea kisses his face.

"I want you to run that sentence back in your head, my guy," Lance suggests.

Thad thinks for a second before looking at Lance. "Fuck you, nigga."

Lance laughs. "I'm like, *'he has to hear how goofy that shit sounded.'*"

They all laugh. Thad's shoulders shake as he barks out a laugh and claps his hands.

"Okay, can I just say how hilarious it is that you call *Friends* vanilla *Living Single*." Jess chuckles.

"Yep, she calls New Kids On The Block vanilla New Edition too." Thad snickers.

Lance wraps his arm around Jess's shoulder, laughing.

Jess asks, "Okay, going back to *Living Single*, Drea, what do you think of Regine's happy ending?"

The server comes with their orders. Thad grumbles a little, making the table snicker. The server refills their waters, then exits.

"I didn't like how they did my girl, Regine," Drea responds.

"Why? She ended up with a rich dude, just like she wanted." Lance cuts into his steak.

"Yeah, but the writers had the opportunity to do the cutest thing. Money wasn't as important to Regine as love was," Drea explains.

Thad takes the opportunity to nab a shrimp off her plate.

"You better leave my scrimps alone." Drea covers her plate.

Thad bites into it. "Mmmm. Garlicy and buttery."

Drea wipes the sauce off his mouth with her thumb before licking it off. "I'mma make you pay for that when we get home."

Thad growls. Drea rolls her eyes.

She continues as she laughs at her husband, "Anyway, where was I? Oh, right. We see that money isn't as important to her as Regine makes it on the episode with Heavy D and Vivica Fox. If Regine only wanted money, she would have gotten back with Darryl after he dumped Vivica at the altar, but she didn't want to mess up their friendship. That proves that it's not just the money. Regine wanted love too. What they should have done was have her get with Russell, then in a funny twist, he wins the lottery. So, Regine gets love and money all at the same time."

"Not going to front, I would have watched that." Lance nods his head.

"Her and Russell did have some good chemistry," Jess agrees.

"That's what I'm saying," Drea says.

"Your thoughts on Toni and Todd," Jess says.

"Oh, God! Don't get her on a *Girlfriends* rant, Jess. I beg," Thad says.

"Okay, so…" Drea ignores Thad.

———

LATER IN THE EVENING, THE FOUR FRIENDS ARE STILL sitting at their table. Their empty plates have been cleared. And now they're just drinking water refills. Why haven't they left? Because Drea's only on season two of *Girlfriends*. Thad begged Jess not to get her started. He shoots her a look that says, *See what you did.*

She shrugs and chuckles before mouthing, *I'm sorry.*

"And I'm sorry, but that whole Stan affair thing with Maya was pointless. They could have conveyed that she and Darnell were having problems without bringing another person into the mix. It was bad enough that he hated her friends and didn't want to see her grow—"

The restaurant manager approaches their table. "Ma'am, I am terribly sorry, but we need to close. We wanted to give you all a little extra time since Mr. Greene is a friend to our establishment, but it's been almost an hour. We will give you each a free dessert, just please. Please let us close," he says.

Thad takes Drea's hand and squeezes it. "My apologies. I'll take the raspberry swirl, crumble cheesecake, please," Drea mumbles.

Everyone else puts in their dessert orders. Thad gives the wait staff nice tips and apologizes.

They all stand outside the restaurant, waiting on Lance and Jess's ride share. Lance and Jess live forty minutes in the opposite direction of Thad and Drea. They took a Lyft to Thad and Drea's house and rode with them to dinner since they live closer to the restaurant and Jess had a craving. Like Thad, Lance will do anything to make his wife happy. No matter what.

Thad is currently trying to do just that as Drea's face is buried in his chest out of embarrassment. "It's okay, baby." He squeezes Drea tightly. "I thought you made some good points."

"You're just saying that," she says in a muffled voice.

"No, he's not, Drea. Come on, it's kind of funny. You were ranting about *Girlfriends* for so long, we got kicked out of a restaurant," Jess says. "That's pretty hilarious."

"I think we aren't addressing the most important

point. We got free desserts! I say the next time we get dinner, someone get Drea riled up about *Insecure* until our whole meal is free," Lance jokes.

Thad, Jess and Drea laugh.

"See, baby. It's okay, and it *is* kind of funny."

"I guess." Drea doesn't seem convinced.

Lance and Jess's ride arrives. They all say their goodbyes, and the Greene's ride drives away. Thad opens the passenger door for Drea before getting in the driver's seat. "Drea," Thad says.

"Yes," Drea replies. She looks less embarrassed but not by much.

"I don't think Joan was unfair to Ellis," Thad says.

"I know what you're trying to do, Thad, and it's fine. I don't need to go through my rant."

"Joan should have been more understanding when Lynn snuck Vosco into the house."

Drea flinches but doesn't respond.

Thad sees he has to ramp it up a bit more. "Peaches and Ronnie wouldn't have been able to carry their own show," Thad remarks.

"What! If Joan's cousin in medical school and her football meathead boyfriend could carry their own show, then—no, no. I am not doing this Thad."

"Come on, baby. You'll feel better once you get your rant out. You were interrupted—"

"And kicked out of a restaurant because I couldn't control myself." Drea looks away.

They stop at a red light, and Thad turns Drea's face toward him. "You don't have to control yourself, and there is no one here who is going to make you feel embarrassed."

The light turns green, and they merge onto the 405, heading toward Brentwood and home. "You told Jess not to get me going." Drea sulks.

"Baby, I was kidding. You know I love your rants." He looks at her and knows just what to say. "I think Joan and William made a handsome couple."

Drea looks at him and says, "How dare you? You know those episodes should be deleted from canon. They were like cousins or siblings or something. It was gross and unnecessary."

"I think it served as the perfect example of how desperate Joan became after losing her soulmate, Brock," Thad offers.

"So what? It was ignorant, and another thing, I know I'm a girl's girl, but those women—with the exception of Maya and Darnell—treated all those men horribly. They are the only girl group of friends where none of them should have ended up with a man. The show should have ended with them all single."

Thad smiles and keeps things going. "I don't think Joan was wrong when she became the 'it' girl. I think her friends just couldn't handle it."

"Okay, now you're starting to piss me off."

"Sorry, my love."

Drea smiles at him. He takes her hand and kisses it as they sit still on the 405 and wait for the traffic to clear.

14

DREA

The bowling ball hits the pins with a thunderous sound. Thad leaps into the air. "Yes! That's what I'm talking about."

"Yay! Go, husband."

Thad takes a bow. "Thank you, wife." He takes a seat and sips his drink. "I haven't been bowling in a minute. This was a good idea for a date night, peach."

"Thank you. And we lucked out. I didn't even realize it was couple's night. You know, I had never been to a real bowling alley until college. Most of the kids I grew up with had game rooms in their houses, so their parties always incorporated the use of them. I bowled, but only in those game rooms."

"Rich kid," Thad teases.

"Shut up!" She chuckles. "And what's this about you and my mom going to the movies?" Drea asks.

"Vivian has been invited to the Dorothy Dandridge retrospective that's happening at the Carter Willems Museum of African American Pop Culture. She has deemed me worthy of being her plus one," Thad answers.

"You are so in. She just might have Dad update his will and include you," Drea remarks.

"Cool. I call dibs on that painting in the foyer," Thad replies.

She laughs as she picks up her ball and rolls it down the lane. Two pins knock down. "Thad! I knocked down two."

"Good job, baby! You're getting better."

"I would hope so after five gutter balls."

"Those don't count. They were practice rolls."

"My scorecard doesn't reflect that."

"Forget that score card." Thad waves her worries away. "We're not keeping score, we're just rolling some balls and having fun." Drea bites her lip. It is obvious she's trying to not blurt out the first thought that popped in her head. "Something dirty popped into your head, didn't it?"

"Yeah, but it was not sexy, so I'm not going to say it out loud."

"C'mon, I'm sure it isn't as bad as you're trying to make it."

"I want to roll your balls in my mouth for fun," Drea confesses, and laughs, immediately regretting it. "See, I told you it wasn't sexy. You look confused, not turned on."

"That actually kind of did it for me." Thad nods.

"That did not get you going," Drea says flatly.

"I mean…it didn't *not* get me going."

"Thanks anyway. You're up, my king."

Thad gets up and stretches. "I guess I can show off my skills for a second." Drea smacks his ass. "Now that *did* get me going. You betta watch out."

She breaks into a fit of giggles and sips his drink before cheering, "Go, Thad. With your sexy ass."

He laughs while holding the bowling ball with his head bowed. He shakes his head back and forth at Drea's silly cheer before bowling another strike. Thad walks back like an action star with an explosion behind them.

Drea claps. He picks up his drink to find it empty. "Really?"

"I was thirsty." She gives him a sheepish smile.

"Stop being cute, and go get me a refill," Thad orders. Drea gets up, and this time, Thad smacks her ass.

She walks over to the snack bar and asks for a refill. Looking around, she notices the other couples. There are two couples playing against each other who couldn't be more adorable. One is chill, taking selfies, kissing and looking cozy. It's clear they're enjoying each other's company, like old friends, while the other couple is seriously making out. They still haven't come up for air. Drea's impressed. They're sucked into their own world so much so that they have to be reminded when it's their turn. It's sweet.

"Here you go, beautiful." The kid behind the counter gives Drea her drink.

"Thank you." She puts a five in the tip jar.

"Thanks." The kid smiles. "You know, I get off at ten."

"Sweetie, I'm here with my husband," Drea informs him.

The youngin' has light brown eyes that pop when contrasted with his darker brown skin. He has an athletic build, a low-cut fade with small waves, the beginnings of a starter beard and a bright smile. Drea admits, if she was fifteen years younger, she'd give him her number. "I can be discreet, shawty."

"No, thank you." She smiles.

"Alright, can't blame a brother for trying. Your man's blessed. Hope he knows that." He winks at her.

Drea smiles. "He does, and thank you." Drea has to admit, while she would never step out on Thad, getting compliments is always nice. It's been happening a lot to them since they got married. It's interesting how different their interactions have been. When people hit on Thad, they tend to be overly eager—for example, Sheila, and Iona, before she realized who Drea was. They foist themselves onto Thad. Drea thinks it's Thad's naturally kind energy that makes him irresistible to all people—and Thad gets hit on by everybody. Men, women, gender nonconforming—you name it. He's always respectful and steers the conversation away from anything flirtatious. Most folks get the hint, especially when Drea's around.

But even the folks that flirt with Thad aren't as bold as the dudes that hit on Drea. Men have zero chill. Especially when it comes to Drea's looks. Her face card never declines, and her body is what a lot of women pay good money to imitate. Her curviness and pretty face have led a lot of men down the path to rejection, some much more harshly than others. The folks who hit on Thad, even on their worst day, aren't as bad as the men who hit on Drea, except for the youngin'. He actually showed more emotional maturity than a lot of other men twice his age, and he couldn't be older than twenty.

She takes the drink and returns to Thad. "Here you go."

"Thank you. What were you and the young buck talking about?"

"He was shooting his shot."

Thad smiles. "Of course he was. Hell, the only reason most men don't come up to you is because I'm around. I repel them, but the minute I'm not there and they have an opening…" He looks in the direction of the youngin' who is now flirting with another woman closer to his age before he turns back to Drea. "I think you get hit on a lot more than you let on, Drea. You just don't want me to know." Thad wags his finger at her.

"There is some truth to that. I would not categorize this as being hit on, but some of the stuff I catch on social media I wouldn't want you to see. Mtindo's IG account has pictures of me, Latrice and Ingrid, and I get a lot of comments about my ass."

"What kind of comments?" Thad frowns.

"I'm not telling you. We're having a nice time, and I don't want to spoil it. But I will say this. You're a man. You know how men think. You know that not all men see women as people, but as body parts. Now use your imagination."

"You know my cousin Tamar works in DC. She can get someone to find those assholes in no time," Thad says, dead-ass serious.

"Speaking of cousins, how's Kofi? When is he supposed to get here?"

"Around May-ish. He has a lot stuff he needs to do before he leaves Kentucky and comes out here." A Richardson cousin is moving to LA and Drea loves how excited Thad is. He told Drea that he and Kofi were tight when they were younger. "And I'm serious about calling Tamar."

"Pick up your ball and bowl, Mr. Richardson." Drea snorts out a laugh.

"Don't laugh at me. I'm serious." He picks up his ball and rolls another strike like it's nothing. *Show off.* "Where do you want to eat after this?"

"I have a taste for wood-fired pizza, and I know you know like fifty-eleven places off the top of your head between here and home."

"It's twelve places, but yes, you're right. We can go to Angelo's. Are you getting hungry?"

"I could eat."

"Cool, roll your last ball, peach, and we'll head out."

Drea rolls her last ball and hits four pins. She runs up to Thad and leaps into his arms. He holds her up by her butt. "Thad, look. Four pins."

"I saw! You have gotten so much better than when we first got here."

"Thank you." They kiss.

THIRTY MINUTES LATER, THEY'RE SITTING AT AN outdoor table with a plastic number fourteen on their table next to their respective drinks. It's a nice night out. There's a breeze, but it's not too cold. They are people watching. Folks are out walking their dogs, which isn't surprising since they're right by the beach. Couples walk together holding hands, families pass by. They both spy a young Black family. The kids can't be more than two and three. They're in one of those side-by-side strollers. As the family passes by, Thad and Drea smile and wave. The parents wave back and encourage their kids to speak back.

"Say hi, kids," the mother instructs.

The two adorable little ones look up at them. The boy has his father's features and his mother's eyes. The girl, on the other hand, is her mother's twin.

One just smiles at Thad and Drea while the other waves and looks confused. Thad, Drea and the parents laugh at the cuties. The parents bid them adieu before walking away.

"Thad."

"Yes."

"I keep going back and forth about kids."

"What about it are you struggling with?"

"Whether to start trying now or to wait like we planned."

"What is your mind telling you now?"

"To start trying."

"Yeah, adorable children have a way of making you rethink things, and those two were freaking cuties." They share a laugh. "I'll tell you what. You decide whatever you think is best, but give it time and take as much as you need. I'm not going anywhere."

"And your mom?"

Thad chuckles. "She'll just have to deal."

"What if I decide I don't want children at all?"

"Then it will just be you and me."

"Thad, are you serious? As much of a dad as you are."

"Since when am I a dad? Do you know something I don't?" Thad jokes.

Drea giggles. "No, it's just something Latrice said."

"She's going around telling people I have kids. I'mma have to talk to her."

Drea laughs loudly. "No, no. It's nothing like that. She told me that you were a father with no kids of his own."

Thad smiles. "That makes sense. I tend to treat the kids like they're my own."

"Especially Quincy."

"Mark wasn't stepping up, and Latrice would tell me, 'Thad, he canceled on Quincy again.' I heard the anger and hurt in her voice. She was trying to keep Mark from drifting away from his son, but he wasn't helping at all. That's where I came in. I was already a presence in Q's life, so she asked me one day, if Mark couldn't handle being a father, could I show Quincy what a father figure looks like?"

Drea's eye light up in surprise. "I never knew she asked you that."

The server picks up their number and places a pizza in front of them. Margherita on one side for Thad and Margherita with artichokes and prosciutto on the other for Drea. They thank him before adding slices to their plates.

"Yep, she called me one day and said that she was

going to need me and Dad to be the male role models in Quincy's life because Mark wasn't holding up his end of the parenting bargain." Thad wipes his hands on a napkin. "Can I tell you something?"

"Of course, husband."

He lets out a slight chuckle. "I was scared when things became more serious between her and Nathan. Don't get me wrong. Nathan is like my brother, and I couldn't be happier for Trice. But things became more serious between her and Nathan around the same time Mark started taking on more of an active role in Quincy's life. I'm ashamed to admit it, but I got scared he wouldn't need me anymore." Thad cringes.

Drea takes his hand. "Thaddeus, you mean too much to Quincy for you to even allow that thought to enter your mind. The boy wears his hair like yours and wants to inherit your shops."

Thad laughs. "You're right—and I know you are—but when you've been someone's person and now they have two other people, you start to question how much they need you. I'm rambling."

"You know I don't mind when you ramble, just like you don't mind when I rant. You know, Thad, you're a big kid yourself. I was just thinking about how your energy attracts people, but I was thinking in terms of flirting. But you really do attract all kinds of people of all ages. You give off that energy that welcomes them to come to you." Thad gives her a weak smile, and Drea looks like a light bulb just came on above her head. "You give off that energy on purpose, don't you? Because of your appearance."

Thad nods. "When I first moved into my house before our current place, I…um…I don't know why I'm admitting to so many embarrassing things tonight, but here we go. I baked pecan squares and lemon bars and went house to house, introducing myself to my new neighbors. Did you wonder why we were handing out full bars on Halloween?"

"Kind of, but I know Trice does that too."

"So does Nay Nay. We know when people see us, we're the nice Black neighbors. We want to make sure that everyone within a three-block radius knows who we are. Especially me. Being tall, dark and—"

"Extremely handsome." Thad smiles and playfully rolls his eyes. "I'm sorry I couldn't help it. Please continue."

"All those qualities and having long locs made me stand out."

"Is that why you cut your locs before Trice and Nate's wedding?"

"Naw, they were getting heavy. I took a shower one day, and the minute they got wet, my neck did one of these." Thad jokingly yanks his head back. Drea laughs. "Could barely lift my head up. That's when I knew it was time for a trim." He lets out a chuckle. "When I was done passing out treats, I felt dirty. Like I sold out to get my white neighbors to—"

"Not call the cops on you. You made sure that these new people who you were living close to knew who you were. That's not embarrassing, or cringey, Thad. That's self-preservation. You were keeping yourself safe. You didn't know those people. We live in an age where white folks are waltzing into Black people's homes and demanding to know who they are before calling the cops on them. You should not be ashamed of making sure you're safe. You aren't the threat. A good number of them are. You were neutralizing a real threat. Do you hear me?" Thad nods, though his head is bowed. Drea lifts his chin and repeats, "Do you hear me?"

Thad takes her hand and kisses her fingers. "Yes, peach. I hear you. Anyway, about the time I was thirteen and my height started to shoot up was when I was first profiled. Apparently, some woman saw me and thought I was a suspect in a carjacking. I was thirteen, not much older than Quincy is now. Police showed up at our house. My mom was pissed. Told those cops they had no business carrying weapons if they couldn't even tell a thirteen-year-old child from a grown-ass man."

"Go, Momma Janet!"

"They saw my dad and realized the height thing was obviously genetic and bid us goodnight. I'm lucky it wasn't worse."

Drea scratches his beard. "I'm so sorry that happened to you."

"Thank you. That's how Lance and I actually became friends. We bonded over our respective encounters with Five-O."

"That's disturbing."

"Yeah. Not something two eighth graders should be talking about."

"I bet you two were trouble when you got older."

"Us? Surely, you jest," Thad jokes, sounding guilty as sin.

"Pfffttt. Lance got drafted when he was nineteen. You were in college. Between your looks and Lance's NBA career, word must have spread around UCLA that Lance Greene's best friend went there. You must have been swimming in pussy."

"None of them were as good as you," Thad assures her.

"You don't have to butter me up. I already know that." Drea waves his comment away.

Thad snickers. "I know. I just wanted to hear your reaction. But to answer your question, yes we were. We were drowning in it, as a matter of fact."

"So, you had a 'hoe phase'?" Drea teases.

"It was more like a 'hoe era,' but yes."

Drea laughs. She gives Thad a curious look. "Thad, can I ask you something? I'd like for you to be honest with me."

"I don't know any other way to be with you." He shrugs.

"Okay, I know that you mainly had casual situations, but with your serious relationships, were you ever tempted to step out?"

"I was, but I never did."

"I assumed you didn't. What stopped you?"

"A number of things, actually. My father's voice in my head for one, and after what happened with my boy, Shaun, I was good. He was with his girl Vanessa for a minute. We all went to UCLA together. He was a football player, All-American, had the NFL checking him out. He pledged Alpha Psi something." Drea giggles. "The point is, temptation was every-where, and he partook a lot. People, including me, covered for him. One day, Van shows up at my place.

Tells me I'm the only one of Shaun's friends who's worth a damn so she expects me to tell her the truth. Is he stepping out? I felt like shit. Years of covering for him hit me like a ton of bricks. I told her the truth. The look of pain on her face was enough to make me never want to make any woman look like that ever again."

"What happened with her and Shaun?"

"She ghosted him. They were supposed to meet up one night, and she just never showed up. Her family and friends were instructed not to tell him where she was. I found out a few years later that she transferred out of state and stayed with relatives. She met some dude, and they got married and have three children. Shaun obviously didn't make it to the NFL. His head was all kinds of fucked up after she left him. He barely graduated. He works for his brother's tech firm, unmarried and still pinning for Van. He likes her messages on social media regularly and wishes her a happy birthday every year. Fucking up something with the love of your life and not real-izing it until it was too late. That was a huge fear of mine. It kept me on the straight and narrow."

"I'm grateful for that cause I would be vindictive."

"How vindictive?"

"I'd hire an attorney from Nay Nay's firm just to

fuck with you, and by the end, I would own all your shops, your Range Rover and your drawers."

"Damn, peach."

Drea shrugs. "Are you forgetting who my mother is?"

"You and Vivian would rip me to shreds."

"Not to mention Latrice, Nadia and your parents. If you cheated, you better just leave the country." Drea sips her drink, looking smug.

Thad grins. "Truer words, my love."

15

DREA

This is not how Drea pictured her first Valentine's Day as a married woman, and her first with Thad. She pictured wine and dinner, roses and a night of hot butt naked sex, preferably on the balcony of a hotel. Not sitting on the couch waiting for Thad to be done with a Zoom meeting while they get closer and closer to missing their reservation. Getting a reservation to any hot spot in LA is impossible, but on Valentine's Day? There isn't a day busier than today. Mother's Day comes close, but the day for lovers reigns over all holidays. And Drea might miss the award-winning cuisine of Langston Walker.

He is rumored to be making an appearance in the

kitchen tonight. Thad has been going through some stress lately, and Drea has been there to make sure he's okay. The issue is, Thad is one of those men who, when you ask him for help, he'll do it, no matter how much he has on his plate. He took on spending time with the kids, which takes time and planning, no matter how many kids are involved. Then he volunteered to help the single mother and widow across the street. Of course, Drea said nothing and offered her support in both instances. She offered to go with Thad, Quincy and Eli, but he knew she had been spending time with the twins and needed an "auntie break," so he took the kids by himself. What Thad doesn't seem to realize is that he needs an "uncle break."

Immediately diving in to help the neighbor wasn't what Drea had in mind. She feels for what Ally is going through, she really does, but Drea makes no apologies for looking after her husband's physical and mental well-being. And she has asked him to fall back, but he keeps saying it's all good. He's currently trying to put out a fire with a wedding party whose hair is getting cut at his flagship shop in April. It's a big, big client, Melvin somebody. He's a Shark or whatever. Drea honestly doesn't know shit about sports, nor does she care. Whoever the guy is, he's ruining her night and adding more to Thad's already full plate. She recognizes how this is affecting Thad, but her patience and understanding for her husband is wearing thin.

Drea folds her arms and crosses her legs. She sees Thad's jaw tick. He clearly noticed the change in her body language. And she's sure the fact that she's staring daggers at the side of his face isn't lost on him, either.

"Will you excuse me for a second, Mel?" Thad says.

"Sure, T."

Thad turns off his camera and mutes himself. He looks at Drea. "Burning a hole in my head with your eyes will not make this go faster, peach."

"Are you sure you're muted?"

"I am."

"This man is getting married in April, so he has a fiancée, correct?"

"Yes."

"Is she okay with him being on a Zoom meeting with you right now?"

"I wouldn't assume she is."

"So, you both don't value your ladies' time?"

"Drea, please." Thad's tone is calm but impatient.

"What? I mean, we only get to celebrate our first Valentine's Day once. Why wouldn't I want to be sitting in our living room draped in couture while you hold a meeting?" Drea knows she should go easy on him, but she has such high hopes for tonight. And she's frustrated, so who better to take that out on than the person who is frustrating her? Hence her snarky tone.

Thad sighs. "Are you done?"

Drea turns her body away from him but retains her folded arms and deep frown.

Thad unmutes himself and puts the camera back on. "My apologies, Mel. You need to add another cousin to the list. Is he getting a cut?"

"Yeah, he's getting the whole treatment, T. And I am so sorry for the last-minute additions."

"It's no problem, but I need to remind you that my flagship shop can accommodate the number of people so far. But if it gets any higher and I have to close another location for your wedding party, I will charge you more. A lot more."

"I got it. Look, man, you go enjoy your Valentine's Day. I'm sure your lady is as angry as mine right now."

"She is." Thad sends a smile Drea's way. Her

frown deepens. *You're not charming your fine ass out of this.* Thad seems to read her mind 'cause he clears his throat and quickly ends the call. "Shall we?" he offers her his arm.

Drea fights the smile on her face and loses. She takes his hand, and they head out to start their romantic evening...

Or so Drea thought. Traffic had other ideas. She isn't foolish and knows LA traffic sucks, which is why she made a reservation for half-past eight. Most folks aren't eating that late. Six or seven tends to be the most popular times for dinner dates. It was a foolproof plan, and a thirty-minute Zoom call fucked it all up. And now Drea's mood is even more sour. It's a quarter past eight, and they're twenty minutes away. LW only gives a grace period of five minutes. So, there's a strong chance that by the time they get there...

"I'm sorry. You missed your reservation window by one minute. We're doing a lottery system for seats," the hostess says.

"What's the lottery system?" Thad asks.

"You take a number and hope it gets called."

"So, it's just a random number?" Thad asks.

"Yeah, pretty much. Three couples have gotten in

so far, and there's only about seven left. I'd say your odds are pretty good," the hostess says.

"What do you say, baby?" Thad asks.

Calm down. Don't make a scene. You don't want to be labeled the angry Black woman who murdered her husband in the parking lot of a high-end steakhouse.

Drea lets in a deep, calming breath, then exhales. "Sure, let's do it."

They take a number, 777. Drea sees it as a good omen and sits in the Range Rover. Thad keeps ahold of the thing that lights up when their number has been called. The hostess took a picture of the couples to keep up with whichever number they got. Drea was not smiling even a little, so when the hostess asked them if they wanted a copy of their picture, she got a sick satisfaction at how embarrassed Thad looked when he saw the look on her face. He must have thought that Drea would plaster a brave face so things didn't look awkward. *Nope!*

"The hostess probably thinks we ran into my mistress or something," Thad jokes, or at least tries to. "Peach…"

"Thad, for the sake of this evening not being completely ruined, please refrain from speaking to me," Drea requests.

"Okay…" He sits quietly and fidgets. His knee

bounces, and he drums his fingers along the steering wheel. It's aggravating the fuck out of Drea. The combination of the sound made by the repetitive movements and his obvious need to talk to her is making her ass itch.

"Fine, Thad. Say whatever it is you have to say." Drea sighs.

"I was just going to say that I can call Nay Nay and see if she has a hookup we can use."

That's actually not a bad idea. Nay Nay has hookups everywhere. It pays in more ways than one to be the divorce attorney to some of the most powerful and influential people in the state.

"Okay, go ahead." Drea relents.

"I'm going to get a smile out of you by the end of tonight, Drea. I swear." Thad smiles.

"Good luck."

⸻

THAD

Good luck.

Yep, that's what Thad is going to need. Did he wear himself too thin over the past few weeks? Maybe. But he's the type of guy who is there when you need him. It's in his nature to help people. It's what Drea commended about him the night they went bowling. Thad's inclination to look out for others has kept him on people's good side, and it's not like he doesn't know how to say no. He's not a sucker. These past few weeks have just been a little hectic. It started when he agreed to take Quincy and Eli to the movies. Mark planned to take them as a surprise. But he ended up having to work late, so he asked Thad to take them, offering to pay for every-thing. Mark moved his activity with Quincy to Saturday. Thad agreed. Drea would get the house to herself for a few hours, and Thad got to see the kids.

Next came helping their neighbors from across the street, Ally and her son, Benji. They lost Ally's husband and Benji's father, Kirk, a few months back. Ally has been handling a lot by herself, so Thad offered to help her. She was going to show Benji basic car maintenance, but she got a last-minute job lined up. Ally is a freelance IT administrator who charges big bucks to big companies who are too cheap to create their own office's IT team. So, Thad volunteered to help. He spent the following weekend teaching Benji how to change a tire, check his oil and change his brake pads. Thad had to split his time in between Benji and getting things finalized and secured for Melvin Sharp's wedding party.

Melvin plays for the Sharks, the same team Lance retired from. Mel recently signed an astronomically huge contract with Big Sneekz, a company started by famed graffiti artist and shoe designer Nomad. He's going to design his own sneaker, and pre-orders have already broken records. This man is the type of client businessmen sell their souls for, and he just landed in Thad's lap. Lance was golfing with him—for a celebrity golf tournament—and Thad had just given Lance a cut. Melvin asked about Thad, and the rest is history. All Melvin has done is add more heads that need cutting, that means his invoice goes up. He's not taking advantage of Thad, and he understands that the more add-ons he has, the more Thad will charge him. To her credit, Drea has been empathetic and has been checking in with Thad regularly. She sees how stressed he is, and has even advised him to take it easy. But it seems she has reached the end of her rope, and Thad is now hanging on for dear life.

He sends a quick silent prayer that his call to Nay Nay works.

Lord, my wife is really fucking angry with me...shit! Can't cuss when I'm talking to God. What's wrong with me? Sorry, Lord. Let me start over. Dear Lord, this is your faithful servant, Thaddeus. Please let this work. There's no earthly reason why it shouldn't, but the way my night is going, I wouldn't put it past anything. Please let Nay Nay answer, and please let her get us in. Thank you.

Thad calls his sister and puts her on speakerphone.

"Hey, big brother," Nadia answers.

Yes! She answered. Please keep it coming, Lord. "Hey, Nadia. So, I need a huge favor. Could you get me and Drea in at LW in Culver City?"

"I thought Drea already had a reservation."

"She did, but we missed it through no fault of anyone's. I mean, think about it, who can truly predict traffic?" Thad says apologetically while looking at Drea. She looks unmoved.

"Okay, it sounds like you fucked up in some way."

"Please stop making my wife angrier with me, and tell me you can help," Thad retorts.

"I'll see what I can do and will call you back."

They wait ten excruciating minutes in silence when Thad's phone goes off. "Tell me some good news, Nay Nay."

"Check your blinky table thing," Nadia says. And sure enough, it's glowing. They got a table! Thad now has to get Drea to agree to give their first-born daughter the middle name Nadia.

"Thank you, Nay Nay. I love you more than Latrice."

"Really?"

"Well, right now I do."

"Whatever, fool. Don't fuck up the rest of your evening," Nadia advises.

"Thanks, Nay Nay," Thad says, sounding slightly less grateful. He takes her advice though. The rest of the evening is clear sailing.

Drea sits across from him and still has a scowl etched into her beautiful face. She doesn't seem to enjoy the evening at all. Thad said he would make her smile by the end of the night, and so far, he's failing.

"Andrea, baby. Please tell me what I can do to get you to stop looking so upset."

"You could listen to me, Thad."

"Baby, I *am* listening."

"No, Thad. The whole purpose of us checking in with each other is to assure that our partnership is strong. We can't do that if we aren't honest. Thad, you do so much. You take on so much. You have a big heart."

"I thought that was something you loved about

me. My energy, remember? How I make people feel like they can come to me."

"I do love that about you, Thad, but I have to be honest right now. I don't enjoy it when your big heart directly conflicts with me getting what I want."

Thad lets out a chuckle. "Peach, you don't think that's a tad bit selfish?"

"I don't care. I have wanted you for years, and now you're my husband. I will protect our marriage from you if I have to. Stop overextending yourself it's making you full of stress. Baby, you practically raised Quincy. You don't have to drop everything and go do stuff with him or Eli or the other kids because you're paranoid Mark and Nate will take your place. You don't have to keep volunteering your time to our neighbors for them to feel at ease. I think between all the candy we handed out on Halloween and you introducing Lance to Dr. Foster's grandson, we're in a good spot for a while. And this Melvin guy. How is he this disorganized for the most important day of his life? Hopefully, he's not this indecisive when it comes time for him to shoot baskets."

Thad smiles. "In his defense, his mom keeps adding cousins to his groom's party."

Drea rolls her eyes. "Thad, don't make jokes."

"I'm not making jokes." Thad gazes at her. "Baby, you have no idea."

"I have no idea about what?"

"The depths that I'm willing to go for us."

"Okay, well, in that case, inform me." Drea scoots closer.

"I will, but first, let me tell you that I hear you. I am listening, and I will cut back on overextending myself. I just want you to understand where I'm coming from when I do these things." Drea nods for him to continue. "Drea, there is nothing I don't do without you and our future in mind. Did I take the kids out because I love spending time with them? Yes, but I'm not tripping off Mark and Nate's relationship with Quince anymore because I know where I stand with him. And you helped me understand that. I also agreed to do something with them because soon, you and I will have kids, and I want them to have the type of relationship I have with my cousins. We're all very close."

"I know. I can't wait to meet everyone at this year's Richardson Family Reunion," Drea replies.

"Well, there might not be one. The weekend that was picked for the reunion conflicts with the new date of a barbecue competition Uncle Levi and Uncle Sly entered. We'll have to cancel it."

"Oh, well, that's unfortunate. I was really excited."

"Yeah, I was excited for you to meet everyone too. There's always next year."

"Wait, are Uncle Sly and Uncle Levi competing as a team?"

"No, they're competing against each other, along with the other finalist."

"Aren't they the two uncles who got into a fight and didn't speak for a year after a game of Monopoly?"

"Yes."

"The barbecue competition isn't going to end well, is it?" Drea asks.

"No, it will not," Thad confirms.

"So, you want to make sure that Quincy and our kids will be close?" Drea sips her wine.

"Yes."

"Thad, that always would have been the case. The Richardsons are thick as thieves."

"Yeah, baby, because we work hard at it. Remember, my father is from Kentucky. We grew up hearing stories of Black families being ripped apart from each other and never seeing each other again. Starting with my great grandparents, we made sure that didn't happen. I don't take anything for granted, especially not my family. It doesn't take much to drift apart." He can tell from the sadness in her eyes that she's thinking of Ms. Olympia. Thad didn't mean to pick at a bad memory. He takes Drea's hand. "I'm sorry, baby. I didn't mean to—"

"I know you didn't."

"My point is family dynamics change. With the baby coming, Trice and Quincy will be spending a lot more time with Nathan's people. Families can grow, causing folks to move. All kinds of shit happens. The folks back in the day laid the initial groundwork to keep the family together. It's up to us to maintain it."

"I get that, but, baby, you aren't solely responsible for maintaining it. You do get that, don't you?"

"I do, and I'll chill."

"That's all I ask."

"And as for the neighbors, that's me doing the same thing *you* were praising me for at Angelo's."

"I know, but I think you might be overdoing it."

"Drea, I'm not trying to add Ally and Benji to our already large group of family and friends."

"Okay, so what's the deal?"

"The deal is, we're going to live in that house a long time. The people in the neighborhood are going to see our children grow up, and I want them to look after our kids like we'd—"

"Look after theirs. So once again, you're getting insurance for our unborn children."

"Yes. Like I said, I don't do anything without thinking about you or our family first."

Drea's exterior has been thawing since he started explaining himself. Her shoulders are much more relaxed than they were earlier. He just may get his smile.

"And the ballplayer?" she asks.

"Drea, that man is paying me a ridiculous amount of money, and all he's been doing is adding to it by adding more people."

"How much is he paying you?"

Thad takes out his phone and sends her a text. He feels saying it out loud would be gauche.

Drea looks down at her phone, then up at Thad. "Okay. Your interactions with Melvin may continue. He's getting married in April, so that's not very long."

"I thought you'd change your mind." He chuckles before speaking to her solemnly. "But again, I do hear you, and I will dial things back. I'm sorry I made us miss our reservation in the first place."

"Thank you." She smiles brightly. *Jackpot!* "Can we exchange gifts now?"

"Sure."

Drea takes out a wrapped box. Thad can tell it's expensive, just from the wrapping. He unwraps the gift. It's a gold pocket watch. "I remember when we were going through your grandpa's things, you mentioned a Bauer pocket watch he had that was lost. Based on the type of pocket watches they made that were popular at the time, I found this and snatched it up during an online auction."

Hans Bauer is *the* premiere watch maker. His shit outsells Rolexes.

Thad has tears in his eyes. "Thank you, peach." He takes her face in his hands and kisses her.

Drea simpers. "You're welcome."

"This is sharp. I'm going to look like a real Mr. Moneybags with this. I can't wait for someone to ask me what time it is." Thad smiles widely. He loves the gift. There's nothing better than when she gifts him with something he discussed earlier. He loves doing the same for her. Listening to his wife, his lover, his best friend, his person, is the most important thing to him, and it's clear how important it is to her as well.

He admires the watch and kisses Drea some more. "Mmm," she moans.

"Now, I have to warn you, peach. My gift isn't something you can hand to someone."

Drea arches an eyebrow. "I'm intrigued. What is it?"

"OH, MY GOD! THAD, YOU'RE CRAZY."

She may be right. Thad's gift is a forty-minute helicopter ride over Los Angeles at night. The twinkling lights of the Staples Center—because fuck calling it the Crypto.com Arena or whatever—and the Sunset Strip are amazing from this high up.

Drea is so excited, she's pointing to landmarks as if she and Thad weren't born and raised in the City of Angels. He holds her close. While he doesn't enjoy having disagreements with her, he loves that they can be honest with each other and talk things out. It truly does make them stronger. Drea feels her purse vibrate in her lap.

THAD

Hey

DREA

Hey, yourself.

She smiles at him.

THAD

> Happy Valentine's Day. I love you, my
> sweet peach.

He smiles at her.
She bites her lip.

DREA

> And I love you, my kind and loving
> king. Happy Valentine's Day.

They kiss.

16

THAD

I t's March and ever since Christmas, Thad and Drea have been cooking together more frequently. Tonight is no exception. Tonight, they are making a baked ziti to drop off at Latrice and Nathan's. Thad has also made cookies. With Latrice's delivery date fast approaching, the family has been making dishes for them to just pop in the oven, so they have less to worry about. Although, with family members like Leon and Amber, they won't have anything to worry about. Leon hired a team of nurses to help them around the clock. Each nurse will work a partnered shift throughout the day for the first year of the baby's life. Thad needs to have a talk with Leon after Drea gets pregnant. *A team of nurses for a year! Yes, please. Sign us up.*

"What are you thinking about, husband?" Drea sprinkles a combination of parmesan and mozzarella on top of the ziti before putting the Pyrex dish in the oven. She pours herself and Thad a glass of iced tea. They take their drinks to the living room and take a seat on the couch. Drea rests her feet on Thad's lap.

"I was thinking about the round-the-clock care Leon is getting for Nate, Trice and the baby."

"We definitely have to ask for that."

"That's exactly what I was thinking." Thad nods.

"Great. We'll ask once we know I'm pregnant," Drea takes a sip before placing her glass on the coffee table.

"We can ask when we make the announcement. Knowing Leon, he'll send a congratulatory text, and I'll just be like, 'So…round-the-clock care sure sounds like something Drea and I could use.' What do you think?" Thad lifts Drea's legs and gets the cookies from the kitchen.

"Or you could just ask him like a normal person, you weirdo." Drea laughs.

Thad comes back, puts down the container of cookies and lifts Drea from the couch before smacking her ass. "The name calling was uncalled for, peach."

"Yeah, but it got my ass slapped." Drea bends over in front of him. "Another, please?"

Thad rubs his hands together and grins like a supervillain, and Drea laughs again. He smacks it so hard that it jiggles, but obviously doesn't inflict too much pain. He pulls down her sweats and kisses her butt cheeks. "Mmmm, damnit, peach!" Thad bites a cheek.

"Aieeyee!" Drea screams and squirms. Thad holds her in place. "I don't know why that still surprises me as often as you do it." Drea giggles.

"The key is not doing it too much. I do it when you least expect it. It keeps you on your toes." Drea laughs as she pulls up her sweats and they sit back down and Thad offers her a cookie. "What were *you* thinking about, wife?"

Drea takes a couple of cookies and bites one. "I actually was just thinking about the Reddit AITA I read the other day. I meant to tell you about it."

"I cannot read too many of those or I'll start to get heated. There's only so many times you can read, *Reddit, my (35M) wife (34F) said I need to help out around the house more, so I fucked her sister. Am I the asshole?*" Thad jokes.

Drea lets out a hearty laugh before becoming

somber. "And the women. Those poor gaslit women."

"Those poor, poor women. That shit makes me sad, but whenever I see an update and it's a woman saying, *Thank you to everyone who replied. I told him I want a divorce, and I'm moving out,* I feel relieved."

"I can imagine those types of stories remind you of Latrice and Mark."

"Yeah, they do. I felt so helpless seeing her in so much pain and not being able to do anything. But our parents told Nadia and I to just let her grieve the end of her marriage. It was hard. Nadia wanted to use her legal connections to fuck Mark's life up real bad."

"I can imagine Nay Nay having to be talked down."

"You have no idea."

"So, what about you? On a scale from one to ten, how badly did you want to kick my brother's ass?" Drea asks. "I'm guessing you had to get talked down from doing something severe like Nay Nay."

Thad's silent for a while. He wants to be honest with Drea, but how exactly do you tell your wife that, for the briefest of moments, after watching your sister cry for hours, you thought about snapping her brother's neck? Thad and Mark are cool *now,* but when Thad happened to stop by his parents' house—and Latrice arrived shortly after him in tears telling them Mark cheated…again—he started devising a plan to make Mark disappear and get rid of the evidence.

"So, what was the Reddit thing about?" Thad asks with a straight face. The fact that he's not trying to make it into a joke or even smiling tells Drea ten isn't a high enough number on the scale because she launches into the Reddit story.

"So, the original poster is a woman, and she's engaged to a dude who comes from a well-off, tight-knit family. They are a bit too tight-knit."

"Drea, if there is something you would like to discuss with me, you don't have to go on Reddit," Thad teases.

"Shut up. It's not about us." Drea playfully pops his shoulder.

"Just checking. Please continue."

"Okay, so the original poster is engaged to this man who is the only male relative in his immediate family. His father died, and his mom never remarried. So, it's him, his sister and his mom."

"I don't think I like where this is going," Thad says.

"You're smart to trust that instinct, my friend.

Anyway, during a family dinner, the original poster's future mother-in-law starts talking about how she's never had the opportunity to travel and how she got married so young and became a mother almost immediately. This leads to a discussion regarding the betrothed couple's honeymoon plans. They tell her that they've decided to go to Madrid. The mom gets super excited for them."

"At least, they think it's for them."

Drea points to him like she's Jada Pinkett-Smith and says, "That part! At this point, the original poster is happy that her future mother-in-law is excited for them. A week or so later, they're hosting an event leading up to the wedding, and mommy-in-law decides to inform the whole family that her son and his soon-to-be wife have graciously invited her and her daughter to go with them on their honeymoon to Madrid. This is the first time the son or the original poster have heard this."

"I'm a pretty laid-back dude, wouldn't you say?" Thad asks.

"You're probably the most laid-back dude I've ever met," Drea agrees.

"One of the things that I hate is when a motherfucker invites themselves somewhere. I hate that as much as I hate eggs."

"And you do hate eggs."

"They're fucking gross. I can't believe people like to eat that shit runny." Thad shivers in disgust.

"I don't care. I will fuck up an omelet." Drea shrugs.

"You nasty."

Drea snaps her head at him. "You love it." She blows him a kiss.

Thad smirks, then licks his lips. "You're right. I do."

Drea bites her lip. "Fine ass making me forget my place."

Thad smiles as he chuckles at her silly ass. "The mother invited herself in front of guests without her son or his fiancée's consent," he answers.

"I love how much you listen to me."

"Kind of hard not to. I've been mesmerized by you for years."

Drea cuddles close to Thad. He kisses her on top of her head. "So, the original poster stands up and announces that no such arrangement has been made, and she's confused why her man's mother would think she was invited. Turns out, the son did ask her and the sister to come along. He felt bad his mom never got to go anywhere. He was going to talk to his fiancée about it and told his mom and sister to keep it quiet. The original poster says that her fiancée accused her of overreacting and that she's an asshole for embarrassing his mom." Thad cracks his knuckles. "Go on and cook him, Thad!" Drea cheers.

"Oh, I'm cooking him, the sister and the momma. Because what kind of Oedipal, *Flowers in the Attic* type of bullshit is that? You have plenty of opportunities to send your momma and sister on a trip. Either of their birthdays, Mother's Day, hell, send them any time they want to go. Why your honeymoon? Because it was already paid for and you just had to add two more people? That marriage is not going to last. The women in his life won't be satisfied until they sabotage it. That is the only reasonable explanation for why they even accepted the invite."

"That's what I was stuck on after I read it. Why would you accept? Apparently, they were all going to fly together, go their separate ways for most of the trip—except for having dinner together every night—which was the mom's stipulation. The original poster explained that her fiancée tried to sell her on the idea by reminding her that all of them would barely see each other."

"We shouldn't be seeing each other at all 'cause

they wouldn't be there. Imagine Nadia and my mom trying to go on our honeymoon with us."

"They'd get so sick of us, they would fly back home after the first day." Drea laughs.

"True." Thad joins her.

"Hell, Nay Nay has been on her phone so much, she probably wouldn't know you invited her," Drea adds.

Thad offers her another cookie before taking more for himself. "What do you know about the guy she's seeing?" he says with gleeful suspicion.

"That's just it, I don't know anything. Nay Nay is keeping whoever he is close to the chest."

"Yeah, I asked her, and she wouldn't give up anything. I was hoping she said something to you or Trice."

"If she had, she would have made me promise not to say anything. And I wouldn't betray her trust." Thad takes back her cookie. "Hey! Give that back." Drea laughs.

"Naw, you ain't even got the info." Thad smirks and hands her back the cookie.

"All I know is his initial is *J*," Drea says.

"How did you find that out?" He bites into his cookie.

Drea breaks a piece of her cookie off and pops it

in her mouth. "I peeped her phone real quick when he sent her a text."

"Being nosy." Thad wags his finger at her.

"Like you wouldn't have done the same." She rolls those wondrous brown eyes of hers. *Never has the song "Pretty Brown Eyes" by Mint Condition been so perfect a descriptor.*

He brushes his hand against the soft skin along her cheek and jawline. "You're right."

Thad follows Drea to the kitchen. She takes the ziti out of the oven. It smells unreal.

"We might have to make another ziti to send them and eat this one," Thad suggests.

"It does smell good, and it's not like they'd know," Drea replies.

"You are bad influence, ziti." Thad stares at the food.

"Did you just call me ziti?" Drea laughs.

"Naw, I said *peach.*"

"Negro. You just called me our dinner!" Drea clutches her stomach and falls to the floor, laughing.

Thad laughs and helps her up. "So, we are eating this one and making them a new one?" He goes to the cabinets to get them some plates. He turns and sees Drea already sneaking a bite.

"No home training." He shakes his head.

"Hush up and give me that plate."

They both laugh. Thad's phone buzzes. It's Nate. Thad answers. "Hey, Nate, we're not eating the food we made ya'll."

"Thad, shush!" Drea frowns.

"Thad, Latrice is in labor," Nathan says. "We're heading to the hospital."

"Okay, we're on our way." Thad ends the call, lifts Drea up and rushes to the door.

"But the ziti…" Drea whines.

"Drea, Latrice just went into labor. We're going to the hospital."

"Oh, my God! Oh, my God. Let's go."

"I am going. You're the one talking about ziti." Thad locks the door behind them.

"Thaddeus, forget the ziti. A baby's coming!"

He carries her goofy ass to the car, gets in the driver's side and heads out.

It's been hours and Drea is asleep on Thad's shoulder. Since Latrice and Nathan are having a baby arrival party next week, only family members are in the waiting room. Momma Ernie, Nadia, Thad, Drea and his parents are all here. Leon and

Amber are on their way with Shellie and Tyler. Quincy sits curled up with his head on Momma Janet's shoulder.

Nathan comes out to the waiting room. "It's a girl!" he yells. "A beautiful baby girl."

The family stands up and cheers. Drea leaps into Thad's arms. A nurse comes by, asking them to keep it down, while other folks in the waiting room applaud.

"Quincy"—Nathan calls out for him—"come meet your sister, Kai."

Kai. Such a beautiful name for, no doubt, a beautiful little girl. Quincy and the grandparents are obviously going in first, but Thad and Drea are itching to meet their new niece. Nathan takes Quincy, Momma Ernie, Poppa Earl and Momma Janet into the delivery room as Leon, Amber and their kids enter.

"Hey, all!" Leon greets everyone. "How's is my sister-in-law doing? Is the baby here yet?"

Thad, who is still clinging to Drea, turns and smiles at them. "It's a girl! Nate just came out and told us."

Amber bounces up and down, excited and clapping. "I'm an auntie!" She and Leon hug.

"Yes! More girls," Shellie cheers. The adults look at her and laugh. "Think about it, between Quincy, big head here"—she points to Tyler—"Eli and Jelani, me and Lettie are the only girls."

"She's right. Thad, you and Drea better get on that," Nadia mocks.

"Hey, Nadia, who's J?" Drea asks. "You know, the guy you've been texting?"

"Point taken. I'll shut up," Nadia replies.

Drea turns to face Thad and beams. He leans in and rests his forehead on hers, smiling back.

After eagerly awaiting Thad, Drea and Nadia enter the delivery room. Latrice looks tired but pretty as always. Thad kisses his big sister on top of her mop of curls and grins at her. "Congratulations, Tricey."

"Thanks, T." Latrice's eyes twinkle. Momma Ernie is holding the little bundle of cuteness. *She has Nathan's eyes and Latrice's everything else. Little Kai copied and pasted her momma's whole face, dimples too.* Thad chuckles.

"What's so funny, Uncle Thad?" Latrice jokes.

"Kai stole your whole face." Thad smiles.

"Dem Richardson genes is strong with this one," Nadia jokes. That's something their grandmother used to say when a new baby was born in the family.

"Yeah, and as crazy about his wife as Nate is, he has no problem with little momma looking like her,"

Leon jokes. Thad and Leon turn to Nate, who is now holding his daughter. The look on the man's face brings tears to Thad's eyes. It's a look of pride, protection and love.

Thad and Drea walk over and look down at the little angel's face. "Hello, Kai. I'm your Uncle Thad, and this is your Auntie Drea."

"Hi, sweetheart," Drea coos.

Kai opens her eyes and looks at them. It never gets old. Looking into the eyes of innocent little ones. Kai blinks and then yawns, making Drea shed tears.

"Quincy, do you think you're ready to hold Kai?" Latrice asks.

"Q, you haven't held the baby yet?" Leon asks.

"I'm nervous. I haven't held a baby since I was four, and my dad was helping me hold Jelani when he was born," Quincy confesses.

"It's not as nerve-racking as it may seem," Leon assures him.

"Come here, Q," Nathan says.

Quincy comes over, and Nathan tells him, "Cradle one arm on top of the other." Quincy does as he says. "Just watch for her head. You'll be fine."

Nathan gently places Kai in Quincy's arms. He looks scared.

"Quince, you got this." Thad smiles at his nephew. Quincy smiles back and looks at his baby sister. She looks up at him…and smiles.

"Mom, she's smiling at me." Quincy has tears in his eyes as he smiles at his mother before looking back at Kai. Latrice tearfully looks at her children and grins back. Quincy gazes at Kai in awe. She smiles at him again. "Hi, Kai. I'm your big brother, Quincy. I'm the one that's going to look out for you. Forever." Quincy kisses her cheek. There's not a dry eye in the house.

THE FOLLOWING WEEK, LATRICE AND NATHAN HOLD their baby arrival shower in the backyard. Crazy to think that seven months ago, Nate and Trice were married in this exact spot, and it's the same spot Thad told his now wife that he was in love with her. It's not a large length of time, but enough to be life-changing.

Thad makes a plate for Drea and himself. The whole crew is here. The MacArthur family, Leon and his brood, Lance, Jess, Nadia, his parents, Momma Ernie, Nate's boy Ronnie and his wife Roxanne, who flew in from Michigan and Greg.

Mark and the twins just came in. The twins run to Drea, and she gathers them up in her arms and squeezes them. Thad hands Mark a drink as they both smile at the little ones' excitement. This is definitely a welcome change from Christmas. The twins deserve to be happy after all the crap they suffered in their short lives.

"Auntie Drea, we want to see to the baby." Lettie jumps up and down, smiling from ear to ear.

"I want to see her cheeks. Babies always have chubby cheeks," Jelani shares.

"Yes, they do! Let's go see Auntie Tricey first." Drea takes the kids to the backyard. Thad and Mark follow.

Latrice holds baby Kai as she talks to Nathan, who is seated next to her.

Drea approaches after using hand sanitizer with each twin. "I hope you two don't mind the interruption, but I have two little ones who want to say hi to baby Kai."

Latrice and Nathan smile at the twins. Jelani sniffs Kai's head, making them all laugh. "She smells good, Auntie Tricey." Jelani smiles.

"Thank you, sweetie." Latrice laughs.

"Auntie Tricey," Lettie says shyly.

"Yes, Lettie?"

"Since you're Quincy's mommy and Quincy's our brother, can the baby be our sister?" Lettie pleads with her big brown eyes.

Latrice gives her a warm smile and turns to Nathan. "What do you think?"

Nathan smiles back at Latrice before addressing the twins. "I think Lettie will make a great big sister to Kai. And Jelani will be a great big brother."

"Yay!" Lettie cheers. She looks at Kai. "Hi, baby."

Thad is taking in the beautiful scene when he feels a hand on his arm. He looks over and sees Drea. "Come with me," she whispers.

Thad nods and follows her to the bathroom. She closes the door, and when she turns to face Thad, she's crying. "Peach…"

"Shhh." Drea places her fingers on Thad's lips. "I'm ready to start trying." The world has gone silent. All Thad can hear are Drea's words swirling in his mind. She's ready to make him a father. "Thad, are you going to say anything? If you're not ready yet—"

He takes his wife in his arms and holds her. He thinks of the past and how foolish they both were to be so scared, about the present and how happy he is and the future and the life he has always dreamed of. A long-lasting marriage and a family with Drea. And now, it's a dream that will finally come true.

When Thad finally finds the words, he says, "We have got to stop making major life decisions at Trice and Nathan's events."

Drea laughs into his chest. "It's not our fault their happiness is so inspiring."

Thad laughs. "That moment with Lettie. I can't wait for sweet moments like that with our kids."

"That was adorable. My heart felt like it was going to burst. These adorable-ass freaking kids we're related to are going to make us bust out with a whole gaggle of little ones. First, Quincy when he held Kai, and now Lettie asking to be Kai's sister."

"Oh, my God. Baby, you saw how I was a mess after that moment with Q and Kai."

"Well, we all were. How could you not be?"

"Right! And Lettie. Baby girl is so stinking cute."

"So. Stinking. Cute." Drea looks up at him. "You ready for a beautiful brown-skin cutie with your dimples and my eyes?"

"Been ready."

They kiss.

17

DREA

It's April fourth and Drea's birthday. This is her thirty-fourth year on this planet, and she's grateful. Today will consist of moments organized by Thad. She has no idea what he has planned, but she took the day off as he instructed. This weekend, she's having brunch with the girls because Thad wanted her all to himself on the actual day of her birth.

Her phone buzzes. She looks down and sees birthday well wishes from family and friends. Her mother sends her a text.

VIVIAN

Happy Birthday, darling. How much money should your father put on the Taylor Made Skincare gift card we're sending you?

Did she say Taylor Made Skincare gift card? Taylor Made skin care and Maya Richards's organic body butters are what Drea lives on. Both products can be a little pricey, so any help with that is welcomed. While Drea would love to go hog wild with her father's money, she settles on a more conservative number.

DREA

Thank you, mom. Five hundred would be great!

VIVIAN

Andrea, why so little? I'll tell him to put two thousand on It.

DREA

Thank you, mom!

VIVIAN

Of course. Enjoy your day. Thaddeus has a full day planned for you.

Before Drea can ask her mother what she means, her phone buzzes again. It's Latrice. She sends a picture of herself and Nathan with Quincy and baby Kai. They had a photographer come over and take pictures to celebrate Kai turning a month old. If there is one label that Latrice will happily wear, it's proud momma.

Drea texts her back.

DREA

> I want to nibble her little cheeks sooooo bad!

LATRICE

Me too. She is too cute. Nathan, Quincy and I just can't stop staring at her.

DREA

> Little momma's probably thinking, 'yeah, I know I'm cute and you all are going to spoil me rotten.'

LATRICE

😹😹 She already has Nathan. Hook, line and sinker. She wrapped her little hand around his finger and he melted.

DREA

> Oh, I can imagine. Nathan gives off serious girl dad energy.

LATRICE

He's going to be snack dad, carpool dad, you name it.

DREA

LATRICE

I'll let you go. Thad has a full day planned for you. You should start getting ready.

That's the second mention of a full day. *What are you up to, Thaddeus Richardson?*

Drea sends a reply asking Latrice to clarify. All she says is,

DREA

> He isn't going to have you two bouncing from one location to another. He's taking you somewhere you'll love.

Drea wants to grill Latrice some more, but she's eager to get her day started. She comes out of the bedroom after getting fully dressed and ready—tight blue jeans, a dragon fruit colored, ruffled, midriff-baring top, and of course, matching stilettos. Her lipstick matches her accents, and her braids are in a high ponytail.

She sees Thad, and he looks good! Drea can feel her mouth hanging open. She's sure she looks like a damn fool, but who cares? If you can't look like a damn fool in front of your own husband and on your birthday, you didn't marry the right person. He's wearing a fitted sky-blue button-down shirt, with tan khakis and brown loafers. His apron reads World's Best Husband. That may seem boastful, but it's no less true. Thad goes above and beyond to make sure Drea feels heard and is appreciated. She never questions his love or devotion to her. That makes him the best in her eyes. Ingredients for a cheese omelet are lying out on the kitchen island. He gestures with his finger for Drea to come closer. She takes a seat on a stool and watches him work. He moves so effortlessly in the kitchen, it's like watching a carefully choreographed dance. His instincts to add a little pinch of this and a little touch of that always makes what he serves taste perfect. She tasted Thad's cooking before they got married, but there's something about tasting it as his wife that makes it heaven on a plate.

He hands her a plate of a cheddar omelet with smoked bacon and melon slices, coupled with orange and guava juice. Heaven on a plate. Drea digs in and loves every bite.

"I love it when you eat like you're high," Thad remarks.

"I swear your food is like a drug. You make, hands down, the best blueberry pancakes I have ever tasted." Drea brags on him.

Thad's face flushes. "Thank you, peach."

"It's my pleasure. You know, the other day I was thinking of how much fun we're going to have cooking with our kids."

"I am definitely looking forward to that.

Teaching our children the art of barbecuing with their cousin Quincy and their Grandpa Earl. You and mom teaching them how to make Haitian dishes. I get excited whenever I think about it, peach. My body fills with an unbelievable amount of joy whenever I think of what lays ahead for us."

"Just when I think I cannot love you even more than I do, you say something so fucking…" Tears fill her eyes.

"Pace yourself, peach. You have a big day ahead of you, and I worked really hard to make sure it feels like this day belongs to you." Drea grins and blushes. She looks down in embarrassment. No man has ever made her blush. Thad lifts her head and kisses her lips. She feels his love, like physically, she can feel his love fill her up. Whenever they kiss, have sex or even just look at each other, Drea feels Thad's love through every inch of her body. It's an incredible feeling that leaves her breathless, weightless and feeling high as hell. "Peach?"

"Yeah." Drea stares at him like he's the only thing that matters in her world. Because he is. "You're so dreamy." Drea breathes out.

Thad smiles, looking like a fucking Disney prince. "Come on, my love. We have places to go."

Drea finishes her breakfast and makes Thad eat

some fruit and bacon. She's started flipping things, now she's the one who checks in to make sure he's eating. The Sharp wedding party is shaping up to be twenty-one clients scheduled to get haircuts, shaves, mani-pedis and foot massages. Thad and his staff, of course, will provide the haircuts and shaves. Thad partnered with a spa owner, Veronique Simms, who owns Serenity Spa and Beauty Clinic. She and her staff will provide the mani-pedis, facials and massages. Thad will also serve tapas courtesy of Esteban's Small Plates. He found out that Melvin loves Spanish food, particularly tapas, so he got on the horn with his friend Esteban—because, of course, Thad knows a guy who serves tapas—and got him to agree to cater last minute. Between the updates with Melvin, and having meetings with Veronique and Esteban, Thad has been skipping meals, hence Drea's concern. It's been really sweet to see that, even after all these years of cutting hair for big name clients, he still gets excited to provide the optimal service to his customers, whether they're new or returning. She loves how seriously Thad takes his work and how much he truly loves his job. Thad once told her the right cut can make someone feel like they can conquer the world, and giving people that feeling is always his goal.

Next on his list of birthday surprises is a visit to the Carter Willems Museum of African American Pop Culture. Drea has been dying to go back for years. She went for a cocktail reception when it first opened but hasn't been back since. The museum takes the visitors through a centuries-long look at all things pop culture—theatre, movies, TV, fashion, film and music—centered around African American history. They enter the museum, and the first thing Drea notices is that they're alone. There are no other patrons here. *Did...did this crazy man rent out the entire —?* Drea looks at Thad, and he smiles at her. "You rented out the entire museum for me."

"Sure did. We can take our time looking through whichever exhibitions you desire."

"You're too good to be true." Drea swoons.

"Baby, come on now. I've told you about making my head swell." Thad sweetly looks away while rubbing the back of his neck. Drea swears on a stack of Bibles when Thad starts acting all bashful, it is hands down the sexiest fucking thing ever.

"Come on, my handsome and thoughtful sweetheart of a husband." Thad chuckles and rubs his neck some more. She loves coming up with silly things to say in order to flatter him. Drea didn't realize how much of a 'my man, my man, my man,' type of girlie she is. Just goes to show she didn't have the right man to bring it out of her.

The two go through the seventies fashion exhibit and end in the modern day. A good two hours was devoted to the fashion section. The Black models' exhibit was amazing. Drea spent thirty minutes watching interviews with Bethann Hardison, Veronica Webb and Beverly Johnson on the screens with the headphones the museum provided.

Next, they hit up music, theatre and film, before ending the day at the TV section. They stand in front of an exhibit for an old TV show from the 2010s called *Doll Face*. It didn't last long, only one season. A lot of people had a problem with it. The premise was about a sex worker who solved crimes. As thin as the plot sounds, it was a good show and had quite a viewership among women, particularly Black women. It got canceled after too many complaints about the graphic sex scenes. *The female lead's character had sex for a living. What did people think they were going to see?* Drea always suspected that folks were pissed about a Black woman lead having sexual agency and being smart to boot. It was like the fucking Ava Doll nonsense all over again. "Did you ever watch the show?" Drea asks.

"Hell, yeah! The writing was amazing. I'm pissed

Tamara Whitehead never got nominated for an Emmy, but I'm glad she finally got recognition with that Oscar nom."

Tamara Whitehead was the head writer on *Doll Face*, and a lot of folks felt the same as Thad. She was robbed and blackballed when she complained about the show's cancelation. But she had the last laugh when her screenplay for *Scattered Ashes* was nominated for Best Original Screenplay at the Oscars almost a year after *Doll Face* ended.

"Now that folks are a little more knowledgeable about sex work, there's a rumor she's going to try and get the show up and running again. What do you think?" Drea asks. She loves getting Thad's opinion on everything. Whether they're talking about serious or goofy topics, it doesn't matter. She'll always want to hear what he thinks.

"As much as I would love to see it, I just don't see it lasting much longer than the first version. People are still pretty skittish about women having sexual agency. I don't see it even getting greenlit. I hate to sound so pessimistic." Thad looks sheepish.

"No, I think you may have a good point. I do hope that her screenplay for *Scattered Ashes* is taught in all screenwriting classes, though."

"It is brilliant." Thad looks around and sees something. "Oh, snap. This was my show."

Drea turns her attention to the exhibit for *Gumshoe,* the show that ran seven seasons that starred former Disney child star and future Oscar winner Robert Emerson. "I loved Gumshoe! The last episode actually made me cry," Drea says. "The look of relief he had when he finally solved Cassie's murder."

"Pop and I had a bet going over who did it. We both lost."

"I never would have guested it was the captain."

"And then when they retraced all those clues, starting from season one." Thad lets out a low whistle and shakes his head. "When I tell you, my mind was blown."

"Me too. They don't make shows like that anymore. Everything is a remake or a reboot. And why is everything only eight episodes now?" Drea complains.

"And why are we splitting seasons? Just play the whole damn season. If you want to create anticipation, then air the episodes week to week, like back in the day. Take risks and stop giving in to everyone's need for instant gratification."

"Here, here!" Drea agrees. She giggles, then takes

him by the hand and heads from the TV section. They've been at the museum from opening to closing. Thad thanks the curator and staff as they leave. This was a full day. "Where to next, husband?"

"Home for a special surprise."

"Okay."

When they arrive home, there's someone already inside, which alarms Drea. But Thad is being chill about it, so it must be part of the plan. He opens the door and none other than Langston Walker is in their kitchen! Drea smiles widely. "You're Langston Walker!" Excited doesn't begin to explain how she feels. They didn't get to meet Langston on Valentine's Day. Even though they did get into LW, by the time they were seated, he had already left. This is so much better!

"I am. Happy birthday!" Langston grins.

"Thank you. It smells heavenly here. What are you making?"

"Steamed mussels with white wine, stuffed lobster tail, filet mignon and a salad of mixed greens."

Drea's stomach rumbles. She and Thad had lunch at the museum café but that was hours ago. "That sounds amazing."

Thad slides up next to her. "I know we made up

on Valentine's Day, but I wanted to make up for the entire evening. I know things didn't pan out how you planned, and aside from scaling back with being too available to folks, I wanted to make sure you got to experience all that we missed that night."

"Thad, you didn't have to do all this!" Drea cries.

Thad wipes her tears. "I told you to pace yourself."

"What else could you possibly have in store for me?"

"You'll see."

Minutes later, they're sitting at the dining room table, sipping wine and enjoying a meal made by Langston Walker himself. Life just doesn't get any better. Drea chews on the filet mignon and lobster and lets out the most satisfying sigh.

"Your thoughts on the food, wife."

"This has to be one of the most satisfying meals I have ever had. It delivers on all levels. The appearance, the smells and the taste. This is the type of meal you have before going to the electric chair."

"That's dark but accurate," Thad agrees. "Did I ever tell you how much I love it when you talk like a judge on a food show?"

"Only all the time."

"Everything I love about you bears repeating."

"I couldn't agree more. I love it."

"Good." Thad raises his wine. "To you, my peach. On this day of your birth, I am grateful for being able to spend it with you, and I look forward to many more."

"Cheers." Drea taps her glass with Thad's. "I love you, Thad. Today was truly wonderful."

"I love you, too, and it's not over. I have one more trick up my sleeve."

Drea bounces in her chair with excitement, wondering what it could be.

After finishing dinner and some birthday cake, they say goodbye to Langston. Drea and Thad are now on the couch, his laptop is out and she's wondering why. It's close to nine at night. Who could he be calling? The FaceTime call is answered, and Drea cannot believe who answers. "Ms. Olympia, is that you?"

"Yes, Drea, baby, it's me."

Thad chimes in. "Ms. Olympia, thank you again so much for agreeing to talk to us so late."

"It's no worries. I can't stay on long, but I wanted to say happy birthday. I'm still in Tennessee, and I look forward to catching up with you both. I see you married a thoughtful man like my Jerry, and you co-own a boutique! I'm so proud of you, Drea."

"Thank you, Ms. Olympia." Tears stream down Drea's face. They end the call, promising to speak again soon. Drea turns to Thad. "How did you…?"

"I asked your father, actually. He has been paying for Ms. Olympia's mother's care for years. When she left, your mother thought that she had quit, but your dad knew how important she was to you. He wanted to make sure her and her family were doing well. He knew that if Vivian knew, she would suspect something nefarious. So, he did it in secret. I don't know why, but something told me to ask him first. I guess I just didn't believe that his closest connection to you was asking you about the weather. Turns out, my hunch was right."

"Wow, I should actually call him."

"You should. I think he'd like that."

"Thank you, Thad. I can't believe how much you love me."

"Believe it, baby, cause I'm only getting started."

18

THAD

It's seven o'clock in the morning. Thad is in the backyard's work out area, sitting crisscross applesauce. He attempts to clear his mind of all negativity. He focuses on the peace he feels as he's surrounded by nature.

The sun is out, the skies are clear, the birds are singing. It's going to be a great day. Everyone who walks into We Cut Heads today will walk out satisfied. The tireless work from me, my crew, Veronique and her crew will not go unnoticed. Esteban has the food handled. We will have a fruitful day. A day that will go down as one of the greatest achievements for We Cut Heads. Black business owners will hear of this day and cheer! He takes a deep breath and opens his eyes. *Yep, still nervous. Damn. I really thought meditation and positive manifesting would work. What is the problem?*

It's almost comical how he still gets opening night jitters when accommodating a large party like today. But this time feels different. Thad still feels like he's carrying a giant weight on his back. Typically, by the time the day of the main event rolls around, he's usually calmer. He likes to keep a clear head and a steady hand, so his crew and the clients are in good spirits. Melvin is getting married in a week. For him, this is the lead-up to the big day. It's a day he will share with the important men in his life. It should be fun and worry-free. But for Thad, it is the big day. He reminds himself that he has some of his best barbers on this team, including his most recent new hire, Ras. And getting this team together was no small feat. All of his employees are A1, so narrowing it down to the five that were selected was difficult. The added stress of Melvin changing the number of folks coming in didn't help. But it is all worth it. Melvin Sharp and his crew are scheduled to arrive at the flagship shop of *We Cut Heads* today at noon. Thad will have the shop closed the whole day. They are offering the Rolls Royce treatment. Cuts, shaves and, thanks to Veronique and her crew, manicures, pedicures, hand and foot massages and facials. This includes face masks, mud masks and face steaming.

Thad will be on hand to make sure everything goes according to plan, and Melvin asked Thad specifically to give him, his father, his future father-in-law and his uncle's their cuts. Mel told Thad that he grew up worshipping Lance, so when he met him at the golf tournament and found out Thad was his barber, he had to book him for his big day. Besides Melvin, his father, future father-in-law, uncles and groomsmen, the shop will also welcome some out-of-town cousins who aren't in the wedding but will be in attendance. Overall, they're going to be working on twenty-five men today.

Thad is going through his phone and talking to himself, reciting the day's events as he re-enters the house. "They'll arrive at noon on the dot. We'll start with the cuts, move on to the shaves, the facials, the mani-pedis and close out with the massages. We have the mimosas, sparkling and cucumber water on deck, along with lemonade. Esteban will arrive with the tapas at three."

Thad enters the kitchen and continues going over the day's schedule. "The shop will stay open until eight. That's plenty of time for folks to get—"

"Morning, husband," Drea greets him.

"Aw, shit!" Thad jumps.

"Thad! What the hell?" Drea's eyes are wide with surprise. "You didn't see me?"

"No, I thought you were still asleep."

"I've been awake for a while. I was watching you stretch and meditate. You looked uneasy, and right now, you look stressed."

"Well, you did just startle me, baby."

"I didn't mean to." Drea puts down her coffee mug and approaches Thad. She slides her hands up from his stomach to his chest before reaching further to scratch his beard. "What's wrong, my king?"

"I don't know." Thad shakes his head. "I'm feeling a little—"

"Out of sorts?"

"Yeah, what the fuck is up with that? I've been doing cuts since I was a kid. Why am I tripping now?"

Drea takes Thad by the hand and leads him into their bedroom. She climbs onto the bed, gets on her knees, reaches out and pulls him toward her by his shoulders. She stares at him like he's the eighth wonder of the world. Thad stares back, pulled in by Drea's power over him. She takes his face in her hands and leans in, so their foreheads are touching.

"Do you know why I call you my king?" Drea asks him.

Thad grins. "I have my guesses, but I'd rather you tell me."

"Simple, because that's what you are. Thaddeus, you rule over all that you do. Husband, son, brother, uncle, businessman and friend. You are a king."

"God, I love you."

"I love you, too." Drea looks at him with hooded eyes. "Take off your clothes."

Thad does as his wife asks. Lifting his T-shirt from the hem, he pulls it over his head. He moves on to his sweatpants, which he pulls down—along with his drawers—slowly while they gaze at each other. Thad steps out of his bottoms. He watches Drea as her eyes roam his naked body. Her fingers gently touch his abs, making their way to his chest, where she rubs her thumbs against his nipples.

"Mmmm," Thad moans. Drea's touch is so... *Oh, my God!* The ripples of pleasure going through Thad's body are so overwhelming his knees almost give out.

"Are you okay?" she asks.

"I'm good, peach." Thad's dick jumps.

Drea giggles. "I love it when your dick jumps." Thad chuckles while he breathes heavily. He's never realized how much he enjoys nipple play until Drea. As if reading his mind, she rubs his nipples in a circular motion with her thumbs. She reveals her nudity by taking off her large T-shirt and tossing it aside. Thad stares at her naked body, and his dick bricks up even more. Drea breathes life into him by giving him soft affirmations into his ear.

"Being nervous is good, you know. It means you care. And you do, Thad. You care about how good a job you do. A lot of people in your position would phone in their efforts. You push yourself. You don't take your skills for granted, and that's why you have a waitlist. You're a king. With a capital fucking *K*. You got this. You're Thaddeus fucking Richardson. The man who opened his first shop a decade ago and has built something to pass down to our kids and Quincy. You broke ground on your sixth shop." She bites his earlobe.

"Huhhh," Thad chokes out. He tries to keep his hands to himself and let Drea take the lead, but he can't help it. He has to touch her. Truth is, it's a miracle he held out this long. His hands make their way to her ass, and he squeezes both her big cheeks.

"I was wondering how long it would take before your hands were on my ass," Drea purrs.

"I tried to let you have it, peach"—Thad kisses

her shoulder—"but I couldn't help myself." He rubs his hands up and down, alternating between her behind and her thighs.

"You're a king." Drea licks his neck, resulting in him letting out a low groan. "You're going to walk into that shop like that king you are and make Melvin and his family thank the Heavens that they chose *We Cut Heads*. Do you hear me, husband?"

"I hear you, wife."

"Good." Drea scoots back before laying down and opening her legs. "Now, come take what you need."

Thad climbs on top of Drea. He takes his dick and taps her clit just like she likes it.

"Mmm, fuck me. Remind me of why this is your pussy."

Thad lets out a growl. His animal side has been activated. Drea's eyes smolder. *She's so fucking sexy.* Then she smiles. Every time he's rewarded with one of her smiles, he thanks God. This time is no exception. *Dear Lord, thank you for bringing this woman into my life.*

Thad pushes his dick inside her, almost passing out in the process. "Ahh! Oh, fuck." Thad shakes, but quickly gets it together. *Don't come. DO. NOT. COME!* Thad grasps Drea's waist while his dick throbs inside her. He moves in and out of her with quickening speed. He closes his eyes and feels every sensation course from his groin as Drea fucks him back. Everything feels like it's in slow motion, even the buildup of his release. Drea's close, she's tightening, and she hasn't stopped moaning since he entered her. He can't blame her. He's doing his fair share of moaning himself. It just feels too good. Thad snakes his hand in between Drea's legs and rubs his index finger in a circular motion on her clit. That makes her come, which makes him come. They both scream each other's name.

"Thad!"

"Drea!"

HOURS LATER, HE EXITS HIS CAR AS FUTURE'S "MASK Off" plays. His employees are outside the shop, waiting for him. It's a quarter 'til eleven. Thad approaches his crew.

"Hello, everyone," Thad greets them with a huge grin.

"Hey, boss man," Carlos jokes.

"Someone's ready," Kesi jokes.

"That's right. Ya'll are too, I hope," Thad replies.

Thad's employees nod and cheer in agreement.

"That's what I'm talking about. We stay ready around here." Thad unlocks the door. Any of them could have opened the door, but they wanted to wait for the "boss man,"—their special nickname for him. All his employees at every shop call him that. They enter and go straight to their stations, getting everything ready. Ras, Carlos, Kesi, Charon and Mac are top-tier talent. He's known them each for years, and knows what they're capable of. He assembled this team by taking one person from each of his shops. Ras's participation was the most important to him. Thad couldn't be prouder of how Ras turned his life around. When they first met, Ras was in a bad place, literally and figuratively. And now he's getting ready to work on the groomsmen for one of the biggest athletes there is. Thad loves his job, and days like today are a huge reason. He smiles. As always, his wife was right. He is a king. With a capital *K*. And the shops are his kingdom.

"Today is a big day. Today, we welcome Melvin Sharp and his family and friends to our shop. They're going to expect the best, and that's what we're going to deliver. I have assembled you all for a reason. Ras, no one handles difficult customers better than you." Everyone applauds Ras. "You are going to be handling Melvin's cousin, Tyron, who has jacked up matted hair and refuses to cut it. Are you up for the challenge?"

"Damn right, boss man," Ras replies.

Mac puts his arm around Ras and kisses him on the forehead. Everyone laughs.

"This is your first time being on a team for a special event. You nervous?" Thad checks in with him.

"Motivated," Ras answers.

"That's why I fucks with you, man." Thad grins. Ras smiles, and his coworkers pat him on the back. Thad goes through the rest of the crew, giving them encouragement and wise words. "Alright, Veronique and her people should be here shortly. Let's get this show on the road." Everyone. "Oh, and one last thing…What do we do?"

"We cut heads!" the crew yells.

"Say it again."

"We cut heads!" they repeat.

"Damn right, we do, and now let's make this money." Thad smiles.

His employees cheer and applaud.

———

A FEW HOURS HAVE PASSED, AND THINGS ARE GOING smoothly, except Tyron still isn't budging on cutting his hair. Thad sees why Melvin wanted him to cut it. Tyron's dreads are a mess. He clearly didn't take care of them. When Thad transitioned from dreads to neat locs, it wasn't arduous because he took care of his hair. He also told Latrice what to do to keep Quincy's hair looking good when he switched to locs. This man's head looks like what Thad's grandma Hattie used to say: *Your head look like somebody done chewed on it.* There are plenty of brothers who have matted dreads, but theirs are supposed to look like that. This is clearly not the case.

Ras lets out a sigh. Thad looks at him like, *Come on, man, you got this.* Ras told Thad that he figured that if he had Tyron get his shave, facial and mani-pedi, then by the time they got to his head, he would have changed his mind. No such luck. Ras nods his head. Thad stands close by and listens.

"Tyron—" Ras begins.

"I'm not cutting my dreads, man. I told cuzzo that I'd wear a hat or something."

How the fuck do you plan on getting a hat over all that mess, bruh?

"Aight, man. I didn't want to have to go here, but do you like women?" Ras asks.

"I love women."

"Okay, picture this. You're in the ballroom of the Park-Barrington full of women looking their flyest."

"Alright." Tyron nods.

"Weddings are full of single women, and these ladies are looking to connect with the right brother. You want to be one of those brothers, right?"

"Hell yeah."

"Then let me get at that head, cause I'm telling you right now, bruh, your head will make those ladies shut you down real quick."

Tyron turns and looks at Ras. He clearly sees that Ras isn't playing because the next words out of his mouth are, "Do it."

Ras nods and grabs his scissors, cutting away at the mess of hair. He looks up at Thad, who's smiling. Everything is running like a well-oiled machine. He didn't need to be nervous. Again, Drea was right, though. Being nervous means you care. Thad made sure everything was on time and ready. Melvin and his people definitely appreciate his attention to detail. He goes into his office and calls Drea.

"Hello, my king," Drea says with an airy tone.

"Keep talking like that and I'mma have to wreck you again when I get home."

"Don't threaten me with a good time, daddy." Drea's voice is the definition of sultry.

"Baby, I cannot go back out there with an erection, c'mon now," Thad teases.

"Sorry. How's the Shark's wedding party going?"

"It's going well. Thank you, Drea."

"You're welcome, my love. When will you be home?"

"Do you miss your king, baby? Cause I damn sure miss my peach."

"I do."

"Mmm. That 'I do' sounds just as mesmerizing as the one you gave me months ago. I should be home by nine. Ten at the latest."

"Okay, I'll stay up and wait for you. I should go. I have an appointment in a bit. With Latrice on maternity leave, it's just me and Ingrid holding down the fort."

"Okay. I love you, Drea."

"I love you, too, Thad."

He reluctantly ends the call. Talking to his wife always makes him feel centered. There's a knock at the door. He opens it, then comes out of the office. "What's up?" he says to Carlos.

"Mel's ready for his cut and shave, boss man."

"Aight, thanks, man."

Thad approaches Mel, who is already in his chair. "Where did you disappear to, Thad?" Mel smiles.

"Talking to my wife." Thad grins. He gestures for Melvin to stand up before he wraps a Sanek neck strip around his throat and ties the cape around him.

"That's what's up. I love calling Theresa during my breaks. It's something about hearing her voice." Mel sits back down.

"Exactly. Hearing my wife's voice puts me at ease. Doesn't matter if I'm stressed or not," Thad agrees.

"I can't wait to be married. How long you been married, Thad?"

"Got hitched back in September." Thad combs through Melvin's hair. "My parents have been married forty-one years. My dad always told me and my sisters that love is too important to just give it to anyone and not to settle. He told me that a man should be willing to lay down his life for the woman he loves. I'd do anything for Drea, and she knows it too."

Tyron chimes in. "Man, I ain't giving up my life for no bitch. That shit's weak. I don't care how long we been together."

"We don't call women bitches in this establishment." Thad states it plainly. He hates it when niggas call women bitches and hoes. He knows that the barbershop is a place where brothers can be them-selves and talk shit, but there are women who work here and Thad wants his employees to be comfort-able, first and foremost. He's canceled appointments of some very well-known men because of how they spoke to his receptionist, Becca, who handles the phones, emails and the waitlist. Being raised by Janet and having two sisters certainly played a role in his way of thinking, but the simple fact is, women are human beings and deserve to be treated as such. There are far too many men who don't seem to realize this. Tyron is definitely one of them.

"C'mon, man. I didn't mean any disrespect. Certainly not about your wife—"

"Oh, I didn't take it as disrespect toward my wife. If I had, I would be getting arrested right now, and you would have gone through that plate-glass window." Thad points toward the front of the shop. "We don't disrespect anyone of any gender in this shop. And for the record, there's nothing weak about what I said."

"Agree to disagree. Do you think your lady would die for you?" Ron asks.

"My *wife* once told me she wanted to die first because she didn't want to feel the pain of missing me," Thad answers.

"Then you got a real one. Most of these females only care about how much money you make and what you can buy them," Tyron says.

"What could you buy someone?" Kesi asks. "Just cause your cousin's in the NBA doesn't mean his money is yours."

"He already knows that," Melvin says.

"Don't worry about it, sweetheart. I got money," Tyron says.

Kesi rolls her eyes. "Well, not all women are like that."

"Yeah, but a lot are. Thad, you got how many shops now? Six, right?"

Thad nods.

"When you first opened and you was getting all that money, how many women were going after your pockets?" Tyron asks.

Thad works on Melvin's lineup with the trimmer. "I will admit, I did run into an occasional gold digger, but Kesi's right. There are a lot of solid women out there who aren't checking for your pockets."

"I guess. She better be fine as hell to get me to settle down. I don't know why you're doing this, cuzzo." Tyron looks at Melvin through the shop's mirror. "Theresa is cool and everything, but think of how much *squish* you passing up." Tyron says *squish* discreetly…or at least he tries.

"Squish? What the fuck is *squish?*" Charon, the other female barber, says. She's currently working on Mel's best man, Bryce.

"You know, coochie," Tyron says, like the answer was obvious.

That's what these young niggas are calling it now days?

Thad laughs.

"Good Lord, just say pussy," Kesi says.

"Okay, think of all the pussy you'll be missing out on."

"You mean possible STIs and accidental pregnancies? No, thank you. Pussy ain't everything, Ty," Melvin says.

"Yeah, but it's something," Tyron replies.

"Look, man, I met the woman I want to spend forever with, who I want to be the mother of my children and who is my destiny."

"That shit sounds corny."

"That's because you're young." Thad has moved on to Mel's shave. He glides the razor along his cheek. "But listen to your cousin. The minute you meet the one, you'll change your mind."

"Doubtful," Tyron says.

Thad and Melvin look at each other in the mirror and share a knowing look. Tyron's young, he'll learn. Thad never had a moment where he wanted to just play around and never settle down. He always saw himself becoming a family man like his father, but he does understand the instinct. Some folks just want to have the freedom of variety with no attachments. Hell, that's practically Nadia's motto—and that's cool —but Thad could never see himself without his other half. Especially now that he has her.

After hours of service, tapas and drinks, Thad is exhausted. His team did it! Everyone was happy with the service. Veronique and her folks made tons of tips, and so did his people. Ras asked to be considered for the next celebrity's big event. Of course, Thad wants all of his crew to have their time to shine, but he's definitely giving Ras another opportunity. Tyron was incredibly pleased with the drop fade he gave him.

Thad walks in the door and presses the buttons to deactivate and reactivate the alarm. He walks over to the couch and sees his sleeping beauty wearing one of his T-shirts. Thad goes into the bedroom and grabs some pj's—a T-shirt and boxers—enters the bathroom and takes a quick shower. He wraps his locs and puts on his pajamas. Finding Drea still asleep, he cozies up beside her and wraps her in his arms. She awakens and smiles at him. "How did it go?"

"It went amazing, peach. They loved everything."

"I knew they would."

"Come on. Let's go to bed."

Thad rises and picks Drea up, carrying her. "I love it when you carry me," she says softly.

"I know you do, peach." He kisses his wife.

19

THAD

Thad drives to Florentino's, his favorite upscale Italian joint. He has at least five favorite Italian places. When he wants to go big and have a fancy dinner, he always chooses Florentino's. He hands the valet his keys and takes Drea's arm. Their linked arms quickly turn into hand-holding as they approach the restaurant. The hostess greets them.

"Hello, and welcome to Florentino's. Do you have a reservation?"

"Yes, it should be under Richardson," Drea tells her.

"Ah, yes. Here we are. Please, follow me."

Husband and wife follow the hostess to the back

of the restaurant. As she leads them to the kitchen, Thad is beyond confused. "Uh, Drea…"

"Don't worry, baby. Just follow her." Drea smiles at him.

Thad shrugs and does as his wife says. They exit the restaurant from the back and go to a building that looks similar to the restaurant, but it's larger, like it hosts…parties. Just as Thad's about to ask Drea to confirm his suspicions, the hostess unlocks the door and opens it. She turns on the light, and the next thing Thad knows, his parents, sisters, cousins, uncles and aunts all yell, "Happy birthday, Thad!"

They're followed by Rachel and Tim, Leon and Amber, Lance and Jess, Mark and Suchi, who all come out clapping. Drea invited everyone. Thad's mouth hangs open. The space looks like an old skating rink—Skate, Rattle and Shake. Thad and his sisters used to frequent it, and their cousins would join them whenever they came into town. It looks almost identical. Thad looks at Drea with tears in his eyes. He told her that the Richardson Family Reunion might get canceled, and she made it happen. He told her about the skating rink and how he missed it from his youth, and she made it happen. Kofi approaches him. Poppa Earl has three siblings. His brother's Sly and Levi and his sister, Bebe. Kofi is Sly's son. He and Thad were stuck like glue whenever his family went to Kentucky or Kofi's family came out here. Kofi is about to open a tattoo parlor in LA, where he recently moved. He already has four in Kentucky.

"Thaddeus!" Kofi yells.

"Kof!" Thad yells back.

They hug each other tightly. "Happy birthday, my nigga. You old as fuck."

"You're only two years younger than me, Kof."

"Whatever, nigga. You still old as fuck." Kofi grins before turning his attention to Drea. "It's a pleasure to meet you in person, Cousin Drea."

"You, too, Kofi."

"How did you manage to pull this off, peach?"

"When you told me that the reunion might get canceled, I got on the horn with Poppa Earl, and we decided that, with June not being a possibility for the reunion, why not make it a month earlier for your birthday? And when you mentioned the skating rink, we had our theme. The owner of Skate, Rattle and Shake has an IG page, so I hit him up. And it turns out, he remembered you, Trice and Nay Nay. He sent me some old photos of the rink back in the day, and I asked Florentino's if they could make their party hall look like it, and voilà! Happy birthday, husband."

"Thank you, baby."

Drea takes him to where there are skates waiting for them. The place looks incredible. There's a section to choose your skates, a bar set up, and right next to it, a buffet. Skate, Rattle and Shake's menu was the typical skating rink fare: nachos, hot dogs, soft pretzels and onion rings, but tonight, the buffet includes some of the finest cuisine on Florentino's menu. Lying out are trays of beef carpaccio, mussels and clams, rigatoni with duck ragu, a charcuterie board, polpo alla griglia—grilled octopus—lasagna and sweet corn risotto. Thad is hungry, but he is dying to get on some skates and get out on the rink. He hasn't done it in a minute and hopes his birthday doesn't end with him having a busted ass—but he's willing to find out. But first, he goes around greeting everyone and thanking them for coming.

"Uncle Sly!" Thad hugs him.

"Hey there, nephew. That is one determined young lady you married." Sly smiles.

"She is. That and much more." Thad looks at Drea in awe. She smiles and bites her lip.

"Damn right, this girl was working overtime to

make this all happen. You make sure you treat her right," Uncle Sly tells him.

"Oh, I'm on it, sir. Believe me."

"Good. How's the barbershop business going?"

"Business is booming as usual."

"That's the Richardson hustle. You got that from your daddy. We all gave it to our kids."

"No doubt." Thad smiles. "Where's Aunt Renee?"

"She's over by the bar with your momma and your Aunt Tootsie. You know how those three get."

Momma Janet, Aunt Renee and Aunt Tootsie all refer to themselves as the RSIL—Richardson sisters-in-law. When they get together, the laughter is loud, and the talking never stops. Poppa Earl once told Thad he was happy that his wife and his brother's wives all got along, but they could be a handful.

Thad shakes his head and laughs, just as Uncle Levi approaches. "Nephew! I hear Quincy is almost about that age to be taught how to grill."

"Yes, sir." Thad hugs him. "He's going to be ten soon, and Pop and I are looking forward to passing down the Richardson family tradition."

"You know your dad's ribs ain't as good as mine. But they're definitely better than Sly's."

"I plead the fifth, Uncle Levi. I am not getting involved in this."

"Fine, fine. You and I both know it's true. Now, when are going to bring this beautiful young lady to Kentucky?"

"Planning a visit once the WWII museum opens. I definitely want to be there."

"Good, your granddaddy would love that." Uncle Levi smiles.

After chatting with a few more people, Thad and Drea take to the rink. Thad holds on to Drea's hands while standing behind her. She's new to skating, so he wants to start her off slowly. "Okay, peach. You're going to place your feet shoulder-width apart and get into a squatting position."

"Okay." Drea nods. "Thad, do not let go of me."

"I won't. I promise," Thad assures her.

"Put your heels together and point your toes out. Then start walking forward," Thad instructs. Drea does as he says. "We're going to move a little quicker and take longer strides."

Soon, the two are skating, not as fast as everyone else—Nadia, Kofi and Tamar—but they're doing pretty well. Drea doesn't feel as stiff as she did when they first started.

"Thad."

"What's up, baby?"

"Look at Suchi. She keeps staring at Kofi."

"I'm not surprised." Thad looks over, and sure enough, Suchi's eyes are glued to Kofi.

"She really does think you have a good-looking family," Drea jokes.

"And you don't?" Thad teases.

"Please, you know damn well how fine I think you are." Drea rolls her eyes.

Thad snickers. "Suchi is his type, and Kofi…how do I put this…?"

"What? Is he a player?"

"I wouldn't call him that per se, but he does love women, and they love him."

"Yeah, the tattoos, his height, face and physique must get him a lot of attention."

"A whole lot. Which has gotten him into some hot water too."

"Let me guess, married women go after him."

Thad nods his head rapidly, making Drea laugh. "Oh, yeah."

"I think him and Suchi would look cute together." Drea rubs her hands together like she just hatched the greatest plan ever.

Thad laughs. "Go for it. Look at you, setting people up like your mom's doing with Mark."

Drea laughs. "She's relentless about that. Call Kofi over."

"Hey, yo, Kof! Come here, man."

Kofi skates over to them. "What's up, T?"

"My wife wanted to ask you something." Thad smiles at Drea.

"What's up, Ms. Fashionista!" Kofi teases. "Came in here with some stilettos on, stunting on folks."

Drea's face flushes, and she chuckles.

"Those are the only kind of shoes she owns. I swear she doesn't have any other kind," Thad jokes.

"That's not true," Drea argues.

"Name another type of shoe you own."

"Slippers. You've seen me wear them at home."

"Exactly. At home. That's the type of footwear you wear in your house."

"Yeah, I was about to say, slippers are basically socks, so that don't count," Kofi concurs.

Drea waves her hand at them dismissively.

"You all moved in, Kof?" Thad asks.

"Yeah, finally. I'll have to have you two over when things settle down a bit."

"Bet. It's gon' be nice having another Richardson man on the West Coast."

"Yeah, I'm glad I got kin out here already. It'll make the adjustment easier. I'm already experiencing culture shock like a motherfucker." Kofi shakes his head.

They all laugh.

"You know what would be a good remedy for that? Meeting someone. So, what do you think of Suchi?" Drea barely hints.

"That was a weak-ass segue," Kofi teases.

"Hush up and answer my question," Drea says.

"You talking about the beautiful brown skin honey with the sweet smile, and the soft eyes right?" Kofi asks.

Thad laughs. *Leave it to Kofi to notice every minor detail of a woman.*

"Yeah." Drea chuckles. "That would be her."

"I was just heading to her when you called me over," Kofi replies.

"Oh! Great. Go, go, go." Drea urges.

Kofi skates over to Suchi. She smiles and blushes as he leans over and gives her a wolfish grin.

"Yay! I made that happen." Drea claps.

"I mean, did you though? He was going to talk to her anyway."

"Yes, but I facilitated it happening faster."

"I'm not sure—"

"Shut up and let me have this." Drea pinches his arm.

"Ow, fine. Mean ass." Thad rubs the place she pinched.

"Say that shit to may face, motherfucker!" Uncle Levi yells.

Thad and Drea turn their attention to Uncle Levi and Uncle Sly. *Jesus Christ. They are too old to be doing this shit!*

"My ribs are better," Uncle Sly says in Uncle Levi's face. Uncle Levi shoves him, causing Uncle Sly to shove him back.

Thad makes eye contact with his dad and Kofi. They all know the routine. When shit gets heated, separate Uncle Levi and Uncle Sly until they calm down. Thad rolls his eyes. It's like dealing with toddlers. Before he, his father and Kofi can get head over, he hears, "You two stop this right now!" from Drea. "You both promised that you would get along and stop this competitive nonsense. This is my husband—your nephew's—birthday. I will not have anybody ruin it. Now, apologize to Thad, and separate for the rest of the evening."

"It's not my fault his ass started talking shit," Uncle Levi argues.

"Are you serious, Uncle Levi? You're a grandfather, for Christ's sake. You really just said, 'He started it!'" Drea responds. "Apologize to my husband, please."

Uncle Levi and Uncle Sly look sheepish and ashamed. "Sorry, nephew," Uncle Sly says.

"Yeah, sorry, Thad," Uncle Levi says.

"Thank you," Thad replies, squeezing Drea.

The rest of the evening goes much smoother. Kofi and Suchi disappeared hours ago, and no one has seen hide nor hair of them since. Thad and Drea skated for a couple of hours, then stopped to have dinner. After a few drinks and chatting with folks, they sit on the sidelines and watch other folks in the rink.

"Thank you so much, peach. This is the best birthday I've had in a minute. This definitely tops Vegas for my thirty-fifth. Don't tell Lance, though. He's the one that organized it," Thad says.

Drea smiles. "No worries, I'll keep my mouth shut."

They watch Lance and Jess out on the rink. Jess holds Lance's hand, and when she cautiously lets go, she lands on her butt and laughs it off.

"I love that everyone is enjoying this. It's like we're getting to be kids again," Drea says.

"That's exactly how it feels. This brought back so many memories. I cannot thank you enough, baby."

"My pleasure, my king."

"Oh, shit! I've been having so much fun that I

forgot to ask about the kids. Where are they? They would love this."

"There with Momma Ernie at Leon and Amber's tonight. This little soiree was for the grown-ups, but I paid a little extra for the rink to stay up so we can bring the kids tomorrow. That is, if you're down. We want our kids to be close to their cousins, after all."

"I'm definitely down." Thad smiles.

He listened to Drea and has been taking it easy on volunteering his time, but it's nice to see that she listened to him too. She's been going with him to activities with the kids, and she brought dinner over to Ally and Benji's when they had to cancel coming over, which was her idea.

Drea kisses him. "It's almost time for cake."

Minutes later, his family and friends are singing "Happy Birthday" to him. Latrice has her phone up, recording. "Make a wish, T!" she shouts.

Thad looks at Drea and smiles. She smiles back. He turns to the cake and blows out the candles. *Drea is my only wish, and she already came true.*

DREA

The summer went by in a flash! Drea looks at the calendar on her phone and cannot believe it's late August already. Her stomach rumbles. She's hungry as hell and has been for the past three weeks. She's thinking of what to order from Chomp—the food delivery service Leon is the CEO of, so she gets *very* discounted food deliveries—when her phone buzzes. It's her dad. She called him a little after her birthday. Thanks to their busy schedules, they've been playing phone tag or texting each other, promising to call the other back. Drea answers and can immediately tell her father is still a little skittish about what to say when the first words out of his mouth are, "Hello Drea," and nothing else.

"Hi, Dad. I wanted to thank you for helping Thad

locate Ms. Olympia. She and I have been talking and catching up. I really appreciate it."

"Oh, right. You're welcome. Do me a favor? Don't mention it to your mom. She was always a little jealous of how close you two were. I'll need to ease her into knowing you're talking again."

"Wow, really?" Drea asks. Vivian Johnson isn't jealous of anyone.

"Yep, she always was. At one point, she wanted to fire Olympia, but I convinced her not to," Greyson says.

Drea is shocked. She's almost as shocked as she was when Mark told her he looked after her when she wasn't paying attention. When Drea was a teenager, she would sneak out the house. Mark was in grad school, but whenever he came home, he'd make sure her parents didn't catch her sneaking out or back in. She never realized the men in her family were looking out for her. She really thought her dad and brother were ignoring her that whole time.

"Thank you."

"No worries."

They're both silent for a bit. Greyson speaks. "It's sunny out today."

This poor man really doesn't know how to talk to me. Drea really doesn't know whether to laugh or cry.

"It is." Drea's stomach growls again and she feels crampy, which reminds her to look for a new OBGYN. When she and Thad agreed to start trying for a baby back in March, they could not have foreseen how difficult that would be. Her OB of five years, Dr. Fredericks, retired, but not before taking Drea's IUD out. And she had to wait until April to get that done. Dr. Fredericks wanted to see as many patients as possible before she hung up her white lab coat in June. Drea was lucky she made the cut. After Dr. Fredericks retired, finding a Black female OB has become more than a notion. Latrice's and Nadia's OB's weren't taking new patients, and Dr. Fredericks referred her patients to another doctor. But he's a man and non-Black. He's probably a great doctor, but just not what Drea is looking for. This has resulted in her not having much luck finding a new one. And with her having irregular periods while trying to get pregnant, the sooner she finds a doctor, the better. Maybe her father calling is kismet. He'll definitely know someone.

"Dad?"

"Yeah."

"My OBGYN retired and I'm looking for a new one, but it's been a challenge. I'd like a Black woman, and I'm not willing to budge on that. Do you think you can help me?" she asks.

"Of course!" Greyson replies cheerfully. Drea's pleased he's excited. This involves schmoozing and dropping his name, two things her dad loves. Drea smiles at the thought. "Hold on one second." There's silence for a few seconds, then Greyson says, "Drea, are you still there?"

"Yes, Dad. I'm here."

"Drea, I have Dr. Claudia Kershaw on the line. Claude, meet my daughter, Andrea."

Theee Dr. Claudia Kershaw is on the line! Drea knew her dad had pull—he's the head of neurology at St. Augustine Medical Center, after all—but to actually be able to call Dr. Kershaw like it's nothing. Her dad has juice. This woman is the OBGYN to movie stars!

"Hello, Andrea."

"Hi, you can call me Drea."

"Hello, Drea. So, your dad tells me you're looking for an OBGYN. I have an opening this afternoon if you'd like to come in. We'll go through the consultation and get you checked out for whatever the issue is."

"Yes, yes! Thank you. What time?"

"How does one-thirty sound?"

"Perfect. Thank you." Dr. Kershaw ends the call. "Thank you again, Dad."

"You're welcome. Drea?"

"Yes?" Drea replies.

"I know you and I were never close, but I would like us to talk more, if that's okay."

"Yeah, it is, and Dad?"

"Yes?"

"We don't have to talk about the weather."

Greyson chuckles. "Right. I'll talk to you later."

"Sounds good. Bye, Dad."

"Bye, Drea."

At a quarter to two, Drea sits in Dr. Kershaw's examination room after having filled out the paperwork to become a new patient. The consultation was pretty quick, thankfully. Drea informed the nurse of her pregnancy plans and irregular period, along with her symptoms. The nurse got her into a hospital gown and had her pissing in a cup right away.

Dr. Kershaw enters the room and immediately washes her hands and puts on a pair of gloves. "Hello, Drea. Nice to meet you in person."

"You as well."

"I have news for you, my dear. You are going to be a mommy," Dr. Kershaw announces. Drea gives her a wide eyed looked of surprise. "I'm guessing this is good news."

"It is. I'm just shocked. My husband and I started trying in May. I've always had an irregular period which is probably why I couldn't tell."

Dr. Kershaw smiles. "Having an irregular menstrual cycle can make it difficult to know if you're pregnant. Did you not have any symptoms?"

"That's just it, I had the usual cramps and salty cravings but no blood flow and that's happened before so I assumed it was business as usual. I've gone without any blood flow for months before. I would have come in once Thad and I started trying but it's been an uphill battle finding a doctor."

"Until now." Dr. Kershaw smiles. Her warmth makes Drea feel calm. Talking to her dad was definitely the right call. Dr. Kershaw continues, "please lay back. Let's get this ultrasound started so you can meet your baby. Now I have to warn you, the gel is a little cold."

"Okay."

Drea lies back, and Dr. Kershaw uses an abdominal ultrasound to check on the little one. Drea is so excited. She can't wait to tell Thad. There's so much to get done, decorating the nursery and registering for baby things—

"Oh, wow!" Dr. Kershaw says. "You're about twelve weeks along." *Twelve weeks! That's three months. Thad knocked me up right away...? Oh, it must have been the night after we went salsa dancing for date night. He was super horny when we got home.* Drea grins at the memory. Dr. Kershaw looks at the screen, "I got more news for you, Momma. Are you ready?"

Drea nods. "Yes, please."

"It's twins."

Drea's eyes widen again. This time they look like they're about to fall out of her head. "Excuse me?"

"You heard correctly," Dr. Kershaw says. "Look here." She points to the two little plum sized images on the screen. "Those are your babies."

Twins! We're having twins.

DREA'S ON HER WAY HOME WHEN HER MOM CALLS. "Hi, Mom," Drea answers.

"Andrea, your father told me that Dr. Kershaw is now your OBGYN! That's fabulous news, sweetheart. She's amazing."

"Mom, I'm pregnant, and it's twins," Drea blurts out. "I haven't told Thad yet, but I had to tell somebody."

"I'm the first person you told?"

"Yes."

"I'm happy for you, my darling."

"Thank you. Twins! I can't believe it."

"Well, they do run in our family. On my side."

"Really? I guess that's how we got Jelani and Lettie."

"No, sweetheart. Twins are only on the mother's side, so that horrific Acacia has twins in her family."

"Oh, who are twins on ours?"

"Your grandmother had a twin sister."

"Seriously! Gram never said anything."

"That's because they were estranged. Speaking of which, I'm glad you and your brother are getting along better."

"Thank you. Me too."

"So, maybe you can convince him to let me set him up with somebody."

"Mom, let it go. Mark needs to work on himself before he gets with anyone."

"He's going to need companionship, Andrea, and someone to help him raise the kids."

"He has Suchi and us to help him with the kids. He'll find companionship when he's ready. Acacia has only been gone for a year."

"Well, at least convince him to have coffee with Gina Chambers. She's been asking about him."

"I'll see what I can do."

"Wonderful, and Andrea? Thank you for letting me know."

"Of course."

"You do realize your baby shower will be at the country club, right?"

"Yes, Mom."

"Good."

Hours later, Drea is putting the finishing touches on dinner—a roast chicken with crispy baby potatoes and buttery baby carrots—she's hoping he senses a theme. She also picked up a cake from a bakery. She wanted to get the ultrasound image onto the cake, but that would have taken a day or two, and she must tell Thad today. So, she settled for a baby decorated on the cake with icing from a piping bag and the message, 'Guess who's going to be a daddy?'

Thad walks through the door. "Hey baby, what are you doing home so early?"

"I had a doctor's appointment, and I decided to take the rest of the day off."

"Are you okay? You didn't mention a doctor's appointment this morning."

"She was able to squeeze me in thanks to my dad."

"Greyson, coming through in a clutch." Thad smiles as he takes his shoes off, then has a seat on the couch.

"Dinner's ready," Drea tells him.

"I'm not too hungry, peach. I'll eat later." Thad turns on the TV to highlights from a USC game. "That Kendrick Wright kid is a beast."

Drea looks at the TV, but she has no clue what she's watching. So, she goes back to trying to convince Thad to come to the kitchen.

"Thad, could you come here, please?"

"Sure." Thad gets up and goes to her, giving her a kiss. "What's up?" Drea takes the cake out of the refrigerator. "Why are we having a cake?"

"Because we're celebrating. Read it."

Thad reads the cake. He looks up at Drea, tears streaming down his face. "We're having a baby," he whispers. Thad grabs her, giving her a tight hug. He gets his phone out and immediately calls his parents.

"Thad—" Drea begins.

"Hi, Thad," Momma Janet says. "Is Drea pregnant yet?"

"Yes, Momma, she is!" Thad cries.

"Oh, my God! I knew it. Your daddy dreamed of

fishes last night. They were fried catfish, but that counts." Thad laughs. "Where's my Drea?"

"I'm right here." Drea joins in. " And—"

Momma Janet cuts her off. "Oh, sweetheart, I am so happy, and I am going to cook a Haitian feast for the baby shower. Earl!" she screams.

"Baby, stop screaming. What's going on?" Earl asks.

"Um, everybody—" Drea tries to talk again.

"Thad and Drea are having a baby!" Momma Janet cries.

"Thaddeus, congratulations, Son."

"Thank you, Pop."

"Your job remains the same. You support Drea and do whatever she asks."

"Got it."

"If that's the case, then can I talk?" Drea asks.

Thad turns his attention to her. "Sorry, baby, we were all just so excited!"

"Well, I have more news. I'm twelve weeks along, and…it's twins."

"Oh, my God! Oh, my God! Twins!" Momma Janet screams.

"Drea?" Poppa Earl says.

"Yes."

"Is our son okay?"

Drea looks over at Thad. His eyes are as large as saucers, and he's silent. "He's stunned into silence."

"Okay, we'll call back later when he's speaking again." Poppa Earl laughs. "Congratulations, sweetheart."

"Thank you, Poppa Earl." Drea smiles, then ends the call.

"Twins," Thad says softly.

"Yes, Thad. We're having twins." He sways from side to side. "Thad, are you about to faint?" Drea asks.

"Yeah," he says, and proceeds to fall backward. The good news is that he landed on a carpeted area.

"Thad? Thad?" Drea kneels and shakes him, but he doesn't budge. "This is why you should have eaten dinner first." Drea continues shaking him.

THAD

It's September 23. Exactly one year ago, Thad and Drea got married. And they're currently lounging on the couch, snuggled up, with Drea sitting on Thad as his legs are stretched out. They're watching *Have Food? Will Travel* and eating Chinese takeout. Why? Because that's what Drea wanted to do.

She pops a fried pork pot sticker in her mouth. "Now that we kind of know him and have tasted his food, I like watching this show even more."

"Do you have a bigger crush on him, too?" Thad asks.

"Yeah, a bit." Drea eats some lo mein. Thad growls. "Oh, stop it. It's your babies I'm carrying, not his."

"That's right. I put two babies in you," Thad jokes with fake bravado. "And on our first time trying too."

Drea snuggles against him, and he kisses her temple. She takes the egg roll out of his hand and bites it before giving it back. "Yep, you put two hungry munchkins in me, and you know, you're talking mighty big for a man who fainted when I told him."

"Drea, I thought we agreed we would never speak of that. It's bad enough my parents told my sisters and Nay Nay's big-mouth-having ass told everyone." Thad shakes his head. "I'm never going to live that down." *I just found out I was becoming a father...of twins! Anybody would have fainted.* When everyone knew Thad was okay, Nadia promptly sent the whole crew an animated version of Thad as a GIF fainting with the word *TIMBER!* on the bottom. He's been getting playfully roasted ever since.

Drea giggles. "I'm sorry, but it was funny."

"Maybe for you." Thad pouts.

"Aw, don't be sad, my king." Drea scratches his beard. Thad responds by shaking his leg like a dog, making Drea laugh.

"Mmm. We should get Jamaican. Spinach patties and jerk chicken."

"You mean for dinner tomorrow?"

"No, now."

Thad takes out his phone and orders more food on Chomp. "It's coming in thirty-five minutes."

"Thank you, husband."

"You're welcome, wife."

"Thad?"

"Yeah, baby."

"Even though it's not Friday, can we have a check in?"

"Of course." Thad pauses the TV. "Are you okay?"

"Yeah, just hormones." Drea's eyes water.

Thad wipes her tears. "Tomorrow morning, you're going to start meditating with me."

"Okay."

"Good, now, talk to me." Thad smiles.

"I love you."

"I love you, too, baby."

"No, Thad. I...I love you so much, and I'm so happy. You're going to be an amazing father. Our babies are so lucky to have you."

Thad wipes away a tear of his own. *God, I love this woman so fucking much.* "You're going to be an amazing mother, Drea. Whenever you're with Kai, the twins or Quincy, I see how much of a great mom you're going to be—hell, you already are. You talk to them, and they're only the size of two avocados."

Drea laughs. "I love that you talk to them, too, and with the silly voice."

"I think they like it too," Thad says in a goofy high-pitched voice. He was going for Elmo when he first did it, but Drea laughed so hard he knew he hadn't hit the mark. Now, they just call it the silly voice. "I love that you've already started reading to them."

"That reminds me, we're reading *Hair Love* tonight."

"Got it."

"Thad, what do you think of the names Addison and Avery?"

"I like them. They work if we have two girls or a boy and a girl. What were you thinking if we have two boys?"

"Avery and Asher."

"Avery and Asher Richardson. That works."

They agreed they wanted the babies to have their own identities and to not be named after anyone. Drea suggested they give the babies *A* names. Thad was all for it.

The doorbell rings, and Drea gets up so Thad can get the door. He gets the food and thanks the delivery driver. He places it on the kitchen island and gets dishes. It's crazy that in five months, he's going to meet his children. He makes plates for them and brings the food over. He goes back to the kitchen and grabs them a couple of bottled waters. Once seated, he contemplates. Maybe he's having sympathy hormones because he's feeling emotional, too.

He begins to talk without thinking. "I imagine where I would be right now if I had remained scared and if I continued to let my previous relationships with women determine my fate. You're my heart's every desire. I don't think I have ever wanted anything as much as I wanted to love you." Drea's doe eyes are wide and filled with tears.

"That was beautiful, Thad."

"So are you, my love."

"Let's have sex now!" Drea cries.

"Your wish is my command."

"Thad! Oh, my God. That was the perfect opportunity to say, *As you wish.*"

"That felt too on the nose."

"I think you should have gone for it."

"Okay, I'll tell you what. If I ever get the chance to give the Inigo Montoya line, I'll go for it."

"Good. Now take me into our bedroom and get me naked."

"Yes, ma'am." Thad picks Drea up carefully and heads to the bedroom.

"Thad, bring the chicken and the spinach patties."

Thad stacks the two plates, holding them with one hand while he holds on to Drea as she lies over his shoulder. "I'm going to sex you now, wife," Thad says in the silly voice.

"Don't ever do that again!" Drea laughs.

"What? You like my silly, sexy voice?" he asks, still using it.

Drea laughs out loud. "Stop, Thad!"

"I love you, Drea," he says in the voice.

"I love you, too, you goofy ass man."

"You love it." Thad puts the plates down and lowers Drea so they're eye level.

She gazes at him. "You're right, I do."

They smile at each other and kiss.

THE END

ACKNOWLEDGMENTS

Thank you Meka James, Jessica Berry, Raeshawn Love, Brynn and Leni Kauffman. This book would not have happened without any of you.

Thank you to all of the ARC readers and those who have purchased, read and reviewed my books for their support. Plenty of people have told me how much they couldn't wait for Thad and Drea's story. I hope you enjoyed it!

Thank you to my husband Joe for his constant support and to my yummy munchkins Michael and Alexander.

I also want to give a special shoutout to Rosie Mayes. Her website is where I got the Cornish game hen recipe Drea uses at Christmas. Support a Black owned business by visiting her site.

https://iheartrecipes.com/

You all will find out more about Thad and Drea twins in 'Tell Me I'm Not Dreaming,' a rom-com anthology featuring Kofi and Suchi coming Summer of 2025.

Nadia's story and the conclusion to the Richardson sibling trilogy is coming in 2026!

Thank you all so much and stay blessed!